HERmione

Also by H. D.

AVAILABLE FROM NEW DIRECTIONS

Analyzing Freud
Collected Poems
End to Torment
The Gift
Helen in Egypt
Hermetic Definition
Hippolytus
Kora and Ka
Pilate's Wife
Selected Poems
Tribute to Freud
Trilogy
Vale Ave

H.D.

HERmione

*with an afterword
by Francesca Wade*

A NEW DIRECTIONS
PAPERBOOK ORIGINAL

This volume was published with the cooperation of the Beinecke Library
of Yale University.

Manufactured in the United States of America
First published clothbound and as New Directions Paperbook 526 in 1981
and reissued as NDP1543 in 2022 (ISBN 978-0-8112-2209-9)

Library of Congress Cataloging-in-Publication Data
H.D. (Hilda Doolittle), 1886–1961.
HERmione.
I. Title.
PS3507.O726H43 1981 813'.52 81-9518 AACR2
ISBN 978-0-8112-0817-8

2 4 6 8 10 9 7 5 3 1

New Directions Books are published for James Laughlin
by New Directions Publishing Corporation
80 Eighth Avenue, New York 10011

To
F……
for
September 2nd

Pandora's Box

It's all over now, I tell myself. Over and done with. What happened, happened. The past is past. Don't delve and dredge. Cut down on nostalgia, that too can be insidious. Concentrate on the present, gird for the future.

But the past will not leave me alone. It pulls me back and under. It surrounds me. The more remote it may be, the closer the encirclement.

A couple of years ago, Donald Gallup showed me around the Beinecke Library. Time was short. The tour had to be brief, a mere introduction. We walked the aisles briskly. He pointed out this and that. Shelves of first editions. And unpublished manuscripts, the contents of the proverbial "trunk." Correspondence: endless rows of filing cabinets packed tight, serried, and labelled Lawrence, Pound, Aldington, McAlmon, Stein, Beach, Richardson, Freud ... on and on. These people seemed to have spent their lives writing letters. I wondered how they ever got any work done. I was overwhelmed by this collective presence, and all the ideas and conflicts and torments. I resolved to come back. I had legitimate entree. I would immerse myself for days, months—years.

I put it off. I wasn't ready. Too much too soon, and, at the same time, too late—and much of it disturbing. Pandora's Box. Leave it be, let it lay. So I left it to the professionals, the scholars. They had the time, dedication, patience—and detachment.

I answer queries and consider permissions requests. I read copies of work-in-progress. Pandora's Box has been opened for me, selectively, and not all at once. I face the contents in the privacy of my home. As I expected, there are skeletons and poltergeists. But uplift too, illuminations. I'm learning so much—a scholars' pupil, trailing them in a postgraduate course of my own.

The autobiographical novel, *Hermione,* has most recently emerged from the "trunk." Completed in 1927. I was present at the creation. Right there, in person. Not there in spirit. Osmosis was absolutely nil. Hush, hush, whisper who dares. "Your mother is working." In her room, behind a locked door. Funny kind of work; endless silence, followed by a barrage of typing. I wanted to be in that room. I resented being hauled away. I didn't know what I know now: that small children and literary endeavor do not mix.

I also know now, with the full weight of hindsight, that I was part of a very bizarre menage. We lived in great seclusion, on the shores of Lake Geneva, Switzerland. I had two mothers. My real mother, H. D., who lived on an exceedingly rarefied plane. And her surrogate, Bryher, who took care of reality.

H. D. was very beautiful, quite magical in appearance—tall, gaunt and graceful, with exquisite bone structure and searching grey eyes. She was also very excitable. Her descents into everyday life were an ordeal. She over-reacted. The least disruption set off total frenzy. I worshiped her. I was in awe of her. Maternal love was true, but she showed it sporadically, in sudden impulsive rushes. We did share quiet tender times. They, I, had to be *quiet,* though.

Bryher's ideas veered between free-wheeling experimentation and old-world discipline. "Hippo, hippo" she would yell, pursuing me with a hippo hide whip. And I was stood in corners, and deprived of dessert like any bad Victorian child. Well warranted, I have no doubt. I was often rambunctious. In their different ways, both mothers gave me a lot of affection. I felt cherished. I just never knew what was going to happen next. Lacking any other frame of reference, I accepted that as the norm.

H. D.'s official name was Mrs. Richard Aldington, mine Frances Perdita Aldington. What of Mr. Aldington, the missing father? Where was he, why did he never come to see us? My questions were always met with a shush and a change of subject.

Bryher was Mrs. Robert McAlmon. He came and went. The mothers complained when he went. When he came, they were a quarrelsome trio. Voices were raised, tables pounded, doors slammed. I liked him. I recognized another loner, not entirely at ease in his surroundings. I tried to console him. I too had a typewriter and a room of my own. I wrote him long letters, "miracles of Gertrude Steinese prose" he later recalled, in *Being Geniuses Together*. I cut out tiny cardboard Christians and threw them to my collection of stuffed lions. His armchair was the Colosseum, he the audience of thousands. Then the adults would break up our game and start arguing again. And discussing matters way over my head. Bandying odd names. Ezra and Pound—separate characters I assumed, since I was not really listening to the context. Joyce and Lawrence, whoever they might be. Sylvia Beach; nice name, it sounded like a tall silvery tree. Frances Gregg. "A very dear friend," my mother had once told me, "beautiful and good, that's why I named you Frances Perdita." I was under a table, probably grooming the lions for their next public appearance, when I was startled to hear Bryher, "Don't mention Frances Gregg, ever again. She is very dangerous."

Physical danger was the only kind I could imagine. She must be around somewhere, prowling the neighboorhood with a dagger, lurking in ambush. We shared the same name, so she was out to get me.

Bryher's edict was enforced. Frances Gregg was never mentioned again.

My entourage dispersed now and then, and inexplicably—packing suitcases all of a sudden, talking about London and

Paris, agitating over tickets. Although they never let me in on their plans, everything was pre-arranged, for then two wonderful old ladies arrived to take care of me—my grandmother, Helen Doolittle, and her sister, my great-aunt Laura. This change of guard transformed the whole atmosphere. They brought calm. They didn't type, they never argued. They were always accessible, and concerned. They listened. They told bed-time stories. They were also very firm. I knew what to expect and what was expected of me. They were so adorable and we had such fun together; I wanted to please them. The hippo whip remained on its hook.

It was a wrench when they left. "Don't cry, we'll be back next year."

In 1927, I was at last considered old enough to travel. I accompanied H. D. and Bryher to London. Robert McAlmon had dropped out of our group. Grandma joined us without Aunt Laura who had stayed home this time. The two of us rode on buses and explored parks and museums. Then, another emotional parting, at Waterloo Station. A train was carrying her off to the States. The boat train. How would they fit it onto the boat; would she have to stay in her compartment all the way? Foolish questions. No one paid them any heed, not even Grandma, flustered, counting up her luggage. It was all very confusing and sad.

She died later that year.

Now she has come back; one of those inescapable voices from the past—in a giant leap and a double loop of chronology. Eugenia Gart, Hermione's mother. My mother's mother, not yet my grandmother. The tale is set in an era before I was born. I also meet "Ezra and Pound" as the impetuous suitor, George Lowndes. And the "dangerous" Frances Gregg, alias

Fayne Rabb—the counterpoint of the love story. Not an easy book. It shifts and jumps, and repeats itself. The voice is frequently overwrought—just like the author's in real life. Yet there is a strange hypnotic force. I'm caught up in the momentum. Then held up by jolts of recognition, clues and double clues, references and cross references—and the play on names.

People are in names, names are in people, she says. And further along: *names are in people, people are in names.*

Names, people; split dimensions. The protagonist is a divided personality, Her and Hermione. Hermione of Greek mythology, daughter of Menelaeus and Helen. Also, most significantly to me, Shakespeare's misunderstood heroine of *The Winter's Tale,* mother of Perdita.

Now, having finished the book, I feel deserted. And haunted beyond the last page. What will become of all these people? There should be a sequel. And, of course, there is. *Bid me to Live,* for one. And more in the trunk. I turn back to the first page, and the dedication. To F...... September 2. To Frances on her birthday. Also Bryher's birthday, shared in armed truce. Astrologers can make of that what they will.

I recognize one certainty in my future. I'll never escape the past.

PERDITA SCHAFFNER

PART ONE

I

one

Her Gart went round in circles. "I am Her," she said to herself; she repeated, "Her, Her, Her." Her Gart tried to hold on to something; drowning she grasped, she caught at a smooth surface, her fingers slipped, she cried in her dementia, "I am Her, Her, Her." Her Gart had no word for her dementia, it was predictable by star, by star-sign, by year.

But Her Gart was then no prophet. She could not predict later common usage of uncommon syllogisms; "failure complex," "compensation reflex," and that conniving phrase "arrested development" had opened no door to her. Her development, forced along slippery lines of exact definition, marked supernorm, marked subnorm on some sort of chart or soul-barometer. She could not distinguish the supernorm, dragging her up from the subnorm, letting her down. She could not see the way out of marsh and bog. She said, "I am Hermione Gart precisely."

She said, "I am Hermione Gart," but Her Gart was not that. She was nebulous, gazing into branches of liriodendron, into network of oak and deflowered dogwood. She looked up into larch that was now dark, its moss-flame already one colour with the deciduous oak leaves. The green that, each spring, renewed her sort of ecstasy, this year had let Her down. She knew that this year was peculiarly blighted. She could not predict the future but she could statistically accept the present. Her mind had been too early sharpened.

She could not know that the reason for failure of a somewhat exaggeratedly-planned "education," was possibly due to subterranean causes. She had not then dipped dust-draggled, intellectual plumes into the more modern science that posts signs over emotional bog and intellectual lagoon ("failure complex," "compensation reflex") to show us where we may or where we may not stand. Carl Gart, her father, had been wont to shrug away psychology as a "science." Hermione Gart could not then know that her precise reflection, her entire failure to conform to expectations was perhaps some subtle form of courage.

It was summer. She wasn't now any good for anything. Her Gart looked up into liriodendron branches and flat tree leaf became, to her, lily pad on green pool. She was drowned now. She could no longer struggle. Clutching out toward some definition of herself, she found that "I am Her Gart" didn't let her hold on. Her fingers slipped off; she was no longer anything. Gart, Gart, Gart and the Gart theorum of mathematical biological intention dropped out Hermione. She was not Gart, she was not Hermione, she was not any more Her Gart, what was she?

two

Her Gart stood. Her mind still trod its round. I am Her Gart, my name is Her Gart. I am Hermione Gart. I am going round and round in circles. Her Gart went on. Her feet went on. Her feet had automatically started, so automatically she continued, then stumbled as a bird whirrred its bird oblivion into heavy trees above her. Her Gart. I am Her Gart. Nothing held her, she was nothing holding to this thing: I am Hermione Gart, a failure.

Her eyes peered up into the branches. The tulip tree made thick pad, separate leaves were outstanding, separate bright leaf-discs, in shadow. Her Gart peered far, adjusting, so to speak, some psychic lens, to follow that bird. She lost the bird, tried to focus one leaf to hold her on to all leaves; she tried to concentrate on one frayed disc of green, pool or mirror that would refract image. She was nothing. She must have an image no matter how fluid, how inchoate. She tried to drag in personal infantile reflection. She said, "I'm too pretty. I'm not pretty enough." She dragged things down to the banality, "People don't want to marry me. People want to marry me. I don't want to marry people." She concluded, "One has to do something."

The woods parted to show a space of lawn, running level with branches that, in early summer, were white with flower. Dogwood blossom. Pennsylvania. Names are in people, people are in names. Sylvania. I was born here. People ought to think before they call a place Sylvania.

Pennsylvania. I am part of Sylvania. Trees. Trees. Trees. Dogwood, liriodendron with its green-yellow tulip blossoms. Trees are in people. People are in trees. Pennsylvania.

three

Pennsylvania had her. She would never get away from Pennsylvania. She knew, standing now frozen on the woodpath, that she would never get away from Pennsylvania. Pennsylvania whirled round her in cones of concentric colour, cones … concentric … conic sections was the final test she failed in. Conic sections would whirl forever round her for she had grappled with the biological definition, transferred to mathematics, found the whole thing untenable. She had found the theorem tenable until she came to conic sections and then Dr. Barton-Furness had failed her, failed her ... they had all failed her. Science, as Bertram Gart knew it, failed her ... and she was good for nothing.

Music made conic sections that whirled round in circles but she was no good for music and in Pennsylvania it had never occurred to people to paint green on green, one slice in a corner that made a triangle out of another different dimension. Such painting, it was evident to Her Gart (static, frozen in early summer on a woodpath) must lead to certifiable insanity.

Seeing in a head that had been pushed too far toward a biological-mathematical definition of the universe, a world known to her as Pennsylvania go round and form worlds within worlds (all green) Her Gart said, "I am certifiable or soon will be." She realised precisely that people can not paint nor put such things to music, and science, as she saw it, had eluded her perception. Science as Carl Gart, as Bertrand Gart defined it, had eluded her perception. Her Gart went on. "I must hurry with the letters."

She flung herself down, the letters flung down with her. Pennsylvania contained a serviceable river, more rivers than one dreamt of, torrents of white water running through deep forests. A river and white streams held nothing ... nothing ... she wanted sand under bare heels, a dog, her own, some sort of Nordic wolfhound; a dog that would race ahead of her while breakers drew up, drew back; she wanted a dog, nothing else, no one else. She wanted to be alone on some stretch of sand with dunes rising at the back and, behind sand dunes, stretches of fibrous marsh grass, Indian paintbrush and the flat, coloured water lilies.

Another country called her, the only thing that would heal, that would blot out this concentric gelatinous substance that was her perception of trees grown closer, grown near and near, grown translucent like celluloid. The circles of the trees were tree-green; she wanted the inner lining of an Atlantic breaker. There was one creature that could save her, a hound, one of her own choosing, such a hound as she had often dreamt of, and one country ... a long sea-shelf. Pennsylvania could be routed only by another: New Jersey with its flatlands and the reed grass and the salt creeks where a canoe brushed Indian paintbrush.

She felt herself go out, out into this water substance. Water was transparent, not translucent like this celluloid tree-stuff. She wanted to see through reaches of sea-wall, push on through transparencies. She wanted to get away, yet to be merged eventually with the thing she so loathed. She did not struggle toward escape of the essential. She did not sigh as people did in those days, "Well, I'll some day get to Europe." Europe existed as static little pictures, the green and mosaic of several coloured prints of Venice and Venice by moonlight. Paul Potter's Bull and the lithographic prints to ruin Turner's victory. Pictures were conclusive things and Her Gart was not conclusive. Europe would be like that. She had felt no rise of emotion at the turn of speech that led "faculty ladies" in their several manners to coo, "Pollaiuolo at Vicenza, no it was Crivelli, don't you remember, at Verona?" Verona, Vicenza, Venice even, were so many boxes of coloured beads to be strung or to be discarded. Her Gart wanted a nobler affinity. She did not know what it was she wanted.

She wanted the Point. She wanted to get to Point Pleasant. She wanted the canoe, she wanted a mythical wolfhound. She wanted to climb through walls of no visible dimension. Tree walls were visible, were to be extended to know reach of universe. Trees, no matter how elusive, in the end, walled one in. Trees were suffocation. "Claustrophobia" was a word that Her Gart had not yet assimilated.

"Agoraphobia" rang some bell when Mrs. de Raub said, "I have agoraphobia, fear of the market place you know." Yet though a distant bell rang somewhere, it followed with no wide door opening. Her Gart had no a, b, c Esperanto of world expression. She was not of the world, she was not in the world, unhappily she was not out of the world. She wanted to be out, get out but even as her mind filmed over with grey-gelatinous substance of some sort of nonthinking, of some sort of nonbeing or of nonentity, she felt psychic claw unsheathe somewhere, she felt herself clutch toward something that had no name yet.

She clung to small trivial vestiges, not knowing why she so clung. Like a psychic magpie she gathered little unearthed treasures, things she did not want, yet clung to. She said, "What made me think of that slipper pincushion with Maria Frederick embroidered in pinheads on it?" She opened eyes that snapped wide open like metallic open-and-shut doll eyes. The eyes were glass now, not filmed with psychic terror. She saw trees now as trees. She said, "How funny...I thought I had got at something and I remembered the green blue ribbon pincushion cut out like a slipper, with Maria Frederick on it."

four

It was obvious she could never find it. It was a root whose fibres held her to a small cabinet, to Dresden china brought direct by European forbears and willow patterns, tribal vestiges. Tribes must hold to relics, a cameo and a miniature with braided locks under glass on the reverse side, and several steel engravings of portraits, now ensconced in their proper galleries. Pennsylvania held her to things of no actual value, small totems that meant some tribal affinities with European races. In Europe were races who had sent out their more energetic and more mystically-inclined offspring, their scourings and their scions to Pennsylvania. In Pennsylvania, Carl Gart had found a sort of peace and a submergence of the thing that drove him, that had driven his people to New England and then West to trek back East. In Eugenia Gart, the fibres were rooted and mossed over and not to be disrupted. If Eugenia Gart pulled up her mossgrown fibres, Pennsylvania itself would ache like a jaw from which has been extracted a somewhat cumbrous molar.

Eugenia was cumbrous with her affinities but she had grown into the subsoil. Carl Gart was comforted, being at peace in the green shadows after the inland prairies and the stark glare of inimical Atlantic waters. In Hermione Gart, the two never fused and blended, she was both moss-grown, inbedded and at the same time staring with her inner vision on forever-tumbled breakers. If she went away, her spirit would break; if she stayed, she would be suffocated.

She remembered the sort of thing that would suffocate her with sentiment; an owl her grandfather had kept in an old loft, a toad her brother had found unearthed near a wellhead in the process of being mortared, a litter of tiny moles about to be crushed flat beneath a garden shovel. She remembered the sort of thing that would mean to her—Pennsylvania. She did not know that Pennsylvania bears traces of a superimposed county-England and of a luscious beauty-loving Saxony. She could not know that the birdfoot violets she so especially cherished had far Alpine kinsfolk, that the hepaticas she called "American" grew in still more luminous cluster at the base of the Grammont, along the ridges of the Jura, in rock shelves above Leman and the Bodensee.

She could not realize that there was affinity with Siberia

when long nights beat them indoors and lamps shining upon tables were the same lamps that made Lithuanians look tenderly across dark tablecloths and that made sailors in Cornwall start, listening to sea-shouts. She could not know that no race is in itself integral but that each has its fibres elsewhere. She only felt that she was a disappointment to her father, an odd duckling to her mother, an importunate overgrown, unincarnated entity that had no place here. She realized in some atavistic cranny of her numbed brain that she would be herself and at peace if she had that great hound. Jock, breathing in her face, was an ungracious substitute ... her instinct was to beat him off as he was not her dog but she saw instantly the inanity of her idea.

five

Jock was the colour of gingerbread, a homely, smutty colour. Moreover he was the colour of Minnie's over-colourful hair. "Minnie is my sister" had been enjoined on her by Eugenia who said, "In our family my mother never referred to Nell or Carnia as daughters-in-law." Minnie, Her's sister-in-law, therefore, by a rule that had roots moss-grown in Pennsylvania, became by some illogical reasoning "my sister." A sister was a creature of ebony strung with wild poppies or an image of ivory whose lithe hips made parallel and gave reflection of like parallel in a fountain basin. A sister would run, would leap, would be concealed under the autumn sumac or lie shaken with hail and wind, lost on some Lacedaemonian foothill. A sister would have companion hound, Hermione's the more lithe, the more regular in fleetness, her sister's heavier for whelping and more subtle and less of a rival in matter of speed, in manner of springing. A sister who owned such a hound … was supplanted by Minnie whose presence poor Jock must inevitably invoke.

Jock on a woodpath meant Minnie lurking somewhere, but Minnie this stifling day, would be sure to have a headache. Secure in her preknowledge of Minnie and her headache, Her took the short way. She cut through undergrowth, stood a moment on a small ridge, looked down at a near springhouse. Flies buzzed negligently over wild carrot, and Queen Anne's lace lay powder-green and powder-mauve in heavy shadow. Across a stretch of meadow were the beginnings of kitchen garden, turned-back hotbed frames, an unpretentious kennel.

Her stooped to the springhouse door, ascertained that the cream in a blue bowl had astonishingly not "turned," saw two flat pie plates sprinkled with raspberries. She stepped inside the door, heard the cold ripple of the concealed runnel that fed the flat dark stretch of springhouse water. Hermione shivered, seeing a face reflected in the water that was almost as unpleasing to her as the thought of Minnie. Forehead too high, hair too lank, eyes that stared and stared, blobs of inconsequent blackness. A face foreshortened in a slightly rippled surface may give back poor reflection. She did not consider this, remembering only that this summer was to have been her glory. This summer was to have been the summer, *the* summer for reflection, for a drawing together … the hard-earned olive chaplet. Nike, Athene gave her nothing … Love had not yet touched her. Gods stood afar off … demigods would have needed no encouragement.

Her bumped her head on the low door, dazzled by the heavy fall of sunlight. She saw a slight trail of dust hanging above the yew trees. Down the road someone had turned, skirting the Farrand meadows. The Farrands even had found Pennsylvania "dull" and "unrewarding" since the death of Russell Farrand.

Her rarely thought of the Farrands, people with too much money. Strung to a pith of loyalty to her "class," she had rarely dared consider what "money" could do. "The Farrands are really nice," Eugenia put in, "though, you know" (tolerantly) "business people."

Business people seldom found their way to Gart Grange. It was Minnie's constant wail that "Aunt Lydia had entertained differently in Philadelphia." There was an Aunt Lydia, or had been, whose only tangible totem was a pin tray and two Victorian silver-topped dressing-table boxes which had appeared some days after Minnie's wedding. Aunt Lydia had promised this, had promised that, had, it appeared on careful scrutiny, an address in *North* Philadelphia which after all (Eugenia said) explained it. Come and go of odd "university ladies," too many sometimes and a dull perception that she, Her Gart, knew the very best people who after all (in Philadelphia) were so distinguished in their modest way and in their European affinities that she knew she would have small hope of cutting through them with any ulterior criticism. There was one thing left her to criticise ... it was Her Gart precisely.

"I know that I'm too old here" answered it. She was too old for this; "Mrs. Tryon have another teacake." Her mathematics and her biology hadn't given her what she dreamed of. Only now she knew that failing at the end meant fresh barriers, fresh chains, a mesh here. The degree almost gained would have been redemption, something she hardly realized, tutoring or something, teaching ... something she had an inkling would bring her in, would have brought her in a "salary." Demigods were far off ... but gods were watching. She had the temerity to boast some sort of odd mind, the sort of thing that, in Philadelphia, could not see cones as of light set within cones, as of darkness. "I failed in conic sections."

The mind, galvanized almost to the point of extinction, had turned inward, had thrust Her Gart backward. The mind that had been a sort of lure, "Come here, a little further," had denied Her. The gateway had been reached but at the last the gate had been slammed on Her. Her did not realize that the watching-near God had slammed a gate so that she should attain a wider vision. In Philadelphia people did not realize that life went on in varying dimension, here a starfish and there a point of fibrous peony stalk with a snail clinging underneath it. Pictures of that sort with a crane shadow passing across a wild cherry half in blossom would have explained something of the sort of painting that she would not have known existed. There was a sort of "composition" of elements that her mind, fused to the breaking point, now apprehended. The catch was that her perception was ahead of her definition. She could put no name to the things she apprehended, felt vaguely that her mother should have insisted on her going on with music.

Music might have caught the trail of the grass as she ran on across the meadow and the deep note made by a fabulous bee that sprung into vision, blotting out the edge of the stables, almost blotting out the sun itself with its magnified magnificent underbelly and the roar of its sort of booming. The boom of the bee in her ear, his presence like an eclipse across the sun brought visual image of the sort of thing she sought for … it had not occurred to Her to try and put the thing in writing.

II

one

Minnie met Her by the steps. Minnie said, "You stopped at the post office," flung out like a sort of challenge. Minnie continued, "Are there any letters?" Her fumbled with the lot, trying not to have to obliterate the memory of an eclipse of the sun by a huge bee (under a magnifying glass) by having to look at Minnie.

A huge bee lifted Her on translucent wings, flung straight upward, her legs either side of the stiff propeller-whirr of the wings, hung down into space. Her saw trees fly past her, trees darting downward, herself static. Trees showed clear in outline, but darker, all one colour, colour of dark cedars. Translucence of beewing veiled the terror of trees' protoplasmic function. Her rode toward a new realization ... "No, no letters," not lifting her face to Minnie.

Opposite in the shadow of the porch, she sensed fragrance, tendrils of honeysuckle blossom, café-au-lait she knew and wax-white like checkerberries. She opened her eyes. At her feet, heliotrope ... Minnie was there waiting for the letters. A face would loom at her, freckles magnified across a drawn pale countenance. She would hate Minnie and lifting her eyes to meet those, round, well-set but drained of any colour, Her would force, "Oh Minnie ... what a *lovely* dress you've got on." Minnie must be flattered, compliment must fly and click and turn heels and bend gallantly. It was obvious that Minnie too was lonely though in an opposite direction. "I think Minnie, there's no letter."

Jock bounded off in the direction of the toolhouse, leapt ecstatically, came back. Her pushed off Jock. Minnie must never see that other people or other people's dogs liked Her. It was inevitable occasion, "Nobody loves me." Minnie had married Bertrand Gart. My brother Bertrand Gart. Hermione hid her brother in her gesture, braced, apologetic, by the porch step. I won't depend on Gart for greatness. Minnie was like some fraction to which everything had to be reduced. Minnie's very presence depreciated the house front, steps, the symmetrical recumbent jade pillars of low carefully clipped terrace. Minnie had on black stockings, white shoes, semitransparent sprigged organdie. Don't let her see I see her ruffles are set crooked. Straighten shoulders, don't let Minnie see how terribly black stockings with soiled white shoes upset me. "What is that … spray thing I mean in your new organdie?" Ringed, washed-out blue eyes, Minnie and her eternal headaches. Escape, escape Minnie. "But there are" (more business) "letters." Hermione handed Minnie Bertrand Gart's letters affecting not to know that Minnie wanted the whole lot, was waiting for the whole lot, had just said, "I'll take the lot to father."

Words that had not (in Philadelphia) been invented, beat about them: Oedipus complex, inferiority complex, claustrophobia. Words beat and sizzled and a word bent backward like a saw in a sawmill reversed, turned inward, to work horrible destruction. The word "father" as Minnie spoke it, reversed itself inward, tore at the inner lining of the thing called Her Gart. It tore her inner being so that she stood stiff, alert, trying in some undefined and ineffectual manner to be "fair." What was it Minnie did to her, reversing machinery so that a simple word "father" wrought such untoward havoc?

"Father" went with a river, a leap out from a boat, a forest where oaks obligingly dropped cups and saucers, acorns and their scattered woodhusks. Cups and saucers set upright

on a flat stone while the wood was ringed with frail lavender, the low leafless Quaker-ladies or as some called them,
bluets. "Father" was a run forward, a plunge backward; that
thing had now no visible embodiment. Nevertheless to hear
Minnie say "father" was a two-edged theft. It stole from Her
a presence that left her (no one else had) alone and that again
stole from her a presence: the thing that would have had that
other hound, twin hounds, fleet-footed, the half of herself
that was forever missing. If her father was also the father to ...
this thing, then the half of her, that twin-self sister would be
forever blighted. Hermione knew she was fantastically overwrought, bending down closer, then hiding her face to explain, "Jock only likes me as I take him to get letters."

Jock sometimes carried a newspaper ... but Hermione could
not trust him not to drop the letters. She tried to concentrate
on Jock ... remembering how Minnie had said "father." It
was still incredible to Hermione, though she tried to fend off
odd superstition, that she and Minnie should call the same
person "father." Hiding her face against the homely ginger of
Jock's soft wool, she tried to dissemble: "Minnie, I *will* take
him to the lake creek, he needs a whole day bathing." Minnie
would not answer. There was no use thinking that she would
ever answer. Minnie was there, a barometer that showed always glowering weather. Her eyes were the colour of mauve
blotting paper that has faded almost white and is smudged
with inkmarks. The inkmarks must be because Minnie had a
headache, rings under Minnie's woebegone, sad eyes. It was
incredible how a creature of Minnie's disposition could take it
out of everyone. She set for them all a standard, "At our Aunt
Lydia's." Aunt Lydia had never even deigned to call on Minnie,
perhaps there was no Lydia ... silver boxes late for a wedding,
don't prove anything.

craving, the craving of the fiend almost for his narcotic. Bertrand later turned to mathematics. Hermione, in the same spirit, later turned to Bertrand's bookshelves. Bertrand had bought her *Jane Eyre*, she would be one with Bertrand. Someone should have told Her that Bertrand Gart's anodyne would be alien to her. Bertrand Gart's incredible gift for mathematics was his anesthesia. Hermione reached out ... but Celestial Mechanics proved a barrier. She had failed, even the beginning, Conic Sections. She had failed to reach Bertrand. She had failed, though she could not have then defined it, to attain the anesthesia that her odd brain sought for.

How could anyone predict that Bertrand would marry Minnie? Nowadays huge volumes predict such things. You may read huge volumes, find names for these things. In those days those astounding Freudian and post-Freudian volumes had not found their way into the common library. Hermione Gart would have been astounded in those days to learn that "Oedipus" links up with the most modern prophets. She did not think of Greek, except in so far as Calypso was the name of an island in a neighboring river where she and Bertrand had once gone to find wild adder's-tongue and maidenhair fern. Pondlilies in the half-stagnant reaches of the little side streams had been connected in her mind with Bertrand. "Bertrand, why is the island called Calypso's Island?" Bertrand had then told Her. "It's the name of a sort of goddess in the Greek Mythology."

The Greek Mythology existed for Her only in the vaguest outline. It existed for Her in so much as Pennsylvania existed. "Bertrand, why do they call mockorange Philadelphus? Is it because it is from Philadelphia?" Bertrand answered every question anyone could ask him. Bertrand said, "No. It's because of Ptolemy Philadelphus in Egypt." Now how did Bertrand know that? Obviously, because he had that flower book on his shelves. Later he began his connecting "link," his theorum of general mathematical biological affinity. "Bertrand ... why do they call mock orange Philadelphus?"

How could anyone predict that Bertrand would marry Minnie? He didn't know many "girls." One day Bertrand called Hermione upstairs. He said "I have something to show you!" Bertrand had a way of producing snakes' eggs like the proverbial magician from the top-hat or raccoons or even minute wild birds or moles which he would manage to extract from nests and put back without Tim the gardener knowing. Bertrand held something in his hands as he had held that tiny mole that day. Hermione said, "What is it?" Bertrand's eyes glowered in a strange way. His face was whiter even than usual. Hermione gave up guessing. He let it slip from his hands. It was the colour of the underleaf of the adder's-tongue they had found on Calypso's Island. It was burnt red-brick colour. Even then, staring, Hermione thought it might yet be some new-found serpent.

She couldn't grasp what it was, even when she saw it. She stared at this thing as if the red-brown strand of poor little Minnie Hurloe's hair had been all the writhing horrors of the famed Medusa. She couldn't even then make any formal gesture. "Bertie ..."

She knew then as she saw it what it must be. She had never considered seriously the little woman that Bertrand had one day brought out to see them. She had patronized Minnie Hurloe, been kind to her since she was so obviously not important. She remembered the little squeal that Minnie had affected at the sight of the raccoon that Bertrand had taken them to see behind the wild-cherry at the far field hedge. Minnie was however not now to be disregarded. In that red lock, was the whole of Minnie Hurloe.

three

Mrs. Bertrand Gart regarded Hermione Gart, standing, head lowered, listlessly shaping an odd assortment of envelopes that wouldn't fit together. One longish yellow envelope protruded ... she lost sight of the others, trying to make the longish yellow envelope fit the others. Her eyes saw nothing but envelopes; Minnie still covertly demanded the lot, wanted to go over them, sort them herself, dash in and out, looking for people, Hermione's little job. Minnie had taken so many little jobs, "But you never let *me* do the flowers." Hermione would not let Minnie take the letters. Minnie would not be able to remember ... anything ... her headache always interfered when there were uninteresting things to do. "I never *dare* take anything."

Minnie stood afar off blighting the garden because once she had almost pruned away a little old-fashioned ribbon-rose that had been put there by Her's grandmother, out of her own garden. Things that needed intuition ... how can you tell anybody? That garden had been a riot of bleeding-heart and columbine; "My mother liked bleeding-heart, columbine and johnny-jump-ups," Eugenia's fervid explanation of that corner. How could anyone tell anyone about things? "Mother wasn't angry, Minnie, it was just a sort of sentiment ..." How could anyone hope ever to explain to Minnie that that particular little bush hadn't ever been touched by anyone, a sort of sacrament, preserving a tiny figure with white cap and apron, snipping with a disproportionate pair of garden scissors. Death was horrible. The old lady had fallen down in the heat, under that same rose-tree.

Death and life were inexorably entangled. The whole place

was a graveyard. Minnie was haunted by things that had no palpable explanation. It was impossible to begin to try to explain to Minnie. Certain days of the year were set aside, inexorable Chinese-like fidelity of Eugenia. Hermione could not keep track of what she called in her childhood Eugenia's "still days." How could, then, poor Minnie?

"No, Minnie, mother's not hurt … it's just … it's just …" It was so impossible to rise from ashes, to drag out things that she herself didn't dare face. Hermione must be loyal to Eugenia; it was impossible to tell Minnie. She compromised, "family matters." Minnie would flare up "You leave me out of everything." Hermione went so far as to chafe the bare hot hands of Minnie. "Don't be hysterical … she lost … she lost a baby." It was impossible to explain to Minnie that the baby was one between herself and Bertrand, a girl, stillborn. "I didn't know there was another baby." "There wasn't exactly. I mean it didn't breathe … it wasn't buried with the others." The whole thing was too horrible. How explain to Minnie a sentiment about a stillborn child?

Minnie was right. In some horrible torturous cranny of her inferior little being, she was right however. There was reason in her hysteria, in her tantrums … but how explain? In order to explain to Minnie, Hermione would have to explain to herself things that had no palpable explanation.

Shadow crept up, heavy metal toward the lawn step. If the shadow crept further it would cut Her down, a black blade of black-scythe, the little old lady haunted that corner of the garden. The little old lady dominated a rose-ribbon, a ribbon-rose forever. Shouldn't Eugenia rather have let Minnie prune the bush down? It was obviously (or had then been) the one untidy corner of the kitchen garden. The kitchen garden was more or less understood to be common property. A little old lady with great scissors ... Minnie. Minnie tyrannized with her eternal headaches, "The specialist said I might die at any minute." Minnie had washed-out, ringed-round pale eyes, the sort of person that would live forever.

Her Gart knew prophetically that Gart would fall, be cut through by railroads, factory chimneys, that Bertrand and Carl Gart (and even the Gart formula?) would be extinguished but not Minnie. The Grange shadow lengthened, came near, it would cut her feet off. Imperiously, without letting Her say another word to Minnie, her ankles dragged Her forward. Her ankles, concentrated terror (that scythe shadow) impelled Her Gart across the wide porch ... a hand, touching the housefront found sanctuary at an altar. Her pushed through the screen door.

III

one

Sanctuary spilled fragrance, the cool hall. There was a squat bowl set on a low corner table. She had set the lilies there herself, remarked that they still stood upright, a shoulder brushing might upset them. Those flat lotus-pod-shaped stemholders were better than the glass ones. Her eyes, too wide, opened, blurred over the impression. Like the first colour-impressionist she saw blobs, perceived matte colour as pure tone. The wood-lilies were thumbed in from a laden palette. Orange was put in, with a thumb, against Van Dyke brown of seasoned woodwork. Her let eyes refocus, saw things clearly, mid-Victorian "interior." The mid-Victorian "interior" became again classic, Flemish, something out of a long gallery, "Flemish school" from those eternal volumes laid flat, with charts and diagrams, on a carpet, threadbare upstairs, downstairs with woolly fringes before an open fireplace. Every sort of school of painting must sustain Her. Twin candlesticks gave out another light, and one pewter platter with dents. The lilies made the place live. Did I stare too hard at Minnie?

Minnie was zinnia-colour, no colour of wild-lilies. A zinnia was a flat vegetable sponge, sucking up sun, never giving out sun. Those lilies were the sun-self, spotted she knew like the wings of beetles. Beetle-lilies. Did Minnie see I saw her black stockings with white slippers? She didn't see I saw her. "She didn't see I saw her" repeated time on end and in time to the giant clock-tick, hypnotized, numbed Her. She needed to be hypnotized, numbed; a growing dislike of Minnie brought with it renewal of rodent guilt gnawing. "But what can one do for her" didn't do much good. "It's this summer weather … she didn't see I saw her."

The screen door hadn't made the customary little click. Her turned back to see to it. Gart lawn made a jade triangle and the box hedge at the back merged so flatly with the forest that forest and box made one barrier; Gart, Gart barrier. Her pulled to the screen door, clicked it inside … must keep it fastened. She waded back down the hall where lilies reflected lilies in bright surface of dark parquet floor. Under her feet there were waxed lozenges of wood, fitted carefully to lozenges of waxed wood. The familiar slippery woodwork brought familiar admonition, "Be careful of the hall floor."

The mind of Her Gart was a patchwork of indefinable association. She must escape Gart and Gart Grange, the Nessus shirt of guilt, phobia, rehabilitation. To be rehabilitated meant tearing fibre and flesh out with the Nessus shirt of "Be careful of the hall floor," and Minnie's "I know you never liked me."

Her Gart clutched at the upright stairpost, it was buoy to her drowning. The floor went round and the smeared-up blobs of impressionistic lilies. She clung to one thing: "This bit of Berne carved wood is pretty." She perceived that she had picked up the little tray for visiting cards, to which the other little table, with wings eternally down-folded, was permanently dedicated. The Berne wood was mellow, contrasted with the lacquer-like surface of the little table, it seemed almost porous; strange tobacco-coloured wood that didn't go, that did go with their house. The European wood seemed soft, permeable, like pine-needles. In contrast, Her thought appositely, their liriodendron and magnolia seemed hard ebony. Trees, trees, trees … this particular plaque of grape and grape leaf was originally meant perhaps for breadtray or fruit platter. The thing had taken on character with years, was right here. Minnie had a way of making Eugenia and her rightness and discrimination wrong. How *has* Eugenia stood it? Minnie was gaping at Her, everywhere she looked was Minnie. Something's happened, something's happened to Gart, everywhere; in the bowl of slightly jaded (she saw now coming nearer) lilies, "I must change those lilies," in the family portrait of Pius Wood (Minnie insisted was *not* a Benjamin West), in the plaque of grape and flat grape leaf to hold visiting cards. Things make people, people make things. Minnie made Gart hallway and the wood lilies and Pius Wood so much junk. She ate into things, predicted inferiority complex, words that had no place in the consciousness of Her.

Words beat and formed unformulated syllables. Her didn't understand Gart and Bertrand and Carl and the acid, acid Minnie that ate into them ... call it life so simply. I'm not at home in Gart. I'm not at home out of Gart. I am swing-swing between worlds, people, things exist in opposite dimension. She waded through more darkness, into another light patch. The dining room was empty. I'll get fresh flowers here too. She struck another swing door with flat narrow hand and plunged into outer darkness. She felt her way along the narrow long passage, automatically with flat hand struck another swing door. It opened outward, revealed space, cool red tiles, brick red that ran toward a funnel of green that was the open window. The unscreened window looked out on green on green on green. "Mandy, I don't see, with that window wide open that way, how you can keep the flies out."

Her stepped precisely on flat tiles, a child game remembered. Her foot was just too long to avoid crack in tile. Her feet had been small in the large square of tile, had been bigger, had almost not fitted. Her feet did not fit any longer into the kitchen tiles. Mandy was stoning cherries. Plunge hands into the wide deep corn-coloured bowl and help Mandy. "Mandy, I don't see how you keep the flies out." Reprimand Mandy, find some excuse to stay here.

She had found the excuse, realized what had brought her, "Oh, your letter." Mandy's letter was postmarked Georgia. It was the usual letter. The carefully-spaced writing was more conventionally careful than any of the writing on any of the letters. Postmarks on letters. There was the usual bundle. She had forgotten what had brought her to the kitchen. It was Mandy's letter.

two

"Here's your letter, Mandy." Her placed the letter carefully beside the deep bowl. Deep bowl holding water, cherries sunk to the bottom of the great bowl, not their black cherries, not their red cherries, not their ox-heart cherries. "Whose are these cherries? I thought we'd gathered all the cherries." "That little back-at-the-hedge tree. No one ever touches it." "That's not a cherry tree for picking. Once Grandmama made cherry brandy from it but it wasn't even good for cherry brandy. That little back-hedge tree isn't meant for picking." "I tell you no black man is ever good at picking. I tell you Tim done miss the best tree."

"Cherry picking isn't rightly part of gardening." Her fell into the rhythm of Mandy's speech, the moment she began to speak to Mandy, "A gardener is a gardener, a black gardener is as good as a white gardener. There's no need *dis*-criminating." Mandy would appreciate that last affectation.

"*Dis*-criminating," she went on with it, let it sink into Mandy's appreciative consciousness (there was no one for appreciating the fine distinctions of the English language like their

Mandy) "there *is* no use. Man is man. A man climbs a tree with a basket, brings it back full, strips the tree of cherries." "You don't know what you're saying. A man ain't a man. A black man is a black man. You don't get no black man rightly to pick cherries." "I don't see that a black man makes any difference." They could go on this way for hours, argue anthropomorphic-ally. Argument took on abstraction like a Platonic dialogue with Mandy, finesse, aplomb, subtlety. "I don't see that a black man makes any difference ..."

Her slipped a white hand into the deep bowl, black arm lifted from the deep bowl. White hand clutched hard smooth pebble-surface of berries, eyes discriminated, "These things aren't worth cooking." "These yere makes better jam than oth-ers." Mandy had her formula. This, this, this. Fish, somedays, weren't eatable. Berries, certain days, weren't worth picking. Sun rose and sun set. The rising of the Pleiades, things out of Virgil, out of Hesiod, influenced Mandy. "Nonsense." The kids, the Hyades, the Pleiades. Things out of Hesiod made Mandy cook beans on Tuesday. "Well, then who in this yere house makes better jam than we do?" "We being Mandy, no one in this or any house. But these are wild things." "Wild black cher-ries picked a'Monday." "Mandy—you're mad, Mandy."

You're not mad, Mandy. Garden cherries were over long since. These were small bitter wild ones. "Not worth cooking." Red-black made mulberry-coloured black-red stain on Her's white wrist. "They're not worth all this trouble."

three

Flat hand beat open the swing door. Darkness. The other door. "I must get some fresh azaleas." Wild azaleas were drop-ping honeysucklelike long florets on the dining room table.

"It's incredibly hot suddenly." Mind swung to and fro. It's hot, it's hot, it's too hot suddenly.

Hermione saw the letter on the top of the fat wedge of letters was addressed "Miss Gart." It was a thin letter, foreign thin envelope, thin grey washed-out sea-colour. She saw the letter was from George. I must have missed it. She swung to and fro in the dining room, the bowl of half-withered azaleas swung to and fro in the dining room. It's from George.

She sat down on a hard upright dining room chair set against the side wall. The screened dining room window showed Gart lawn this side of the stable wall, grey as covered with sea mist. It's too hot here. Gart is set like a bowl in this wood. It's too hot here. A canoe seemed rippling between weeds. If I could go alone to Point Pleasant but Eugenia's given the cottage to Minnie for the summer … Hermione wanted to go alone, to get away from this thing (huge scrawled-over handwriting taking up, in one sentence, the whole of a wide square of distinguished thin sea-grey paper): "Hermione, I'm coming back to Gawd's own god-damn country."

"George is coming back." Hermione spoke lifelessly to Eugenia. Eugenia was sitting in the little morning room that was no more than a glassed-in conservatory sort of odd-cupboard, except for the little shallow step down, almost part of the dining room. Her had caught that glimpse of Eugenia as she looked up from her letter. She said, "George is coming back," and trailed lifelessly after her own words toward Eugenia out of the dining room into the little morning room to get away from the dining room wall that was swinging, swinging, that was swinging a bowl of half-wilted wild azaleas with it.

"It's incredibly hot." "Yes, isn't it? George who?" "George." She had forgotten the name of George. "Why *George* …" "Not that incredible Lowndes person?" "Yes, wasn't he? I mean incredible." "Why has he written to you?" "I don't know." "Where has he written to you?" "Why here, to the Grange, Werby, Delaware County, Pennsylvania." "Stupid. I don't mean—I mean where was he written *from?*" "Why didn't you say from? He's written me from—from Italy." "I remember—" Eugenia would be remembering. Everyone remembered something. Mandy remembered Georgia. "Venice that spring—" Everything was something to everyone but nothing was anything to Her.

I am Her. I am Hermione. I want to get away to the sea. "Why must Minnie have the cottage?"

Hermione picked up the thin grey envelope lying in the creased summer material of her flowered dress. A tiny bow of the same flowered material chafed at her throat. She pulled at the round opening of the same material, fanned herself vigorously with the thin wide square of foreign paper. The wind made only the slightest little flutter of the ribbon on her undergarment; things stuck fast, she remembered she had on only one straight one-piece undergarment, the dress was almost thick enough not to see through.

She felt now she mustn't get up, Eugenia would be sure to see she had no petticoat on. She felt too the whole linen one-piece dress would bear imprint of her hot sides, her back ... her legs stretched under the one-piece summer garment ... "Where from?" Her Gart started upright, stopped erratic fanning. "... from? Why, the Grange woods, I ran back the short way ... the cream hasn't even curdled." "I said Lowndes, where," Eugenia shouted as if Her were a little deaf, staring with wide eyes as the deaf do, "has this Lowndes written you *from?*"

"Oh—from—" Her Gart turned over the bit of paper. It occurred to her again that it was incredible (Eugenia was right) and preposterous that George should say just that, "Gawd's own god-damn country." Her shoulder blades jabbed uncomfortably as she let herself plop back into the wooden armchair. The arms of the chair were cooler than her hot arms. She rested her arms along the chair arms, the letter waved negligently up and down in one hand. "How should I know, mother?"

"Well, darling, can't you read it? Where does he say he's staying." "He doesn't say where, mother." "Well, where is the letter postmarked?" "I think it's ... I think it's Italy. I suppose he's still in Venice." The name did nothing to her, recalled nothing but some tiresome prints in the volume of the Schools of Painting that she didn't care for, and a general feeling of a crowd, the sort of thing she had avoided priggishly, even in real childhood, shoot-the-shoots, carnival of Venice. Say "Venice" and you say "Carnival" and are pushed into an open rowboat to bump and shriek, shooting shoots, with other preadolescents. That hadn't lately happened ... Venice did *nothing* to her.

Not so with Eugenia who sighed, "Venice." Eugenia went on sewing. She dropped her sewing. "Are the other letters for your father?" "I think so." Her mother counted out the letters, "There're none for Bertrand." "But Minnie's had hers." "Here's one here—girls at Bryn Mawr." Someone from a long distance said "Girls at Bryn Mawr." It was Eugenia speaking.

"I think this is for you too. It looks like one of your girls at Bryn Mawr." Her took the envelope with its stereotyped, carefully "cultivated" writing going off at the edges. Nellie Thorpe. "It's from Nellie Thorpe."

four

Nellie Thorpe in her hand. George. Two people utterly inapposite, never coming together at all in any compartment of her compartmented mind. My mind is breaking up like molecules in test tubes. Molecules all held together, breaking down in this furnace heat. She went into the hall. The screen door was open again.

She closed the screen door with an irritated hopeless gesture, slam-and-bang-to and trying it again to make sure there wasn't any odd misfitting rough edge, said, "It's *agacé.*" The thing annoyed her, *agacé* is the word. George was *agacé* by this, by this in what he called Gawd's own country. Gawd's own god-damn country. *Agacé. C'est agaçant.* The screen door was horribly *agaçant.* She found the stairhead, her usual formula of running fingers over the carved plaque of grape and flat leaf. Her wrist was still smudged with wild cherry stain. I must get some fresh azaleas. In her room, she decided not to throw herself on the bed, she would drift away. She would feel heavier seated stonily upright before her own desk.

From her desk, set square in the middle of her desk, Eugenia looked at her. There was a dart in her hair fluffed out, smooth above small ears. The dress was cut mathematically square. The 1880 coiffure was Hellenistic. Eugenia was not Hellenistic, she was Eleusinian. Eugenia is Eleusinian. My father is Athenian.

From the downstairs hallway Jock was barking, slipping of claw feet on polished wood, scuffling and thud—it must be Mandy chasing him from the kitchen. I told Mandy she should shut the window. Jock like a greyhound would be pulled out like a reflection of Jock seen in rippled water. Jock and Jock would be lightning succeeding lightning in angular bright pattern. Jock must have leapt through the window. I told Mandy she should close it. The broom, it must be the broom, went thud and Jock the other side of the slammed-to screen door said ouch-ouch dramatically. Mandy shouldn't hit Jock that way. It's so insulting to him.

There was a small red Temple Shakespeare one side of Eugenia's picture, the other side was a blue book matching it. The *Mahabharata?* One of those translations anyway. Temple Shakespeare. I am out of the Temple Shakespeare. I am out of *The Winter's Tale.* It was my grandfather's idea to call me something out of Shakespeare. Her picked up the limp volume. Leather was limp and smelt of innumerable compartments in her odd mind. Leather, smelling like that, wafted through and through innumerable compartments bringing dispersed elements and jaded edges together, running like healing water across an arid waste of triangle and star-cluster and names of biological intention. Atoms were held together like limp grasses gone arid, filled with healing rain drops. *Lilies of all kinds* ... I am out of this book.

She picked up the other book. It had a like effect upon her but more potently. Water lying filled with weeds and lily-pads ... lilies of all kinds ... became even more fluid, was being taken up and up, element (out of chemistry) become vapour. The water lying so pure became vapour, she would be lifted up, drunk up, vanished ... I am the word AUM.

Hermione dropped the volume. This frightened her. God is in a word. God is in a word. God is in HER. She said, "HER, HER, HER. I am Her, I am Hermione ... I am the word AUM." This frightened her. She slid out of the chair before the desk, still clutching her letters, seated herself in the other little low sewing-chair (in which she never sewed) pulled sideways, three-quarters facing the window. Her back was to the desk, to Eugenia, to the *Winter's Tale,* to the other little volume. She tried to forget the other little volume. "I am the word AUM" frightened her. She tried to forget the word AUM, said "UM, EM, HEM" clearing her throat, wondered if she had offended something, clearing her throat trying to forget the word ... I

am the word … the word was with God …. I am the word …
HER.

Hermione Gart hugged HER to Hermione Gart. I am HER.
The thing was necessary. It was necessary to hug this thing to
herself. It was a weight holding her down, keeping her down.
Her own name was ballast to her lightheadedness. She would
be heavier somehow sitting in the low chair than flung tossed
down like some tree branch on the wide bed. I am Hermione.

George is George. George or Georgio. George is not Georg
(she pronounced it Teutonically, heavily stressed *Gay*-org).
Georg is too hard, he is not Georg. Georges (she softened it
in the Gallic manner) better suits him. He is possibly Georges
but he is nearer Georgio. There is something harlequin about
George making him write simply that on a beautiful light
piece of foreign paper. He might have said so much on that
sea-grey slip of paper. The paper had been so light, slipped
in somehow between the letters; now she realized why she
had not given over all the letters to Minnie. She must have
somehow known the thin letter was there, slipped sidewise.
She must have somehow sensed it. She had not handed over all
the letters to Minnie, standing there by the lawn step, covertly
demanding them. She had not given in to Minnie. She usually
did give in to Minnie. It was easiest in the long run to give in
to Minnie. Minnie was obsessed with Minnie. We are all obsessed with something. I am obsessed at this moment by the
fear of loosing an … obsession. She opened the second letter.

She began somewhere about the middle, "I never know
what to call you, you are fey with the only wildness that per-
tains to ultimate solution—," Hermione turned the page,
skipped to the end, "so you must come." She turned back,
tried to gather the gist of the matter without being too bored
to read it, "Go straight to the telephone." She gave up, started

over again—"You are fey with the only wildness." Oh here was what it all was, there was someone else who was fey too. "Now get this into your human consciousness if you are so far human as to use a telephone, I am 2231 Spruce. Go straight to the telephone—come to see me—to see a girl I want to see you."

Hermione Gart flung aside the letter. A bird rustled the deflowered tendrils of the wisteria, the mock orange bush beneath her window was now, too, all but over. "To see a girl I want to see you." No, she wouldn't see that pseudoliterary little snob, Nellie Thorpe. "To see a girl I want you to see—go straight to the telephone." George had written on that other bit of paper, "I am coming back to Gawd's own god-damn country" like a harlequin.

IV

one

Gart and Gart sat facing Gart and Gart. Bertrand Gart picked up the salt cellar, was making a pattern with it and the pepper pot and his little pearl-handled fruitknife. He dropped the pearl-handled fruitknife, picked it up again and ran it along the edge of the damask wall-of-Troy pattern on the table-cloth. Hermione watched him, watched Eugenia, slid covert glances at Minnie. Minnie would be too immersed in soup to notice. "I'm sorry mother but you know I can't eat thick soup." Minnie would or would not say that, the soup wasn't so very thick. Celery was the salty thing that flavoured it. Mandy dried their own celery-root, made a sort of dried herb lasting through the summer. Eugenia didn't like it. Eugenia hadn't noticed it. Carl Gart was dabbing at his white Pericles moustache with a table napkin. The table napkins had rose-pattern, didn't match the tablecloth. Minnie was saying "It wasn't Jock's fault. It was Mandy's."

Mandy was coming back. Don't, don't let Mandy hear you. Mandy hated Minnie. Shoving dishes at her, there was always that moment of waiting … Mandy hadn't heard her. "Coppard tells me the Copenhagen volume hasn't any more than the last series of Minnenberg's." "Minnenberg found his line *after* the younger Coppard." "Coppard had the elements but Minnenberg made the final constation." "Minnenberg simply picked up the thread where Coppard dropped it. He went on and on with the same pattern." "Coppard is pure design, Minnenberg mere pyrotechnics." "Coppard missed out through lack of knowledge of psychology." "… his thought applied on

33

the plane of minus-plus as Dorrensten presented it." "Newton made gravitation accessible to mob mind with his ripe apple. So Coppard designing the parallel of plus-minus (with of course the usual sheer mechanical devices as applied in textbooks of, say, chemistry) made the ultra-violet rays come along in line with mathematics. I mean it's simply linking up the thing with mathematics."

"Mother. I said it wasn't Jock, but Mandy." "Shh-shh, don't let Mandy hear you." "If you would keep the salt in the oven, it wouldn't get so grey. Grey salt. If you would tell Mandy to keep the salt in the oven ..." "The usual demonstration wouldn't be applicable ..." "I know it's Coppard's doing ..." "There was the obvious allowance to be made. Coppard was a Dane. Minnenberg a German." "We don't agree on that mere nationalistic question. After all ..."

"After all" went trailing off into names, people, places. Hermione gave up following. It always ended in "after all" waving like a banner in the torn air. The air was torn, frayed by the sharp electric thought-waves of Gart and Gart facing each other across a narrow strip of damask. They hurl things at one another across the table-cloth like two arctic explorers who have both discovered the north pole, each proving to the other, across chasms of frozen silence, that his is the original discovery. They would drag up people, things from Ptolemy to Pericles to Phidias (no not Phidias) to ... up, up, up and down, down the line till one was dizzy. There was no use trying to follow Gart and Gart into the frozen silence ... "Mother you might make her." "I can't insist. Mandy has quite enough work." "It's so odd your idea of servants. She ought to wear a white cap. Now Mrs. Banes was saying ..." "Mandy looks trim enough in her dark handkerchief." "You ought to get someone younger." "Mandy's young enough for us here."

How long would mama stand it? Eugenia, Hermione knew, would go on, go on, go on keeping up a secondary line of dialogue with Minnie, for the moment Minnie was left to her own devices Hermione knew, Eugenia knew, Minnie would nag at Bertrand. She was now nagging. "*Bertie.* You are so awkward."

Bertrand Gart had sliced a neat knife-edge into the worn thin linen of the cloth. A neat knife-edge slipped into the wall-of-Troy tablecloth. "*Bertie.* We were never allowed to play with knives as children." Minnie accused Bertie of this, of that, getting it across to Eugenia that Bertie hadn't been brought up properly. "He never hangs up his towel in the bathroom. It's the *wives* who always suffer."

two

"I wish you would come with us." "Thanks, Bertrand." "I wish you would come along to Point Pleasant with us. You *used* to like it." "I do like it." I wish you would come with us ran rhythm with their rockers (I wish you would come with us) on the dark porch—I wish you would come with us. Did Bertie really wish that? Bertie. I called Bertrand Bertie. I never call Bertrand Bertie since Minnie started calling him Bert. Bertrand. Bertie. I called Bertrand Bertie. "I wish you would come with us." Words went on and on across the darkness and a great giant wing brushed down from the dark corner, just lit by some upstairs window, a triangle of light across the upright far pillar of the far end of the porch.

"Minnie wants us to have the whole thing wired in, netted." Her said that from somewhere to Bertrand for there was no use, no use at all saying anything to Bertrand about anything that mattered. "Minnie wants—Minnie says." Minnie was so near, she was probably leaning out of the upstairs window listening. Minnie was always listening. Minnie must be listening somewhere, she was everywhere, she was always listening.

Clear throat, Em, Um, Hem. Aum. It was AUM. I am the word AUM. God was in a word. A moth was responsible for that giant cloud darkening the clear cut-off edge of light that cut across the far end of the porch. "The upstairs window's open. It must be Minnie upstairs."

Say "It must be Minnie," drag in Minnie. Minnie was always listening. "Minnie wants the thing wired." It wasn't Minnie upstairs. Minnie, a grey-white elemental, emerged inexplicably from behind a pillar. She left the light on upstairs so we would think she was in her room. Minnie crept toward them. Minnie *had* been listening.

"When are you and Bertrand going to the cottage?" "Eugenia says immediately. Day after tomorrow even." "Oh, it's so ho-ot to talk of packing. Oh it's so ho-*ot*." "Yes. *Isn't* it? Isn't it suffocating?" "I suffer so. None of you realize how this heat affects me." "Yes. The heat. Isn't it too terrible? Eugenia was saying that she wanted you to get off, to get away immediately." "Oh—*mother*." "Yes. Eugenia was saying—."

Rock, rock in the rocking chair, rock, rock in the rocking chair. A great beetle flung in, humped against the window at the back of the rocking chair. Beat his nose on the wire screen, fell with a thud, recovered, crawled limply and darted off miraculously recovered, in another direction. "Now why did that beetle go in that direction?" "Wh-aaat?" "I said, mother was speaking of it." Minnie had hypnotized her into saying mother. The person Minnie calls mother is not my mother. My mother is Eugenia. "Eugenia was saying ..."

Rock, rock, skrun-ccch. "You've stepped on a beetle." "I haven't." "Don't tell me it's a tree toad." Rock, rock, skrun-ch.

"This place is simply crawling. I think it positively evil to allow it." "Yes. I was saying to Bertrand that you thought we'd better have it wired in." Rock, rock, skrunch. It was the noise the rocker made on the uneven floor. There was no one rocking on a beetle. "These chairs creak so. Mother really ought to have them seen to."

"Mother really ought to have them seen to. Now I was saying to mother …" rock, rock, scrun-nn, scru-uuunch "that she ought to have them seen to. Tim does nothing. Tim does simply nothing." "Yes Mandy was saying to me today that Tim does simply nothing." "Now why was Mandy saying that about Tim? Tim told me that Mandy—" rock rock, scru-uunch "Tim was saying that Mandy—" rock, rock, "Tim was saying that Mandy—."

How dare she, how dare this little upstart gossip, butt in, interfering with their household, how *dare* she? Shut up, shut up Hermione, don't speak, don't speak, Hermione. You started it, Hermione. You should never, Hermione, have said that Mandy said that Tim, that Tim said that Mandy, that Eugenia said that Mandy.

But what was there to talk about? Gart and the formula? As soon as she began on the formula Minnie would fly into a temper. "You leave me out of everything, you leave me out of everything." Minnie would fly into a temper, "just because I am a *poor* girl." Poor girl. Orphan Annie. Orphan Minnie. Nobody would mind anything if—rock, rock, scru-uunch—she knew how to sew on ruffles. "I know. I know these darkies are so dreadful."

Darkies are dreadful. Darkies are dreadful. Mandy is adorable. I adore Mandy. How Mandy ha-aates Minnie. Hermione hugged this to herself. Keep quiet, don't say anything. Talk down to Minnie but let Minnie think she is talking up to Her.

Let Minnie think she is talking. Rock, rock, brrr—"It's the telephone."

three

Sauvé. Bien sauvé as George would say. Hermione banged the screen door. Curiosity was holding Minnie together. Minnie would decompose, drift off into decomposed atoms if curiosity didn't so hold her. Minnie should have said (Minnie always did say) "Oh, my head, can't you ever shut the screen door quietly?" Hermione would have said, Hermione should have said, "I'm awfully sorry Minnie but you know this door swings and won't fasten till you bang it."

Usual dialogue was for the moment suspended, it would all come later. Words said over and over, over and over. They were a stock company playing in a road show, words over and over. All very well cast for the parts, can't get out of this show, it's too fu-uunny. I'll never get out of this show, it's too funny, Eugenia with her 1880 Hellenistic beauty made a drudge for this thing. Me, me, me Hermione out of Shakespeare made a doormat for this little cheap dressmaker's-sort-of-assistant person who can't even hem a ruffle. Funny show, for Gart and the formula. Because *if* Minnie has hysteria, Bert will sit up all night with her instead of hatching molecules, all so-oo funny.

"What are you laughing at?" "It's so-oo funny, Eugenia." "Are you answering the telephone?" "You ca-an Eugenia if you want to," was new variant on the old dialogue. Hermione had slipped in all unnoticed by the audience, a new line—"You can Eugenia if you want to." She repeated it. "You can answer the telephone, Eugenia, if you want to." "But you *know* I hate the telephone."

Brrrr-rrr. It was the telephone. "Isn't anybody going to

answer the telephone?" "Shut the screen door, Minnie. You know how the June bugs swarm in." Now this was one on Minnie. Minnie had to shut the door. Hermione saw Minnie, grey elemental behind the grey gauze of the wire netting, elemental held together by her curiosity. Why didn't Minnie walk in? Now this was one on Minnie. Minnie didn't dare let them see she was eaten up with curiosity. Minnie's pet formula (how often had they heard it?) "Now *I* am never curious."

Brrrr-rrr. Minnie would die of this. Minnie would be found dead if the telephone went on burr-ing and nobody answered it. "Come, come Hermione. Stop giggling. It's what your grandmother used to say when I acted like that" (so Eugenia acted like that), "there's a black rose growing in your garden."

four

"Ye-e-e-e-*es*." Hermione clung to the wavering receiver like a sinking man to a floating, vanishing life belt. Tiny spar floating on the top of things, spar on the top of things, something floating on top, outside the thing that she was sinking into, that was drawing her. This is a tiny thing: I am holding on to something that may in time lead on to something—"Yeess—" holding on, who is it? Far and far a voice out of something, out of nothing, holding something, holding nothing. "Oh it's—*George*."

Back beat of waves beating now against her, this isn't fair. I have the whole of the ordinary forward beat and the whole of the sideways beat of waves to fight against, to fight alone against, this isn't fair. Back beat of waves beat against her and in the beat and the whirlpool, the things came clear; there is that eternal three-legged stain at the top of the wall where the picture moulding used to be where the roof leaked last year.

Mother must see to it, mother must see to it. "I didn't know you were here." "I'm not here"—more cryptic, why couldn't he be natural on the telephone? It was bad enough to hold on to the telephone, to say in herself "Mother must see to it," to feel outside Minnie listening, to feel the nervous strain of Bertrand outside with his thin dynamic hands opening, shutting, his thin fine fingers opening, shutting, never quiet, his thin hands tonight with the tablecloth, wall-of-Troy pattern on the tablecloth. Carl Gart had lifted a napkin that had rose-pattern that did not match the wall-of-Troy. *There's a black rose growing in your garden.* Why didn't George leave her alone to it? Why hadn't George left her alone to it? "I mean, I thought you were in Venice."

Words make tin pan noises, little tin pan against my ear and words striking, beating on it, bella, bella, molta bella, bellissima, you are, he was saying bellissima and he must see Bellissima. Why didn't he talk English on the telephone? Anyway, far away the voice of George making circus tent noises, little far away miniature Punchinello shouting outside a tent, Bellissima.

"I mean, I can't. I can't possibly see you." Now why couldn't she possibly see George? It was evident that she couldn't see George, but why couldn't she see George? Now just why can't I see George tomorrow? ... "The heat is too, too awful." Yes that was it, he wanted trees and the moss, trees and did she remember the perch in the live oak (he remembered it was a live oak, he hadn't known it was a live oak till she told him) and the stream that said ... that said ... George was talking some other language. He wanted trees, because it was hot, he wanted her because it was hot. It was hot. "It *is* hot." "It *is* hot" said in answer to something she didn't understand, didn't help her. "If you ring off, I'll simply ring again and again and ring at one and two and three and at dawn precisely."

She heard the words far and far, little circus tent flap went flap-flap and outside it was Punchinello, a harlequin sort of person with patchwork clothes with patchwork languages, bursting into Spanish or Italian or the sort of French that no one ever tried to think of speaking. *C'est agaçant.* "*C'est agaçant*," she managed over the telephone pronouncing it distinctly, "I mean I'm horribly sorry. It's far too late tonight and tomorrow—" Tomorrow. There must be something. "Oh. I *am* so sorry. It's terribly *agaçant*. There is a woman simply won't be put off. Nellie Thorpe, you never I think met her. I had her letter with yours. I only just had yours." Followed long tirade. He left letters to be posted after he left the pension and letters to be posted immediately and he had tipped the boy too much or he hadn't tipped the boy enough and the letters that were to be posted after he left were posted the week before he left leading to countless difficulties. *"Agonante"*—and the letters he wanted posted immediately, ecco, Bellissima, were left till after he *had* left. "Then I'll see you *next* time."

five

"George. It was George on the telephone." "So I gathered." "It was George." "You said he was in Venice." "You said he was in Venice" brought that odd tone into Eugenia's voice.

"You said he was in Venice" brought back odd things, things that had all along been half-accepted and so the more difficult to reject openly. When Eugenia said "You said he was in Venice" in that tone of accusation, Hermione knew she must formulate George Lowndes. It was going to be very difficult to formulate George, to concentrate enough to get an image of George, to say, "I hate George" or to say, "I love George." She perceived heat lightning wavering above the Farrand oak trees and realised that now was the moment for some definition.

"I did say I *thought*, Eugenia, he was still in Venice. I said there was no postmark." Her Gart felt she was groping toward some ill-defined landmark, toward some sort of path out of this dangerous shut-in Pennsylvania, herself bewildered path-finder in some new unchartered region of thought, of aspiration. It is true "Venice" had meant nothing but George might help her get out. Was it possible that she wasn't quite a failure? "I intend to ask George." The thought of George sustained Her for a moment. She perceived Eugene glaring. Her said, "Just why do you hate George so?" "I don't hate, as you put it, George Lowndes. Have I ever *not* made any of your friends welcome," made things again incalculable, though Eugenia, to be quite fair, was no worse than other people.

People hated George. George was *agaçant*. But people should hate with reason. There must be a reason. There was a reason for Mandy to hate Minnie. There was, as far as Her-mione could follow, no reason for Eugenia to hate George so. "*Just* why do you hate George so?" "I don't hate as you put it George Lowndes. It's his odd way. I don't mind people doing things. It's the way they do things." "Things? What things?" "Oh Hermione—out-*rage*-ous—all the university ladies knew about it." "Because the university ladies knew that George had a—had a—a person to his room, it's an outrage, not because George had a person to his room but because the university ladies *saw* him have a person—anyhow who saw him?—to his room." "Hus-ssh." "Yes, I do know. Yes, I do see—but—" (was it too late?) "Yes I do know Tim *is* awfully lazy." Now how had Minnie got there?

Minnie was standing by the little table under the picture of Pius Wood,. pretending to look up something in the telephone book. How long had she been listening?

"I heard you say George has come back. I couldn't help hearing. You do shout so." "Yes, George has come back." "I always liked George Lowndes. You should never listen, *I* always think, to what people say about other people. All the ladies at the university always gossip. I was saying to Mrs. Banes the other day that I never knew such gossip for a lot of supposedly *cultured* people." Parthian shaft left Hermione staring, her jaw metaphorically dropping, at Minnie ascending the curved staircase, going up prim with self-determination, with an ultraconscious look to her back, *I* never listen, *I* never gossip. Now why has she gone off that way with the telephone book? I've forgotten Nellie's number.

V

one

She could flounder toward constructive reality which none of them then had. For them, there was no vantage point of Jazz, no sounding board of Middle West and the alien American growth of their thin strip of Europe had not then been recognized, as such. They were in fact American, had not yet been repudiated.

Their type of mind was still recognisable, a later blare of mentality left it almost extinguished, as stars just not seen in daylight. They were Nordic, they were New English, they were further extinguished by Germanic affiliation. They budded from a South German affiliation to be blighted with the cross-purpose of New England. Into it, Minnie stepped, nonchalant and aggressive. She was their first "American."

Minnie was some two generations rooted, might technically be termed that. Minnie was American, might theoretically have been of another continent. Jazz and the prelude of the Midwest had not yet managed to drive that thin Atlantic coast wedge right off into the ocean. The Midwest in all its two generation affiliation was not yet so predominately "American." Minnie Hurloe was technically of another center. She was different. They did not know what it was, they had no words to say it. Eugenia at best might mutter, "Bertrand's wife had an unhappy childhood." They were too loyal to discuss this alien prodigy. They did not even understand that it was alien.

It was before the days of their capitulation. The term "alien" had not yet been invented. "Aliens" in Europe, now "alien" in America, they yet had peculiar standards. But they had no word for those things; they were not English, were not German, they were not according to the later formula "American."

Americans rooted in the subsoil yet had peculiar standards; the deeper rooted, the more flamingly parasitic they seemed. Hermione flaming up into some uncharted region of "America" was so far more American than the later-day Midwest, that she, so to speak, fell ridiculously over backwards to preserve her own integral uprightness. She had a way of saying, "It doesn't matter what you are so long as you are yourself." She did not know what *gnothi seauton* meant, perhaps had not even caught the tone of its peculiar syllable. To know herself she would know Minnie, would know Bertrand, would know America. There was no one to tell her that America reaches round and about and that ghosts live even in America.

America has its Hinterland, as yet, be it precisely stated, vaguely charted. There are today not a few signposts, set by valiant pioneers in that Hinterland of imagination. In the days of Hermione, signposts were yet unpainted. Bastards like herself, alien to either continent had yet no signposts. The later generation found their way about, put all their energy into "life," had no crying need for definition. Her's energy must go groping forward in a world where there was no sign to show you "Oedipus complex," no chart to warn you "mother complex," shoals threatening. "Guilt complex" and "compensation reflex" had not then been posted, showing your way on in the morass.

two

Nevertheless there remained strains of tardy civilization common to both continents. There were teacups, tea-handles, even there was such an anomaly as a teacozy that day at Nellie Thorpe's. Nellie Thorpe had a sister Jessie, who had had a picture exhibited somewhere in Paris. Said picture was perched upon the grand piano, perky little exhibition number guaranteed its reliability. Because after all, it might just have been a pewter platter set there, against a drop of velvet, so intimate its highlights, so infallible its painted-in dint of pewter shadow. American art ... Paris. The thing, had it been ironical, would have been *coup de grâce*. So too would the clatter about Nellie's table, which could hardly have been distinguished from that of Chelsea or certain sectors of the Rive Gauche, in anything but a possibly even more over-stressed self-consciousness.

There was perhaps, to be fair, no other "attitude" for them. The ground under their feet had not yet been sufficiently stabilized to guarantee the later leap into nothingness as from intellectual asphalt. They remained part still of the almost but not quite "set" intellectual utilitarian asphalt. They could not radically leap away from standards that were not altogether there to leap from. States of mind correlating the pewter platter carefully highlit against the fall of prescribed velvet were not yet catalogued and consequently to be disclaimed as "sterile."

Their states of mind were not then apparent to them. They did not see that their carefully grouped "literature," "music," "art" criticisms were as carefully highlit, as Jessie's picture. Jessie stood out among them as becomingly shoddy, was superior in an inferior manner, appearing Anglo-shabby, her heels deliberately left to shambles though her one-piece shantung costume almost succeeded. "Paris?"

Jessie Thorpe almost succeeded where the others failed, she failed where they almost succeeded. The Rive-Gauche touch was refreshing as an arum in the desert but her air boded inferiority, Nellie having becomingly attained an acquired Bryn Mawr touch. But both Nellie and her sister were running true to type, there was no hint of externalised America in them. Nellie's literary pretensions were also niched, had acquired a pleasant semblance of reality, her form of pewter against velvet. Nellie had had an essay actually commented on by the *North American Quarto* though "not actually accepted." Nellie's sister had, by that pewter plate, the so much further attained. Though Jessie was perhaps older, and years then so awfully counted. One was labelled by years as classic art collections are by centuries. This year was by that time the so much more important than any later stretch of vague ten years or even vaguely fifteen.

All this, Hermione Gart vaguely sensed, vaguely knew was there, she vaguely met it halfway as she stepped from an asphalt grill into the cave area of Nellie Thorpe's half-dismembered town house. The family had gone, Miss Nellie the maid explained was waiting upstairs. Hermione knew they had been talking of her as self-conscious; she stumbled through the doorway. It was Nellie's own voice saying "Such clever people … and at the end, Hermione failed completely." The schoolmarm slightly acrid superiority of Nellie's voice was cut across by Jessie's "She's far too perceptive for your subliterary Bryn Mawr, Nell."

three

Perception, perceiving, having perceived, being perceived. None of this thing termed "perception" seemed to have entered consciousness with the somewhat problematical exception of Nellie's sister, Jessie. Jessie saw just around the corner.

Nellie could see as far as the room wall and the fact that it might be "distinguished" to have a pewter platter, exhibited in some little sub-offshoot of some minor French Academy. Perception might have been perceived but it wasn't at that moment.

That moment was prolonged for an exact re-evaluation of the room and its contents by Nellie Thorpe who had realized by a fraction of a second too late that she might have made a blunder. Nellie Thorpe hesitated, then decided that she could not now redeem a possible error in "taste." She rallied to her predicament; "My dear ... this is the other creature that I wrote you is fey with the same sort of wildness."

It appeared that the girl thus indicated, was anything but that. She was stonily incarnated. She sat somewhat withdrawn but forced straight into the core of a predicament, she rose valiantly. She moved with a stolid directness that made the rest of them seem like so much sawdust. They were that, mental scatterings of ideas, whittled away from Europe. The girl said "How do you do," in a somewhat ironical imitation of Nellie's Bryn Mawr manner. She sat down opposite Her Gart at the little table.

There was nothing however of her reality in that girl. The mind of Her Gart jibed off from "fey with wildness." The phrase was typical of Nellie, of her pseudo-affectations, of her knowing air of accepting things she didn't in the least realize meant things that, if she had recognized, she would have rejected. Nellie was taking stock of her immature blunder. The two she observed didn't in the least look "fey." She might do anything, said Her Gart to Her Gart, but she couldn't get me out of concentric tree-circle on concentric tree-circle. The trees were gelatinous and she wanted a wall of breakers. There was nothing however to do now for it. Her Gart regarded the new acquaintance across a table and regarded a centerpiece. The thing was fringed, had hieratic center still demonstrably quattrocento through untidy scatterings of teacups. The fringe was linen thread knotted with peculiar deftness. Hermione pulled at it. "Oh, what a pretty teacloth."

"Yes. Isn't it. The last time, no it was the time before last, we were in Florence—Aunt Jessie insisted on matching the little tray cloth we had got from the time before *that*" and so on and so on and so on. Throw out a little word, that was tact; tact is throwing out a little word and the thing goes on and the thing goes on.

A convex Victorian mirror above the head of the girl opposite showed Nellie and Hermione tilted sidewise, making an exaggerated puffed out little Dutch group of them, table and cloth and careful lines of the oblong pattern where the folded cloth had been carefully unfolded, making two careful lines, bisecting teacups clustered and teacups scattered ... someone was interfering with the teacups.

"Yes, it was rather a blow. I mean getting just so far; rather brilliantly they said, and then utterly, utterly coming down on everything. I failed," she flung it out, "utterly." Someone was asking her what she would take up next? Did one take up something next? What did one take, as they say, "up" after one had been banged on the head and sees triangles and molecules and life going on in triangles and molecules. "Oh—it's too—too late." It was really too late to take, as they say, "up" anything. "Are you eighteen or twenty-one?" said some ironical cold voice.

Nellie's saccharine Bryn Mawr voice tried to turn away the other voice that again said, "Your incredible Bryn Mawr, Nell." Nellie was saccharine, the other voice protested and Nellie went on being tactful. Tact, tact; tact is throwing out a word at the right moment. It was someone else's turn to talk. The girl opposite wasn't being tactful. Nellie's sister was descending again, soft edges to the grim voice. "Are you just eighteen or all of twenty-one?" Now the saccharine voice again and the other voice was badgering Nellie. One really couldn't be bothered listening.

Nellie was trying to turn away Jessie's slightly husky-at-the-edges voice. A face went with the voice. A face drew out of people grouped like teacups and people bisected by long lines of blue curtain hanging from miles above one's head, from a ceiling miles above one's head to a floor miles below one's feet. The floor was polished and showed diagonals of the blue curtain in space between chairs going down and down. Bits of the floor went down, reflected between table legs; long lines of pure blue. Think of long lines of pure blue. Across the table, with its back to the little slightly convex mirror, facing Her Gart and Jessie, was this thing that made the floor sink beneath her feet and the wall rise to infinity above her head. The wall and the floor were held together by long dramatic lines of curtain falling in straight pleated parallels. Answer the husky voice that speaks to you. Don't look at the eyes that look at you. "A girl I want to see you." The girl *was* seeing Her.

four

There are of course bits of colour to be thrown down like counters in a banking house, or chips across a poker table. All your life you will retain one or two bits of colour with which all your life will be violently or delicately tinted. You will have an infinitesimal grain of purple dye or a flat counter to hoard or to risk in one reckless spend-thrift moment. There are gamblers of the spirit as there are gamblers of the mind, passions of the psyche as well as passions of the body. All of life may be spent looking in vain for a counter that might bring glory or fame or wisdom which at some off-moment you may pick up unexpectedly—from the gutter—then you save it or you spend it. Take Nellie Thorpe's room for example.

There is a bowl of peonies on the piano, slightly edged off toward the shadow by the blue-curtained French window. There is Jessie's counter, one pewter platter that had brought Jessie fame, there was Nellie Thorpe's Essay on the Bi-lingual Division of the American Literary Consciousness lying carefully uncreased in the Via Tornabuoni leather portfolio with the singing boys of Donatello embossed on the upper cover. There is a scattering of cups and crumbs and a nonrelated body of choruses, off in the shade of still another sister (married) and two other classmates of Nellie's, almost strangers to the group proper and this other "fey with wildness," who knew Nellie at "High School."

Gambler's luck was with Her. She had the gambler's instinct but it was only at that moment that she recognized it. She was not made for any of these groups, even the slightly meretricious sympathy of Jessie couldn't draw her into another cycle of one-step-removed America which was not just what she wanted. Gambler's luck pertained to this obvious situation. Keep in with this set, Nellie, Jessie, the others who merged in and through the eternal faculty ladies and their related groups here and abroad, Rome, Oxford, Munich. Keep in or keep out. Accept values as all these people see them or accept value in one gem, one strip or stripe of colour, accept red as you get it, in coral or blue as you get it, perfect star sapphires in eye-sockets.

The gambler's instinct, however, was not at the moment so transcribed in consciousness. It was a premonition rather than a recognition. Her Gart recognised a sort of prickling across cheekbones, which caused no rise of colour, but if anything an intensification of a somewhat congenital pallor. Hermione did not see the girl that Nellie had asked her to see. She did not actually hear the words she uttered. She did not apprehend her, she possibly perceived her. She went on talking, not knowing what she said, she seemed to explain herself not knowing why she did it.

"I failed," she flung it out again, "utterly." Would "I failed utterly" keep people from repeating as they would keep on, Tibetan prayer wheel, "What are you going to do, what are you going to do, what are you going to do now?" What was "now" and what was "doing" and what was "what" precisely? Words went round, had odd ways of tacking off, billowing out, full sail. If she could have gone to Point Pleasant, listened to the sea, everything would come right. Point Pleasant with Minnie wouldn't be Point Pleasant. Escape through barriers ... if she could see clear for one week, for one day. NOW was raging down on her like a great lumbering bullock, something dangerously half-formed, depending on its intuition, half-formed, half-baked. Nellie's sister would keep on insisting "You'd better join our little group in Paris." Nellie's sister had a blatant assumption of finality, something crude and forthright, she didn't presume. Nellie was so obviously a climber.

"Climber?" "I said 'Climb,'" (I didn't know I had said anything) "I will have to climb out of my own predicament."

VI

one

Something beat about Her but she could not comprehend it. Something conforming to a giant night-moth, something Bertrand had said about "violet rays in line with mathematics." Something formulated, then uncurled its formal moth-wings, so that the room was a room with set chairs and tables, to be moved about and rearranged like dollhouse furniture.

The people in the room were assorted, out of different boxes, yet all holding to some pattern, they had the same trademark of nonentity. All people, Her Gart realized (as the thing whirred like a dynamo and yet was delicate and would evade one like the underbelly of a night-moth) have the same sort of trademark. Her Gart realized, while this went on, what Bertrand had meant saying, "violet rays in line with mathematics." The thing whirrrred like a bird on its way into bird oblivion, it was in line with something ...

Nellie went on talking. The sister of Nellie propounded a sort of mild "French" joke which people pretended to get the point of. From the top of the piano, the pewter plate still gave back its pewter highlight and painted pewter shadow. Facing eyes that come "in line with mathematics," Hermione apprehended, but did not grasp, a thing that whirred like a bird up, up into a forest of metallic leaves and a forest of leaves that waved like seaweed under water. She saw the girl who was "fey with the same sort of wildness," then she came to, like coming out of ether. Someone was saying, "Oh, yes, *Diana of the Cross-ways*" and with the automatic click-click that had gone to so much of the outer mechanism of the thing called Her Gart, a voice answered, "No ... it was *Richard Feverel.*"

It was Her Gart saying *"Richard Feverel."* Something as unrelated to a giant moth-wing as a saltcellar is to a petunia took up that strand; she contributed her counters to the play of conversation with as good a grace as any. Yet all the time something nonrelated caused a queer sort of blurring-out of image. She couldn't think and talk and see and be, all at the same instant. Hardly knowing that she WAS, she let go more than one half of Her. She returned to a room where people sat on chairs (the sort that come with the dollhouse furniture) and she repeated with as good a grace as any, *"Richard Feverel."*

Hermione realized that she was still sitting before a table whose tray cloth Aunt Jessie had especially bought in Florence. Hermione focussed to that edge of cloth as her eyes in summer woods had managed to formulate one leaf, out of all gelatinous-green, so here she endeavoured to find a flaw or torn thread in this work. She found one peculiar knotted inch of fringe-end. Her fingers clawed the thing straight. Then she dragged her eyes off the tablecloth, dragged eyes up convex surface of a teacup, dragged eyes up into space that ran on and on across the room behind the back of the creature that had spoken. Hermione forced eyes back till they met eyes ... "Oh, Meredith! Do you read him?"

two

One conversation of all the conversations may retain significance; by one leaf you may judge the contour of a great tree, whether it be oak, or beech or chestnut. One conversation can give clue to the whole insistencies of a forest; analyse it and you will find whether the tract of oak wood may or may not, at some specific later date, be blighted. Analyse pulp substance of green gelatinous woodleaf and you will find worlds revolving and a continent of armies, massed to slide along ridges of leaf-vein or to swarm in battalions into another exact triangle of wood fibre. Here a patch of brown may show the invidious canker or here some sodden bubble under the living texture may foretell a waterlogged anaemia. One conversation in a sodden jungle (her yet unformulated consciousness and her consciousness of America) gave her a clue to a new race and a new revaluation of the forest. The jungle must be weeded out surely... but the soil was ripe for a new sort of forestation.

The real sort of grace of God that was there was not this febrile garden-growth from England. George Meredith was a somewhat waterlogged and pollared British by-product, an offshoot of an insular and specialized race consciousness. George Meredith set a sort of standard for them and by that standard they must repudiate the forest. For how could they live then in that uncharted wilderness? The mind must have its landmarks. Theirs were false ones.

Nevertheless they clung to the lifebuoy, the sort of thing that might possibly mean (they didn't know it didn't) England. It did not mean that they wanted to be English, it did not even mean that their would-be standardization at all approximated the thing that Nellie stood for, with her Anglo-shabby air of trite repudiation. We are American, therefore we read Wilkie Collins and George Meredith, but rest assured, these in our lighter moments. Down and down and further, there were other kinships. The girl with the wild eyes that were the only sane eyes (possibly except Bertrand's) that Hermione had yet seen, said, "What about Dostoevski?"

Dostoevski rang no bell. A conversation that should have slipped on oiled grooves, inevitably to Turgenev did no such suave thing. A voice somewhere (Nellie's) should have taken up that odd name, that word that sends out a fringe, somewhat untidy aura, the very contour of a forest, but no Nellie chirped up, "Our Dostoevski is Walt Whitman and our Turgenev is Poe." America had its Dostoevski, its Poe, already its Dionysian and Apollonian were specified but Nellie and Jessie and Hermione didn't know that. The conversation jibbed at Dostoevski as a little summer sailboat at a log flung across a tide river. They skimmed the edge of their continent, how could they have done other? Dostoevski was a shaggy word, it did not suit them. They came back to Meredith. A high pitched and intense vibration, the married sister this time, insisted that they do so. "What was it you said about the *Diana of the Crossways,* Miss Gart?"

Her Gart, now definitely included in that resurrection-of-the-dead conversation, answered, exact automaton, "I said I liked *Diana* but I said I liked George Meredith with reservations." "In what sense exactly, reservation?" Nellie Thorpe had neatly clicked her counter. "I mean a friend of mine—a man I know—George (he is George too) Lowndes, have you heard of him? he writes; George Lowndes says Meredith shows in every other syllable that his father was a tailor." "Tailor? Does he? I mean was his father in that sense a tailor?" "Well, you know what I mean. I mean I don't exactly know what I do mean. But it's wordy. I mean, it's words and words—not like Henry James."

"Oh *James*—who reads *him?*" One I love, two I love, three I love. Do you see me? No. I do not see you. Play hide and seek behind Henry James and Meredith. "I mean, Nellie at Bryn Mawr wrote *brilliantly* about him." Nellie had written brilliantly about Henry James, done a thesis, taken a degree.

Degree, degree, degree ... Hermione went up like the mercury in the thermometer. Degrees, degrees … she would burst out of the top of herself like the mercury in the thermometer. Mercury in the thermometer rises, rises … What does it feel like when it can't rise any higher and is there, pulsing, beating to express degrees beyond the degrees marked carefully in fine spiderweb of silver on the glass tube? Mercury that felt expression … beating, pulsing; I am feeling degrees of things for which there is no measure. "It *is* hot. Terribly."

"But *you* with that lovely place in the country—" "Yes, *you* with that lovely place in the country—" "—can't feel the heat—" "—as we do." Everything people say rhymes in *rhythms,* you do, do—you, do re mi fa so la si do. "Did you *never* take up music?" Someone else was talking to someone else about taking something as they said "up." They were always taking things up or why didn't you take things up, this up or this up or this up. Life was going on in circles, people placed like tea-cups in clusters, changing molecule clusters because it was so hot and someone said, "Is the dust worse or is the heat worse" and someone said, "But there is no dust in your street, Miss Thorpe." This street is so secluded and someone said "They have tarred the whole front of Chestnut Street; Philadelphia is shocking in the summer. Now I have a friend in India"— impressive pause—"in India. That is she is English, what they call Anglo-Indian"—impressive pause—"*she* says it is far, far more repellently hot in Philadelphia than in India." "Oh but in India," a voice said, "there are snakes, there are vipers and scorpions" and then someone went on dramatically about someone whom they knew who had wintered (impressive) at Luxor, up the Nile and the snakes—something about someone calling snakes from little walls and sand caves and porches out of temples with a reed pipe.

three

Precinematographic conscience didn't help Her. Later conscience would have. She would later have seen form superimposed on thought and thought making its spirals in a manner not wholly related to matter but pertaining to it and the peony petals magnified out of proportion and the people in the room shrunk to tiny insects while the teacups again would have magnified into hemispheres. This teacup would have fitted that teacup, each of the two nonentities talking to its nonentity, had mind fitted like a teacup. Nellie and the James subject, Jessie and the second of the Thwaight twins were equally nonimportant yet matched in a nonimportant manner. The married sister was removing a spot of sticky mille-feuille from her starched jabot, and at the moment talked to no one. Jessie and Nellie and the married sister had kept some six or eight nonrelated sets of people talking, each self-considered intrinsically significant, when all the time, they were minute and flyspeck size and the peony petal had lifted, spread surface over all.

She saw the room as a room, the people as people, the teacups as small cups placed upon small matched saucers, the mille-feuille plate as a plate with pattern round the edge, the piano as a piano, no more, no less, the girl facing Her as a girl facing Her with rather staring slightly rude eyes and an irreverent manner. Her Gart saw the girl as that, all the time realizing with an instinct that was at the time submerged, that she had seized on her pearl-of-price thought this time; as it happened, it was a pair of exactly matched star sapphires.

four

"Who is George?" "George—I don't know." "You said he wrote or knew people who wrote or something." "Oh, he knows people who write. He writes." "What does he write?" "He writes about—about Castile, I don't know. He wrote a sort of treatise on something between Castile and Cadiz. I mean he knows languages." "Does he travel?" "George? He is—I mean he hardly ever doesn't." "Where does he go?" "Oh—he went to Algiers, I have a photograph of George in a fez." "It doesn't sound like George." "No—it isn't. George isn't the least bit like that. It doesn't suit him." "What then is George like?" "Oh, I don't know—rather like Aucassin and Nicolette. I mean he once said I was." "Like—" "One or the other. Aucassin, you know, and Nicolette, you know." "I don't know." "Well—that sort of thing. He got me the copy from the Portland Maine shop, you know that shop." "Yes, I know. What else do you read?" "Read? Oh I read Ibsen, Maeterlinck, all of Bernard Shaw." "Do you like Maeterlinck?" "*The Bee—yes,* George said it was nature faking." "Did you think it was nature faking?" "A little—it didn't quite ring true. But then the French is easy." "Do you read much French?" "No, George bought me—a set of—I mean Dante's *Fiori* or I mean Saint Francis and the Beata Beatrice. I don't care for the *Paradiso.*" "Queer, now I like the *Paradiso.*"

"Your mind seems to have a definite octopus quality. Do you assimilate anything?" "Assimilate?" Her Gart came to as from an anesthetic. Just what had she been saying? She seemed to have answered this odd girl, word for word, click, snap and click, the exact requisite counter, the same game but involving something very different from the casual afterdinner sort of auction-whist her words meant with these others. Her words now were a gambler's heritage, heady things, they would win for her, they would lose for her. Now as she realized that these very words must stand forever, her counters win or lose, she realized there was a general flutter as of some new people coming and of some of the rest going and Nellie had pounced down on them.

Her cheekbones felt as if they were tinted with the most hectic point of the Indian paintbrush; colour seemed to have drawn a cycle across a world, to have marked out a zone, a continent. There was a zone she had not explored. She could use the same counter, the same sort of password that she used with all these people, but she had passed out in a twinkling of an eye into another forest. This forest was reality. There, the very speaking of the words, conjured up proper answering sigil, house and barn and terrace and castle and river and little plum tree. A whole world was open. She looked in through a wide doorway.

Nellie said, "Now you two, you mustn't monopolise each other any longer. Come, Her Gart, there's Adelaide Noyes who terribly wants to meet you."

VII

one

She wanted George as a child wants a doll, whose other dolls
are broken. She wanted George as a little girl wants to put her
hair up or to wear long skirts. She wanted George with some
uncorrelated sector of Her Gart, she wanted George to cor-
relate for her, life here, there. She wanted George to define and
to make definable a mirage, a reflection of some lost incarna-
tion, a wood maniac, a tree demon, a neuropathic dendrophil.

She wanted George to say, "God, you must give up this sort
of putrid megalomania, get out of this place." She knew sooner
or later George would begin his prodding and sooner or later,
she must make up her mind. She wanted George to make the
thing an integral, herself integrity. She wanted George to
make one of his drastic statements that would dynamite her
world away for her. She wanted this, but even as she wanted it
she let herself sink further, further, she saw that her two hands
reached toward George like the hands of a drowned girl.

She knew she was not drowned. Where others would
drown—lost, suffocated in this element—she knew that she
lived. She had no complete right yet to this element, hands
struggled to be pulled out. White hands waved above the
water like sea spume or inland-growing pond flowers ... she
wanted George to pull her out, she wanted George to push her
in, let Her be drowned utterly.

George was the only young man who had ever kissed Her.
George was the only person who had called her a "Greek
goddess." George, to be exact, had said ruminatively on more
than one occasion, "You never manage to look decently like

other people. You look like a Greek goddess or a coal scuttle."
George said she looked like a coal scuttle. He also said she
looked like a Greek goddess. There was that about George,
he wanted to incarnate Her, knew enough to know that this
was not Her. There was just a chance that George might manage to draw her out half-drowned, a coal scuttle, or push Her
back, drowned, a goddess. Regarding him, very hot on the
woodpath, Hermione became almost collegiate of the period,
almost a person with hair up and with long skirts. Her became
almost Hermione as she looked at George with his collar torn
open at the throat, turned-back Byronic collar, clean shirt,
hot underarms in great symmetrical patches. There were
clean wet patches under the arms of George, his coat was left
somewhere. "Where did you leave your coat, George?" "I've
forgotten, Bellissima. Now *is* this the forest of Arden?"

George said, "Now is this the forest of Arden?" She looked
at George; pedantically, she replied, "My little body is a-weary
of this great world." She swerved, she would yet dramatize herself, she turned as with stage gesture toward stage trees. But
Orlando couldn't save Her, Rosalind couldn't save Her. The
trees were not forest of Arden, they were not so far incarnate,
were of another element. Trees swung and fell and rose. Trees
barricaded her into herself, Her into Her. I am the word Aum,
I am the word Her. Her was received into trees that swung and
billowed and swung. Trees formed upright shafts and rose upright into shafts that held crossbeams of trees—George was
saying "Crossbeams of trees. A forest's so damn Gothic."

two

His voice was low, sursurring, (it was his word) somewhere.
His voice when he wasn't being too funny, wasn't showing off,

was simple accompaniment to trees above her head, to herself, revitalized, born into trees. "We aren't in any Gothic setting, George" she wanted to say but didn't say. "It's under water" she wanted to say; "It's under deep-sea water," she didn't say. Her eyes half-closing saw George gone tawny, leaf-colour, his hair is the colour of leaves drifting down, he had drifted down from trees. She did say "It's your hair George." Hair now started upright to her vision as she opened wide eyes; Harlequin was facing her on a narrow wood path. George was Harlequin though for a moment he had swung back. For a moment George had swung back through a swing door and back and back. George was wavering with his green eyes and his odd Gozzoli features, his curious beauty that made people hate him, his odd tawny hair gone (in small rings) hot on his damp forehead. "Why is it that I can't *love* George Lowndes properly?"

"This is the forest primeval, the murmuring pines and the hemlocks," (George intoned dramatically; she knew why she didn't love him) *"bearded with moss and with garments green, indistinct in the twilight."* She knew why she couldn't love George properly. George gone tawny, hair the colour of vermillion seaweed, wash of vermillion over grey rocks, the sea-green eyes that became seagrey, that she saw as wide and far and full of odd sea-colour, became (old remembered reincarnation) small and piglike. George being funny is piglike. His eyes are too small in his face. His teeth are beautiful but when he is being funny he unnerves one. George back of George, George seen through a screen door, George gauzed over by lizard-film over wide eyes, George seen with perception was wavering tall and Gozzoli-like with green jerkin. Almost this is the forest of Arden.

George in torn-open collar and throat long and angular rising out of torn-open collar and with throat flung back and square lean chin thrust out against a tree bole, made this almost the forest of Arden. Almost Hermione was out of Shakespeare with George, words running through her mind, there was a smell of leather, of morocco bindings about George Lowndes. Almost this is the forest of Arden and Orlando stepping out with agile feet across leaves strewn across a narrow woodpath. Almost she was lost, stepping back and back into the pages of some familiar rhythm, *now this is the forest of Arden.* Almost her long legs were bound in Elizabethan trunkhose and almost in her hand, under her hand was a silver chain which almost she was about to drop about the throat of George, of Orlando kneeling, *wear this for me one out of suits with fortune.*

George Lowndes with his throaty sursurring gone funny, George being funny, nasal intonation, being funny, *this is the forest primeval,* brought back hunched shoulders, little desk, hard seat of little desk and the heated scrape of slate pencil across slate surface. Numbers jogged and danced and long division made a stop in her brain ... George, so beautiful, healing her by his presence was a hideous harlequin being funny on a woodpath. "Noaaw this is fawrest *pri*-meval."

three

It was the forest primeval, it was not the forest of Arden. George almost made it the forest of Arden. If at that moment, George had made it the forest of Arden, Hermione out of Shakespeare would have been again Hermione out of Shakespeare but this time Hermione from the *Winter's Tale* (who later froze into a statue) would have been Rosalind with sleek, deer-limbs and a green forester's cap with one upright darting hawk quill. Almost, Oh almost, almost this is the Forest of Arden. But not quite. This forest could never be affiliated with that forest. Back and back, hiding among tree trunks, abreast, crouched low among the sassafras and among the trailing vines of wintergreen, there were knees and brown flanks and the long low swirl of stone arrows that cut them forever and forever from the country they had that once repudiated. Repudiate the Forest of Arden and cling to the memory of that Forest as a man clings to the memory of his mother or a mistress he has outgrown. Almost, almost Hermione was Hermione out of Shakespeare ... but not quite.

Words were her plague and words were her redemption. George with his parody of their New England poet was cutting her again from moorings; she could not join on to benignity in a white wig, to Father Christmas dressed up to imitate an earlier Chronos. Longfellow was Father Christmas, he was not their primeval Father, he was not their authentic intellectual progenitor. George linking up to Castile, with his run of "foreign" literature, was not progenitor to Hermione standing dazed upon a woodpath. Almost, almost she heard words, almost, almost she discerned the whirr of arrows ... almost, for a moment, George had made it come right, saying "You are a Greek," saying, "You are a goddess." Almost for a moment, repudiating that earlier mystic genealogy, her soul had gone further, almost she had found her mother—wood-goddess on a woodpath. Almost words would work charm ... but not yet. George had broken charm, chanting in harlequin nasal those words out of New England, "Naw this is the forest primeval."

four

Charm broken, snapped like a snapped bowstring. She saw where she was. She giggled, lifted the hair from the nape of her neck, shook out the half-dozen bone hairpins. She bound the hair tighter, noted George even could not make an "occasion" of this somewhat nursemaid rhythm she made of this theoretically feminine (of-the-period) gesture. George might have wished there were more coquetry in her, or George might have been relieved there was not. George stared at her. His eyes widened in his face, now he was nearing seriousness, they were no more piglike. George said, "What do you do with yourself, Hermione?" He called Her, Hermione. She said, "Sit down, George."

Hermione realized George wanted now to help Her. She tried to reach forward to some stabilized world they might create between them. Her head now was simply hot, she felt a tight band about her forehead withdrawn. She felt no whizz of the stone head of an arrow. She said, "Do with myself?" She thought; said, "I don't exactly know George. There's always lots around the house. Minnie is ill so much. They've gone now to Point Pleasant. I read." George said, "What do you read?" She tried to drag out some consecutive classroom relay of catalogued information. What now had she been reading? "I don't know, George. I am the word AUM."

George said, "What?" "Those little Wisdom of the East books, they seem to be the only thing that fits here. You know—I am the serpent so-and-so, and the certain such-and-such an elephant, naming said beast." George turned facing Her, rubbed cheek against a tree trunk. "Don't talk," he now said, "don't talk," but she talked. She said, "I told you on the telephone I was going to a party. I went to a sort of party. Everyone there did something. People are always doing something."

She now braced herself decisively against her own tree. She rubbed her shoulder blades against that small tree. Small hard tree trunk (as she rubbed her shoulders to more raw reality) swayed a little, upright swaying little tree swayed. She was stronger than the upright little tree. She was stronger than anything. She was too strong. She wished she were not so strong, blighting things, people, herself, Eugenia. She wished she could love George. "I don't know why you hate George Lowndes so" was the nearest she had got to loving George Lowndes. Corroding "I don't know why you hate George Lowndes so" and corroding answer, "I don't hate George Lowndes," except between her and Eugenia. Something crept, always crept between her and everybody ... everybody?

"I met a girl at that tiresome Nellie Thorpe's I told you I was going to see on the telephone?" "Did you?" "Did I what?" "See her on the telephone?" Harlequin squinted down at her as she glanced swiftly up into the eyes of George. The eyes of George squinted down and she saw the nostrils of George the other way round like photographs in the two huge volumes of sliced things on ceilings. Perspective was in sliced things on ceilings. George had been to Europe, had come back and gone back again and had come back again. Why didn't George stay put, stay there or stay here? George, in perspective, was a figure in the Pitti Palace or something in the Riccardi Palace; he had seen the Ducal Palace, the Riccardi frescoes, not only poured over them in enormous volumes with coloured plates laid flat on the floor since the time she could remember.

George was out of the Famous Painters' Volume, was right, seen that way; from the bottom of a well, he loomed again beautiful, constructed, made. George was made. He tricked up the George that was there all the time, in harlequin words, harlequin language. Was George made? Was there a George at all? "Is there a George at all?"

"You're nothing, George. I mean precisely nothing." The branches swayed in back of George. He was part of the branches. Why wasn't he part of the branches? Her thought, panther-lean cat, strode up ahead of George. Her thought was swifter than George's witty, tricky thought. Thought chased thought like two panthers. Her own thought, swifter than the thought of George, was there beyond him. "You'll never, never catch me." Her faced George with that, standing on the narrowest of woodpaths that twisted (she knew) a narrow trickle of earth-colour across the green and green that was the steady running of swift water, the steady sweeping and seeping and swirling of branches all about her. If George would catch her, then George would be, might yet be something. "It's too hot, Hermione."

Heat seeped up, swept down, swirled about them with the green of branches that was torrid tropic water. Green torrid tropic water where no snow fell, where no hint of cold running streams from high mountains swept down, was swept into and under branches that made curious circle and half circle and whole circle ... concentric circle of trees above her head (how can anyone ever draw trees?) half circle of a (she saw) beech branch arching earthward. Tree on tree on tree. TREE. I am the Tree of Life. Tree. I am a tree planted by the rivers of water. I am ... I am ... HER exactly.

Her caught Her to herself, swirled dynamically on flat heels and was off down the trickle of earth-colour that was the path cutting earth-colour through green pellucid water.

VIII

one

Conversation went on in several layers. There was one gramophone disc, so to speak, of a conversation that she could put on at any moment.

She did not think about the girl she had met at Nellie's. She had not again seen her. Conversation returned like something forgotten, like echo in delirium. Conversation that said, "You have an octopus intelligence," and staring up into trees with George lost or forgotten or simply mislaid somewhere, Hermione let octopus-Hermione reach out and up and with a thousand eyes regard space and distance and draw octopus arm back, only to replunge octopus arm up and up into illimitable distance. Something in Her should have warned Hermione. Something far and far that had to do with some scheme of biological mathematical definition had left Her dizzy. It had not occurred to Her to try and put the thing in writing.

Writing was an achievement like playing the violin or singing like Tetrazzini. It had, it appeared, nothing or very little to do with the fact of cones of green set within green cones. Writing had somehow got connected up with George Lowndes who even in his advanced progress could make no dynamic statement that would assure her mind that writing had to do with the underside of a peony petal that covered the whole of a house like a nutshell housing woodgnats. Woodgnats without wings buzzed continually; Dostoevski had not entered into general conversation. George Lowndes, the high-water mark of the intelligentsia of the period, proffered Shaw, Maeterlinck, Bertrand de Born and, half-apologetic, the unexpurgated *Morte d'Arthur.* Writing had no mere relationship with trees on trees and octopus arms that reached out with eyes, too all over-seeing.

two

Hermione, thrown flat on wood moss, regarded green seawater that was parting, that was sluicing apart like crude description of the Red Sea parting. George, standing on dry land, severing sea from sea, was man on dry land, no proper deep-sea monster. George let light through to fall on her face. She waved back the light, fastidious as a gamine in a cellar. Under the sea, deep down in her deep-sea consciousness, she was putting out premature feelers; octopus became potato in a cellar. George stepped through suddenly as through an open stuck-fast cellar window. George stepped through a flap of branch that she had thought closed her away from any possibility of George Lowndes ever finding Her. *"The hounds of spring are on winter's traces,"* said George Lowndes.

"The hounds of spring are on winter's traces," repeated George Lowndes. He let fall red-sea on red-sea which now became simply simple theatrical swirl of green baize curtain. The hounds of spring are on winter's traces caught up to Her, gazed down and down; it was not the ginger of poor Jock gazing. The hounds of spring are on winter's traces and she looked up into the face of George Lowndes that went on now embroidered on the neat fold of a curtain "... the mother of months in meadow or plain, fills the shadows and windy places with lisp of leaves and ripples of rain ..." and George stepping forward was George, heavy foot was heavy on moss, he left a print like Tim left on their carpet. Hermione recalled Tim and that day and rain and slush dripping on the carpet. He was lugging in

their Christmas tree ... "*And the brown bright nightingale amorous. Is half assuaged for ... for ...*" It was George about to bend, he was near, he was coming nearer, he was small, he could never, never come near for Hermione looked far and far and George was a midge and a leaf was the size of a house and an acorn-cup would shelter herself ... for ... I am a tree planted by the river of water. George did not know that, was midge under peony, I am the word tree. He shall have a new name.

I am in the word TREE. I am TREE exactly.

Hermione sat bolt upright. George was going to sit, had sat beside her. "You said I'd never catch you." "Well *did* you?" His arm sudden about her snake form gave the lie to her swift thought. Her thought was panther-swift, had swirled away long before George made that so sudden suave gesture. George is tricky, unreliable. Her thought preceded her into forest branches. George could never love a tree properly.

Kisses forced her into soft moss. Her head lay marble weight in cushion of forest moss. Kisses obliterated trees, smudged out circles and concentric circle and the half-circle that was the arch (she had seen) of a beech branch sweeping downward. The kisses of George smudged out her clear geometric thought but his words had given her something ... *the brown bright nightingale amorous ... is half assuaged for ... for ...* her name is *Itylus*

three

Smudged out. I am smudged out. Concentric circles that are the trees going round and round are smudged out. I am smudged out. TREE is smudged out. Other circles going round and round in the back of my head are not touched by this spongy sort of thing, across slate, this wrong sort of sponge that smudges over, rules out concentric circles that are George, that is the recurring, rather chivalrous really, kiss of George. George is kissing me, almost Orlando; Orlando kiss doesn't affect the back of my head.

The back of marble head pressed down down into moss, down down into moss wasn't affected in the slightest by recurrent, rather charming really, kisses of this George. "Georgio." He said "Hermione" softly sursurring it, rather nice way of speaking when he wasn't being funny. George was it was obvious, not being at all funny. Her head pressed into the moss saw that George wasn't in the least bit being funny. The back of her head in the moss was pressed out, rounded out, round marble-polished surface in the soft moss.

Polished surface that was the slightly convex mirror hanging above the left shoulder of the creature sitting opposite. She knew the name of the creature seated opposite who had made walls heave and walls fall and straight lines run to infinity in the polished surface left between groups of people talking, teacups talking, people coming and new people and the teacups taking different form, changing interrelation as the heat beat and beat and beat (they could feel it) on the pavement outside the carefully curtained long French window. People were in things, things were in people. Names were in things, things were in names. Pennsylvania. People should think before they call a place Sylvania.

"People should think before they call a place Sylvania." Hermione saw a thin claw-like hand pressing against the blue stuff that was the clean sweet fresh stuff of the summer shirt of George. Underneath her hand there was the clean sweet flax-blue shantung, fine nice shoulder beneath the thin shirting. Hermione slipped a long hand into the open space of the wide flung wide collar, felt a smooth surface of polished clear smooth marble. Long dynamic hand ran across the smooth narrow surface, felt thud-thud, heavy thud-thud of rather too heavy bursting heartbeat. Thud-thud, heaving like the heavy foot that had trod heavy on the fine moss. The thud-thud was heavy, did not go with the sursurring of his voice when he wasn't being funny, did not go with the green of (now they were right) grey-green forest eyes. The eyes when he said Hermione that way were green and grey.

four

He had joked about something she had wanted to tell him? What was it that she wanted to tell George?

As she looked up into eyes that were grey, that were green, she recalled the dynamic splendour of two gambler's gems, star sapphires, she recalled the tilted mirror that was the back of her head and in that mirror, she saw little stark shapes passing. The front of her head turned and looked into the back of her head as a child may do, astonished to find things turned round in a mirror. Her discovery was a gambler's heritage. She did not know that all her life would be spent gambling with the stark rigidity of words, words that were coin; save, spend; and all the time George Lowndes with his own counter, had found her a way out.

The hounds of spring are, indeed, on winter's traces. Her mind, could she have so formulated thought, would have conceded: I have tasted words, I have seen them. Never had her hands reached out in darkness and felt the texture of pure marble, never had her forehead bent forward and, as against a stone altar, felt safety, I am now saved. Her mind could not then so specifically have seen it, could not have said, "Now I will reveal myself in words, words may now supersede a scheme of mathematical-biological definition. Words may be my heritage and with words I will prove conic sections a falsity and the very stars that wheel and frame concentric pattern as mere very-stars, gems put there, a gift, a diadem, a crown, a chair, a cart or a mere lady. A lady will be set back in the sky. It will be no longer Arcturus and Vega but stray star-spume, star sprinkling from a wild river, it will be myth; mythopoeic mind (mine) will disprove science and biological-mathematical definition."

She did not think this for her mind was too astonished to perceive how she could turn, perceive as a mirror the whole of the fantasy of the world reversed and in that mirror a wide room opening. She could not say how or when she saw this; she knew it related back to an odd girl and Nellie and a group of non-related midges and a group of gnats enclosed in an acorn spread across by one pink peony. She could not have revealed herself to George who had made harlequin joke of something she had been just about to tell him. George had said, sometime back, mock ironically, "Did you see her on the telephone?"

She could now answer but she did not, "No I did not see her on the telephone but in a sort of mirror television." She did not say that, for she was suddenly overcome with the enormity of her discovery. *The hounds of spring are on winter's traces* let her fall forward, there was hope in block of substantiated marble, words could carve and set up solid altars ... Thought followed the wing that beat its silver into the seven-branched larch boughs.

Breath came in short gasps. Georgio was kneeling, Orlando gesture, by her. Georgio was shaking her, saying "Come, come," seriously. George was shaking her, her head (marble weight) lay heavy on his shoulder. The back of her head that was slightly convex, that was a polished surface, that was a mirror holding a Dutch-group, a picture, rested heavy on his shoulder. She shut out larch boughs and the bit of jagged open space and little Christmas tree tinsel glitter that was sunlight flung like Christmas tree tinsel here and there tangled and matted and sometimes strewn on carefully, across the seven-branched larch boughs. She shut out larch boughs and odd triangle of sunlight that seemed to fall as from the edge of a half-open shutter. Her head rested heavy, dehumanized on George's shoulder.

five

"But you can't go on this way." "Which way?" "You can't come in late and tired and ill from the woods." "Ill?" "Oh Hermione. Oh my dear, *dear* child." Eugenia saying my dear, dear child didn't mean that she was dear, didn't mean that she was a child.

Now why had Her let her catch her? Eugenia had caught Her, whirling on forest heels, whirling down the hall, about to leap up three stairs, whirl up, up a forest fountain into her own room. "But Her-mi-o-nie. You are late." Late, late with forest edges to everything, edges of moss about the worm-eaten picture frame, above the little table, worm-eaten edges, moss about the plaque of flat leaves, grape and grape leaf brought from Berne by Eugenia on her honeymoon.

"But you're late and what have you had for dinner? Did Mandy save your dinner" and she was caught; swirl about on flat fountain heels and follow Eugenia prim into the living room. Dusk now filled it. Have I sat long enough waiting to bounce upstairs? Am I grateful enough to Eugenia? She hasn't really been a bit horrid about my being so late with George though she hates him. "But you can't go on this way" was a merely mechanical device, something you said automatically to your own child.

"But you can't go on this way." Eugenia would say that again and she would say it again. I will give her, Hermione said, seven times to say it. She has said it seven times. Now she can say it another seven times. If she says it another seven times...

"Well, *what* are you thinking, darling," "I don't know, Eugenia." "I've been hurt you know Hermione by the way you call me Eugenia." "Shall I call you Gart then simply? It's rather confusing calling everybody Gart. You're Gart and Minnie is Gart and papa is Gart and Bertrand is Gart. I am Gart too, I suppose. If I say Gart everybody will run including Jock and Mandy for I suppose Jock is rightful Gart and Mandy..." Hermione didn't know what she was saying, didn't care. Eugenia wouldn't listen anyway. She went on.

"Mandy belongs to us. Mandy belongs to me. Mandy is mine. This business of the United States, United States of America doing away with states being separate with separate states and each state with its own laws is what is responsible for all this mob rule." (Get her off, hare and hounds, *you can't go on this way*.) "You get no sort of cohesion out of a thing so immense. You can't expect every one of us equally to sympathize with Southern Spanish California and New York Dutch and Middle Western and French from Louisiana. This thing that any one can say *united we stand* is all rot. We can't stand united. Divided we would probably stand. You're defying laws of science," (hare and hounds) "mathematics and chemistry by trying to mix such mobs heterogeneously. You can't expect things to go on forever this way. You'll get mob rule and then mob rule and then mob rule."

"How can you stand George Lowndes?" Eugenia hadn't heard a word of what she had been saying. "How can you stand George Lowndes?" Hermione would have to find some other weapon. Eugenia had found something else for "But how can you go on this way?" Hermione was saved this time. She had stopped saying "But how can you go on this way" and she was saying (she would, would go on saying) "How can you stand George Lowndes?" Eugenia's head rose from the dressing-jacket frill of ruffled spotted dimity (Eugenia called it spotted dimity), hands moving back and forth, quietly, monotonously, back and forth, back and forth.

"Why are you always knitting? Only old ladies knit and knit like you do." "I am an old lady. I can knit in the dark. I can't sew in the dark. Your father likes the light concentrated in a corner. He can work better if I'm sitting in the dark." Father, your father. Eugenia sitting in the darkness, the green shade, fixed now here, now there over the just one blazing electric light, just one concentrated circle of light across the half of a desk, strewn with papers, only Gart's papers were always piled in little heaps, folded up in little bundles.

"Did you catalogue that last lot of papers?"

She had catalogued the last lot of papers. Hermione said "Yes, I catalogued the papers." Papers, periodicals, papers from Munich, thicker volume from the Institut de France. France. *C'est agaçant*. France. French. She had catalogued the papers, printed their numbers on the slips of cardboard, small filing cabinet, her job, doing it automatically. It was easier to do these things than not to do them. She was hypnotized by these things. How long would she go on this way? I am a failure. She must pull herself out, pull herself out of something. She must pull herself out of this at just this moment. "I must go upstairs, mama." She must get up now. She must get away from Eugenia sitting in the dark like a great moth, dimity dressing jacket, feet crossed on a low pouf thing, hands knitting, hands, hands … knitting. Eugenia worked her old charm. She hypnotizes me.

"You never listen to what I say, mama. Your throat looks so pretty coming out of that ruffle … like a moonflower. You're soft like a moonflower. You shouldn't be called Gart. You're round like a moonflower with a sort of stamen pistil sort of thing, the sort of throat that you have rising out of a moon-ruffle." "Hermione. You say such pretty, odd things. You ought to go on writing." "*Writing?*" "Those dear little stories you did …" "Oh, mama, that's not *writing.*" "You ought to do something, Hermione. You're looking odd and worried and distracted and not right here." Hermione didn't say "Why didn't you let me go away then, alone then, to the cottage."

Watching hands. Hands in the darkness, hands in the darkness … you have no midwife power, you can't lift me out of this thing. Oh, hands in the dim light, for Gart wanted one heady downstream just there, on just his papers, Gart is too terribly in me, light concentrated on just his microscope or on just his little dish of sizzling acids. Light must be concentrated under a green cone, a cornucopia, like you hang on the Christmas tree, cornucopia, horn of plenty, she had told them, Demeter hand hanging little horns of plenty on the tree and always enough horns of plenty to go round. It was right. Oh, she's so horribly right. Then what is wrong with everything?

Screw of light that always had been there, burning incandescent in the room, the middle or the side, by the open window, by the doorway, Carl Gart calling to Bertrand across the hall where they had turned a sort of butler's pantry sort of little slice of a room into a laboratory, little room upstairs that ought to have been an extra linen cupboard turned into a darkroom, rooms eating out their slow and comfortable existence like black acids, rooms here and there, another slice in the cellar for aquariums and Eugenia moving through it powerless, all-powerful … one should sing hymns of worship to her, powerful, powerless, all-powerful … and what am I between them?

I am broken like a nut between two rocks, granite and granite … "I told you that I met that girl at Nellie's." "Yes. Why don't you have her out here?" Why don't you have her out here? Why don't you have her out here? Out? How did one get her out? "I've forgotten what her name is. I mean I don't think I ever knew her name. I don't know what her name is."

She would get upstairs somehow for one did get upstairs somehow. The way of her getting upstairs remained unsolved, insoluble, but one always did get upstairs somehow. "I must go upstairs" … for a name, having said that she was nameless, branded itself, indelible acid, fire, across her flaming spirit. Her spirit quiescent, snuffed, so to speak, out by this hypnotic movement of hands, of hands in darkness, of hands in half-light, of hands crossing hands and making a pattern like moonlight across the black leaves of swamp, of March lilies … *of all kinds, the fleur de lys being one* … her spirit snuffed out by Eugenia flamed and flared by Gart … the spirit pouring down its incandescent splendour was like Gart collecting all the light to fall just there on just that microscopic slide or just that bowl of little sizzling acids. The spirit and the bride say come. The spirit and the bride say come. *Her name is Itylus.*

Why didn't George leave her alone to it? Why hadn't George left her alone to it? There's a black rose growing in your garden. Black rose (the outer hallway) opened to receive her, Hermione out of Shakespeare. George had bent forward, George had leant forward, George had appeared above her like a bit of a jagged edge (showing behind a cornice) of the Ducal Palace. I have never been to Venice. I have, in fact, never been anywhere. I would rather go to Point Pleasant alone with a big dog, only Jock isn't my dog, a silver hound that would scrape sand pattern, that would make pattern of dog feet in the wet sand and deeper dog feet in the dry sand and round sort of cone-shaped hollows in the very dry sand sifting through baked seaweed at the highest tide line.

The highest tide line ran almost to ribbed grasses that caught wind that hiss-ss-ssed like quiescent and friendly serpents. The girl with those cynical eyes said she was glad I hadn't been to Luxor. Up the Nile. Everybody is taking things up or going up ... upstairs is all I'll get to and I wonder if I *will* get upstairs.

I am glued to the heart of this black hall, this black rose, this thing that beats down on me, it must be the heat. Everybody cares for something but I don't care for anything. I don't care a bit what her name is. It's funny, I don't know what her name is for George was heavy and the sun caught that jade light in his eyes. For a moment he was tawny with his sticking-up hair and his harlequin features blurred out, cut across by jade light from green eyes. His eyes were green, sea-green and wood-green but he would never love a tree. I am a tree. TREE is my new name out of the Revelations. He shall have a new name ... written on his forehead. The mark of the beast. I have the mark of the beast. I would rather go off alone with a sort of a Jock who was my dog not Minnie's than to have ... than to have ... the temple on the Nile. I am out of the Temple Shakespeare, a small book with leather and George smells of morocco bindings. His heat was symmetrical ... patches under hot arms ...

Now lightning showed her a mirror, the plane square above her dressing table, patches of silver that were the polished backs of brushes and polished handmirror (Mandy was always at them). Lightning pulsed (it's only heat lightning) above the black line that was the forest where it was banked against their lawn. We are set like a problem on a blackboard. The house is columns of figures, double column and the path at right angles to the porch steps is the line beneath numbers and the lawn step is the tentative beginning of a number and the little toolshed and the springhouse at the far corner of the opposite side is bits of jotted-down calculations that will be rubbed out presently.

Gart lawn outside the window lay black and luminous, a square this side of the lawn step, a symmetrical square the other side. Gart lawn lies like everything else in and about us, too clear, too perfect; lying there it makes two blackboards across which in a moment lightning, white chalk, will brandish its symbols (give the answer perhaps) from some cruel and dynamic unseen hand making circles across blackboards.

The sky too is a blackboard, smudged here and there with grey whisps of cloud seen from the underside like half-smudged-over chalk marks on a blackboard gone grey with marks and marks. Someone should take a wet sponge and wipe it all out, make it quite black, not smudged at edges with cloudy chalk stuff.

Suffocating ... it's suffocating. It's like breathing in a crowded schoolroom ... the whole place is crowded; schoolroom full of chalk, full of dust, "But you Miss Thorpe, don't know what dust is." Nellie Thorpe in the right street, in the wrong street didn't know what dust is. "But you Miss Gart in that lovely country." Gawd's own god-damn country. George had come back, why had George come back to Gawd's own god-damn country? She had asked George why he had come back and the smudges of anemone-coloured smudged kisses answered her. His mouth is the colour of a burnt-out red hibiscus. George doesn't know what trees are.

Herself flung down, white branch, wilted on the wide bed, repeated from somewhere like some formula remembered from a forgotten textbook, "George doesn't know what trees are." Herself, branch wilted, repeated this, "George doesn't know what I am." Her hand flung out on the long narrow too-soft pillow sank down, down into the pillow. Her hand was something apart, weighted, a weight of broken-off hand flung down, sunk, smudged out in the soft too-hot down of the long pillow. My hand is a marble hand sunk into the pillow. This afternoon (was it this afternoon?) her head had sunk back and back into moss. She tried to visualize moss under a head that became heavier and heavier. It seemed that her head must sink down into the pillow, through the pillow, through the mattress beneath the pillow. It seemed that her head must sink down through the boards under the mattress, the movable lath-like boards that ran across the bed from side to side of the bed like boards laid across a stream for feet to walk on. She could walk across a narrow log flung across a wide stream. She had so dared walk across the very narrow almost-sapling that spanned the wide shallow stream, the almost-river that had edged Gart woods, that separated Gart woods from the Werby meadow. The Werby meadow ran on across leagues (it seemed) of land, on, on to the Werby station.

"Werby the horrid name of the horrid little station." Werby station lay the other side of the field and she had skirted the field, thinking vaguely that George would get as far as that, then turn tracks, go back, look for his coat, find his coat, see Werby station and go straight back on the about-8:30 train to Philadelphia. George had followed her somehow—*the hounds of spring are on winter's traces* and somehow George had guessed that she would dodge across the railroad tracks (had they done it last year?) into the Farrand forest. The Farrands liked her plunging into their forest. The dogs knew her. But the Farrands and the dogs were away now (Wolf and Freya). They used to take the dogs to Maine with them before they went abroad. Wolf and Freya loved the Maine woods, great hounds (Jock was at Point Pleasant), enormous hounds; they took the dogs, Minnie had taken Jock too with her. Everybody had something; Minnie had Jock.

George was like a great tawny beast, a sort of sub-lion pawing at her, pawing with great hand at her tousled garments. George had been like a great lion but if he had simply bared teeth, torn away garments with bared fangs, she would have understood, would have put narrow arms about great shoulders, would have yielded to him. George was neither beast nor man, was not attuned to high beating intellect that had raced ahead of him, that he had not caught for all his wit in finding her flung down under the seven larches, the seven small larches making a circle where moss spread in a circle for Hermione to lie on.

Hermione tried to visualize moss under her hot flanks. It was too hot ... was it less hot with or without a sheet. The sheet made creases like white hot metal, white hot creases for iron to flow down. The sheet was iron upon her. She flung off the iron metal of metallic white sheet ... buzz ... ping ... a mosquito flung brass weight against her, giant mosquito as big as a chicken hawk flung against her face. She felt the weight of his weighted heavy gauze wings, wings like grey wire gauze, his wings cut her cheek, gauze of metal cut her cheek bone. Hand lifted automatically from the pillow, bang, jip ... but she hadn't got him. Her own hand (bang-jip) against her cheek-bone was less heavy than that edge of wing that had brushed her. Bang-jip ... but she hadn't got him. He was away, sitting somewhere high above her, as big as a chicken hawk gorged on her own blood. She scratched the bitten bare knee ruefully. She became angry with just this thing ... there is a limit. There just *is* a penultimate limit.

She sat up in bed, her two arms encircling her bare knees. She pulled her thin garment down tight about her bare knees and sat up in pulse-pulse of lightning like some carved heavy marble, suppliant praying with head bent down on swathed marble knees. Knees in the white pulse-pulse that was the pulse-pulse of heat lightning above the sharp edge of the black woods, made her white, a marble, seated in anguish, a young suppliant with knees covered with marble folds of cloth, of carved stone. She sat, an image on a headstone in the pulse of heady lightning.

Turned to stone, turned to stone ... who was turned to stone for something? I will be turned to stone but buzz-zz ... zzz ... saved her from that predicament. Weighted hand (Hermione's?) raised fire and lightning of anger and fell angry, heavy, passionate on the nape of her own neck. The exposed naked nape of her neck at the base of her head (noble suppliant marble head on bare marble) was ignobly gouged by this ignoble creature. She could visualize the mosquito flown off again somewhere as huge, seen under some horrible magnifying glass, sitting leering at her with his enormous mammoth jaws ... with front legs toward her raking from a black arena.

six

"Did you?" "Did I what?" "Sleep well?" "Did *you?*" "Did I?" "Sleep?" "Oh moderately." "Did anyone—" "Did anyone what?" "In the whole world sleep at all last night, I wonder."

Thunder reverberated across wet lawns, shook the middle forest, prolonged itself like some beast growling under deep-sea water, shook the water above their heads, broke through it and let down more water through a funnel. Water poured through a funnel on the roof above them, slid off gutters, made a sheet across the window, darkened the dining room and blotted out the dining room silver. Silver forks, spoons, a bowl on the side table became lost in silver, mist in and out, a sheet of silver hung permanently across the dining room window. Window tight-fastened, odd shut-in feeling on a summer morning. Outside the odd tight-fastened window, a sheet of thin metal hung wavering ominously. "I feel we're shut up inside a submarine or a bomb that will burst suddenly."

Brrrr-ooooo-ommm—the bomb burst suddenly. "This is ghastly. I thought the storm was over." The silver went platinum-white in the succeeding sudden flashes. "The whole world's blown up suddenly." The silver went lead, less than silver in the reassuring heavy downpour that almost drowned the distant BRRRooming drum, reassuring drum of raindrops beating; we're coming to help, we're coming to help, we're on the way to rescue you from lead and shot and silver turned to gunfire … "It may be over sometime."

Brrr-oo-mm seemed driven off somewhere, heavy brroom was gradually beaten back, became faint beneath the steady alert drum-mmm of heavy tropic waters. "It must be a cloudburst." Tropic water receded ever so slightly, they were as it were lifted up from underwater to a higher layer of water. They were still deep underwater but breath came more naturally, not gasp on self-conscious gasp (one listened for one's breathing) while the heady brrr-ooommmm was hanging ominous just above them. "It's like the flood exactly. The animals went in two by two ... will you pass the honey."

"I'm glad you can eat, Hermione. This air is stupefying." "I'll open the window, mama." "Oh you can't yet Hermione ..." But Eugenia was braced for fresh effort by that idea, lifted the handle of the coffeepot, poured out coffee slowly, seemed returned to life by that familiar action, looked up with a smile in grey-green underwater features. "It's funny your smiling that way. It's like a face seen under bottleglass. We're all green like faces under water ... no. Not all green ..." Mandy was standing with them. "Mandy's different ..." "Sh-sssh ..." Mandy (exquisite bronze) was a brazier burning in that bleak room. Mandy was bronze like a brazier (they—Hermione, Eugenia—were bottle-green) but Hermione couldn't say it. Eugenia was shushing at Hermione, not wanting her to say it. I can't say Mandy is a bronze. I can't say Mandy looks like Etruscan bronze dredged from the mid-Ionian with colour flashing against her polished bronze ... I won't say Mandy is like a bronze giving out iridescence like a flying fish, there is a blue-green iridescence across the copper polish and her face is fixed like a bronze face, her eyes are set in like agates in a Mena-period Egyptian effigy. I won't say that. I must say, "What Mandy—not more hot cakes?"

They (Eugenia, Hermione) were flung now into profound intimacy like shipwrecked mariners after the heavy sweep of waves has numbed them past consciousness of former quarrels, in the tiny morning room. The morning room stood square against the elements. It endured like a lighthouse set edge-square with rising waters. The lighthouse little morning room showed an edge of Virginia creeper, hectic prematurely brilliant colour, that beat against the sea-washed window like seaweed flung up from dense mid-waters. "The Virginia creeper, mama's touched already." Swing swing of vermillion-tipped first autumn leaves against a rain drenched window. "Good Mandy. Put the logs *here*." Hermione bent to newspapers, matched dried handful of odd shavings. A tiny flame burst up; forest worshiper, fire worshiper (Hermione) enclosed as in a ball of glass, bent to revive life. Eugenia's face was pale, tipped at the chin edge by phosphorescent line as the light crept up, little live flame into the midst of water.

Unless you are born of water ... unless you are born of water ... they were born of water, reincarnated, all their past million-of-years-ago quarrel forgotten in the firelight. "I never remember such a storm at this time. I mean it's so uncanny happening at this time of the morning."

Hermione had drawn away, forgotten herself. Eugenia had drawn away forgotten herself. Eugenia forgetting herself spoke to herself. "Your father was *afraid* (the flood the year before had cracked Bolton's bridge) that the doctor wouldn't help us." Eugenia was speaking from somewhere outside herself, beyond the window, slashed with its hectic vermillion leaf-flash, fins of tropic sea fish, seen through tidewave of tidal waters. Eugenia had forgotten Hermione. "It was such a funny *time* to have a baby. I don't know why but it seemed a funny *time* to have a baby. It seems odd having a baby (I don't know why) by daylight. It seemed such a funny *time* to have a baby."

"It was all over in a few hours ... it was so funny. It was all over in a few hours. It was so odd. I had you in the morning."

The morning stars sang together. Words of Eugenia had more power than textbooks, than geometry, than all of Carl Gart and brilliant "Bertie Gart" as people called him. Bertrand wasn't brilliant, not like mama. Carl Gart wasn't brilliant like Eugenia. "*Then* the doctor came. But she was such a dear nurse, so much better than the doctor, she was like a mother to me ..."

Demeter (such a dear nurse) lifting the tired shoulders of a young Eugenia had driven the wind back, back ... the house was sitting on its haunches. The house sunk down on its haunches. The house took a deep breath settled down, decided to settle down for another re-incarnation. It was Eugenia who had saved it.

"The house has decided not to be blown away, mama." Eugenia looked up with an odd start. "Oh, what were you saying to me? What was I saying?" "I wasn't saying anything, Eugenia. You weren't saying anything. I said the house has decided not to be blown to splithers. There's not even a window broken." Purrr-rrrrr, the giant voice of a giant panther gouged with destruction, storm blowing over Gart and the lawn and the little springhouse and the toolhouse set down like numbers, had smudged out numbers and the blackboard and the grey slate of lawn were washed clear, clear for another number, for another set of numbers. Giant hand had brandished its weapon, chalk of brilliant sizzling white fire had written insoluble words across the densest blackness. Carl Gart, brilliant Bertie Gart (as people called him) had no power against the numbers. Demeter ("such a dear nurse") had driven the raging storm back ... had saved them from the numbers.

"But you're crying, birdie." "Oh no. No ... never mind, Eugenia ... the heat ... last night ... upset me."

She went out odd and unseeing. She couldn't see anything. Her eyes were statue's eyes, blurred over, eye-spaces where eyes should be. Her eyes were a blank covered with a white surface, a statue with eyes of a statue seeing nothing. The early Greeks painted eyes in their statues (coloured prints in the two huge volumes); before that, Egyptians coloured dark wood images, beautifully cut and modelled with eyes of stones. A beautiful stone shining (the print was beautiful) and enlargement of the two agate-dark dark eyes with bright very-white white around them. Mandy's eyes are set in her head like those eyes. I can't see things. I'm crying ...

She saw things. She realized she had suddenly stopped crying. She saw Carl Gart in high storm boots, rubber boots pulled high almost to his waist like the lifesaving people at the lifesaving station at Point Pleasant. Carl Gart dripped pools of water on the polished hall floor, pools of water ran from his shoulders, his white Pericles beard emerged white and frost-stiff from beneath the wide rim of his felt hat drawn like an assassin's over his deep eyes. His eyes were blue under the hat like an assassin's hat, under the hat like a helmet, like a fireman's hat, like the cap he wore in the little old daguerre-otype. Carl Gart (in the daguerreotype in blue uniform and little buttons) had an odd young chin, unfamiliar rather child-sweet chin, chin rather insignificant (he was only seventeen) beneath the beak nose and the young eyes that stared and stared out of the mirror surface of the old daguerreotype.

"You're wet, father." Carl Gart stood, like Proteus, dripping water. He would see that Hermione had been crying. She had stopped crying suddenly at the sight of Carl Gart in his assas-sin's hat pulled over eyes that were (she knew) too-blue under the white eyebrows above the beaked nose, above the clever little Pericles white goat beard.

He said, "The thunder got 'em."

Hermione said "Got what, papa?" though she knew from

the odd careless way he said it, that the storm must have leaked into the cellar or into the outer toolhouse and broken something. Something too-precious only brought that too-casual, slightly flung-out tone to his monotonous pure utterance. The little laugh was like a horse that neighs. "The storm sprung a leak in the tool-house but that didn't so much matter. But the aquarium in the cellar was simply flooded out. The thunder got 'em." He said "the thunder got 'em" like a formula.

She said "Got what, papa?" knowing what it was they had got. "The old five year experiment. Bertrand will feel it badly." He laughed his little horselaugh. "The whole lot swam out, flooded out, the cross section and the cross hatching were simply flooded out." He seemed to think this funny. "Now Bertie and I will begin another breeding. That took ten years, fifteen in all if you count the first experimental failures."

Water dripped from his gumboots. He was rescuing people in a high storm. Something had broken something ... "Oh, *mama* will be *heart*-broken ..." "Your mother takes these things too seriously."

seven

The sun, after an amazing unprecedented thunderous week, came out making gold runnels in thick jade, making heavy gold layers of light on jade temple fronts. The heavy bull-like forehead of an oak tree was set with a great heavy knob of gold, and gold was set most cautiously and discreetly (yet with immense extravagance) across the pillars of outer porches that were birch trees. Gold was laid discreetly ... it was gold across silver really. "The world's changed utterly."

Static, upright, parallel, the static upright tree shafts held parallel (or seemed to hold parallel) crossbeams of polished oak wood. The oak wood was unpolished when she came to look at it, great hulk of a tree trunk, rough hippopotamus tree-hide, tree-hide furrowed like a mountain on the moon. The tree trunk was furrowed, a territory, a continent, a planet. Hermione ran her fingers along a mountain range, the furrowed tree trunk, ran her finger along the damp rain-soaked bark, ran her finger along ... "Then you will come with me?" "I said I would come if I could come." George Lowndes was waiting for her to say "Yes, I will come." "I'll have to get the tickets."

"Well why don't you get your ticket and leave me out of it?" "I can't leave you out of it." "Why can't you leave me out of it?" Words from a child's primer, words for a beginner, a Slav, a Russian, a Hindu learning to speak English. She ran words along like a child reading out of a first primer, like a Hindu learning to speak English, "But why can't you let me stay here?"

"I can't let you stay here," he went on like the next line in the Reader for Small Children, "because—*be*-cause I can *not* let you stay here." He answered her in tone, in time, in rhythm and simple beat, do re mi fa so la si do. He ran his words together, he separated his words. "Do you *re*-alize what this week has been without you?"

"A week? A week without you. Has it been a week without you?" Has a week been a week that is not somehow broken slashed and tattered by George and his odd disassociating harlequin way with everything? "Is it a week without you?" He said, "You rushed me to the station without the decency of offering me my dinner. You rushed me to the station ... said in a week you'd tell me." "Did I say in a week I'd tell you?" "You said Georgio if you catch the 8:15 to Philadelphia you can come back in a week's time. If you miss the 8:15 to Philadelphia then you can come back—never." "Did you catch the 8:15 to Philadelphia." "I *did* catch the 8:15 to Philadelphia." "*And unto the church in Philadelphia, write*—what did they write unto the church in Philadelphia?" "Hermione, you *will* come?"

One I love, two I love, three I love ... how do I know what I love? I love Eugenia but I can not stay here. I love Bertrand and Minnie stays here. One I love, two I love, three I love. Her finger came to a full stop in the mountain. "This is a mountain on the moon, George. This is the moon, George. Why should we go to Europe when we can travel on the moon, when we can follow tropic rivers through our oak wood, when we have the Farrand forest that is like the Chersonese before the oak trees rotted? In Greece, the old forests are dead, in Italy ..." "Italy—" he caught her hand raised upward to oak beams laid parallel on polished tree shafts, "In Italy, Hermione will find the heart to love me."

"But you can't *marry* George Lowndes." "On what compulsion must I—I mean mustn't I—tell me that?" "Be serious. Do you know what you are saying." "I am saying George has been asking me to marry him." "But you can't, you can't possibly." "Why, just why can't I possibly?" "Well, there are—there is—why—you can't—there are the university ladies." "What have the university ladies got to do with me, with George Lowndes?" "Why, why—why—Hermione, you know—surely you're only joking—surely you must remember—" "What? What exactly mama?" "That horrible—well—fiasco—you remember." "But I thought that was all forgotten and anyhow everyone knew George took the poor creature to his room to feed her." "People don't take people to their rooms to feed them. You're out of your mind, Hermione. Mrs. Lastrow was saying to me that everyone cut George Lowndes." "Why, why did everyone cut George Lowndes?"

Hermione heard Hermione speaking, saying something out of a play, words had been written for her, she was repeating words that had been written, "They cut him because he's getting on, because he's had his books published. They're all a set of provincials." "*Provincials.* You're getting on famously, Hermione. George Lowndes is teaching you, actually *teaching* you words, telling you what to say." "George isn't. He never tells me what to say. I never say anyhow what anyone ever tells me to say. Do you think I have so little spunk, so little character that I would repeat (like a foul parrot) words, words, words out of someone else's mouth, spew back words that have been already chewed and chewed? Your so-called university ladies are like a lot of old cows spitting up cud that's already been chewed into a foul mass years back. Have you nothing better to discuss than poor George Lowndes?"

"Poor George Lowndes. I thought you said he was getting on famously, that all London, Munich, Paris and Berlin were at his feet, that he was chanting his verses to crowded houses, at tea parties—" "I didn't say anything of the sort. I said that Yeats had praised him in a review, that Madox Ford wanted him to help in a new book he's doing, that—" "That, that, that … Hermione this will *kill* me."

"Now why will it kill you, mama?" Best have it out with mama, go on shelling peas (she was sitting on the porch floor) for Mandy. Dinner will be late. Mandy had missed her usual train back. Best go on shelling peas. "Well, you had the decency at least *not* to ask him to dinner." Go on shelling peas. "I asked him to come tomorrow instead. I told him it was Mandy's afternoon out and I asked him to come tomorrow." Go on shelling peas. One I love, two I love, three I love. I don't really love now anybody.

It's horrible. Why, why couldn't George have left me to it? I can't go away with George, I can't stay here without George. Something is so horribly rotten in the state of Denmark.

"These peas are half of them waterlogged, the whole vegetable garden was like a swamp till this morning when the sun so obligingly came out again after a week of this diluvian weather." "There's too much for Tim to do on the place. The garden alone is one man's work." "I helped all last week." "Yes. It's good for you to work, house work, garden work. After that horrible fiasco of yours at Bryn Mawr" (Eugenia had fiasco on the brain) "and all the disappointment and now poor Carl." Go on shelling peas, go on shelling peas. All life is so horribly disproportionate, we never know in this Uncle Sam country where we are, brilliance and destruction, we live in a sort of thunder storm, with heat and cold and intersecting rays of lightning.

God, some sort of Uncle Sam, Carl-Bertrand-Gart God, shut us up in a box, with temperatures too high and temperatures too low to breed new specimens like Bertrand Gart, like Carl Gart in their aquariums. There is only one solution ... there is only one solution ... "Shall I go on shelling peas for ever?" "Aren't you almost through?" "I'll never be through. I think I'll never finish." "But you didn't *have* to do it." "No, but if I didn't you would and you've too much to do anyhow. Why can't you and father give up this house?"

"Give-up-this house?" "Yes. Why can't you and father just give things up, just scrap everything?" "Hermi-o-nie? Are you mad my dear child?" "No. Where is this all leading us? All leading you?" "I'm not at the age to be led, Hermione; your father and his work are more important." "More important than what exactly?"

Cruel, cruel, be cruel, be cruel. Drag tatters of red and blue and striped shiny black and stained cherry-coloured satin ribbons and beggars-tatters around Hermione. Dance and sing and whirl round and round on mad heels. George Lowndes is right precisely. "George Lowndes is right." "In what exact particular?" "Why don't you see? Don't you see? This *is* the forest primeval. Why don't you see—don't you see? There are numbers fencing us in. We are being fenced in with numbers, one I love, two I love, three I love. Rich man, poor man, beggar man, thief. I mean years are like a lead fence." "What years Hermione?" "All years—what *is* the year anyhow? I mean what particular year is it? I come up against a lead block in my brain when I try to remember anything. Years are about our necks, years are making a fence, each year a bit more of a fence. George Lowndes is right precisely."

Drag tatters, a new garment, drag something distinctive and different about whirling mad limbs. Thought goes up and up in spirals like a water spout. "The whole vegetable garden was a mire. He ought to buy some pigs to root there. The sweet peas won't come right again this summer." This summer, what *is* this summer anyhow? The year, this year, makes a new row of spikey spokes to the fence that is hedging me in, things are too much, things are too much. Will I go on shelling peas forever? "Rich man, poor man, beggar man, thief," she counted green peas in a pea pod, "doctor, lawyer, merchant, priest." "It isn't merchant, priest, it's merchant-chief." "Well anyhow I'm going to marry a priest or a merchant-chief when I marry George Lowndes."

When I marry George Lowndes, when I marry George Lowndes. "And when exactly are you going to marry George Lowndes?" Eugenia spoke ironically, she was speaking up nicely, they were making snap and spark between them,

George Lowndes the flint for spark and snap and steel sparks flying. Eugenia was never sarcastic. Eugenia was now sarcastic.

"Don't you know what marriage *means,* Hermione?" "Marriage means me whirling like a waterspout, swirling out of everything, whirling over fences, out, out, out of the forest primeval" (she achieved the exact George Uncle-Sam-in-whiskers voice). "Pri-meval" (she repeated it), "I am going to whirl out of this the forest primeval, the murmuring pines and the hemlocks bearded with moss and with garments green indistinct in the twilight. I am indistinct in the twilight. I am going to swirl out, out." "With what are you going to swirl and how are you going to swirl and where are you swirling to?" Eugenia roused was spark to flint, flint to spark. Eugenia roused was being ironical. "I'm going to swirl to Europe. Doesn't everybody go there on a honeymoon? Didn't *you* go there on a honeymoon?" "How are you going? Has he any money?" "Money? I had—hadn't thought of money. Yes he has a little money. A driblet (he calls it) from an aunt. Oh, we won't have much. We won't as a matter of fact have anything. He said we won't need anything." "You can't live on nothing." "I can live on sunlight falling across little bridges. I can live on the Botticelli-blue cornflower pattern on the out-billowing garments of the attendant to Aphrodite and the pattern of strawberry blossoms and little daisies in the robe of Primavera. I can live on the doves flying (he says) in cohorts from the underside of the faded gilt of the balcony of Saint Mark's cathedral and the long corridors of the Pitti Palace. I can gorge myself on Rome and the naked Bacchus and the face like a blasted lightning-blasted white birch that is some sort of Fury. That face on a plaque that is some sort of Fury." She was standing with the bowl of shelled peas under one arm, dramatically held aloft like some young hydrophyte.

She held the bowl against one hip, stood with one foot elevated. Sunlight fell across the tossed mouse-hair of Hermione tucked short and unimpressive into a moire band of narrow ribbon. Her face was a face of some young Pythian priestess. "And I can live on *nothing*."

"You can't live on nothing. Your father won't permit it. Do you think your father and I would have such inhumanity as to let you—to *let* you marry a man of George Lowndes' reputation and marry a man of George Lowndes' reputation on simply nothing?" "You mean if this man George Lowndes had a heap—had I mean a steam yacht and a million of dollars you would let me?" "I mean the thing is unsuitable and you're mad altogether."

"Father. I am going to marry George Lowndes." Carl Gart looked up from a superimposed bit of glass on a bit of glass that had already squashed flat a bit of alga. The thing, she knew, would look odd, unholy in its beauty under the microscope that one thin hand was screwing, adjusting to his vision. Carl Gart pulled away his eye from the microscopic lens and with an effort jolted himself back, with a jolt brought himself back to—"Eugenia." "I'm not Eugenia, I'm Hermione."

Carl Gart saw a tall creature, his own daughter, with odd unholy eyes. Eyes shone odd and unholy in a white face. "I said father that I'm going to marry." Carl Gart brought his mind by a superhuman effort to readjustment to the thing before him. He saw an odd fury-ridden creature with white face and flame-lipped face and a face where two lips were drawn tight almost like dead lips across a skeleton. He saw ridges in the face, fine bones beneath the face. "You're—you're thin, Hermione."

"I'm not any more thin than I always am, father. I'm no more thin than you are. We are thin, father." A long skeleton hand was screwing a little round wheel; screw a little round wheel and I know you are great, I know you are as abstract and as beautiful as white bones bleached in sunlight. The mind of Carl Gart was white bones bleached in sunlight but the mind isn't everything. "I'm going to marry George Lowndes, precisely."

Carl Gart readjusted the microscope to exactly suit his vision. His mind hovered like a desert eagle before his dual beauties. Like a desert hawk that sees here (this side) a skeleton of a dead horse and there (that side) some low flying swooping sister eagle, Carl Gart wavered. The mind of Carl Gart wavered before the vision in the lens beside him and this other vision ... Hermione sitting here beside him, sister eagle, brother eagle, twin eagle mind, Hermione. Bertrand was patient but uninspired. Hermione has some odd way of seeing ... she had failed him. "I mean—what were you saying, daughter?" He called her daughter like a Middle West farmer, like someone out of the Old Testament, like God saying *daughter I say unto you arise.* He called her daughter out of some old, old volume ... she left the room ... defeated.

Mechanically she went to the telephone. Mechanically she rang up the operator, mechanically she said hello,hello, hello. Voice far and far at the end of a long wire, somewhere far and far a voice would speak to her, the voice would say, "You are one damn fool Bellissima, you can't let me down this way" and she would say "But you must never come again George" and George would know she meant it and she was hanging on, hanging on to a tiny spar above the seething waters and George would utter commonplaces and the voice would shout back "This is the forest pri-meval, the murmuring pines and the hemlocks."

The murmuring pines and the hemlocks would be murmuring all the time over the other side of the creek that was almost a river. The creek was spanned by the narrowest of bridges, an almost-sapling across which her feet would run, had run, would all her life run like a forest cat, like an older forest cat, like a cat gone thin and thinner and more gaunt and more dehumanized. For "I can't marry you now, George" she would say for George, with his ribbons and his tatters of learning, was the one thing to save her from this dehumanizing process and she wasn't strong enough to do it.

Little bridge led from here to another world, a world where people lived in a soft aura of mist, of fog. George said in England there was no summer, no winter, just one low mist that was fog, that was a low horizon, no thunder and snow blinding her and heat and cold that some Uncle Sam Gart sort of person brandishing sizzling lightning would force down, would force up to 200°, 300° or whatever it was Fahrenheit, to some odd centigrade she had forgotten. Super-boiling point, freezing below freezing on the thermometer. That is how we live here. On the other end of a thin wire, a thin telephone wire there was a long space of green grass and through it crocuses bloomed in February. In February, George said, the crocuses in Hampton Court made streaks of pale yellow like the flaming footsteps of some pale Aurora. George did not say like the flaming footsteps of some pale Aurora; Hermione said that saying hello, hello, hello mechanically.

"But my dear child …" This was not George but a timbre, a little voice outside a tent, a shouting of a Punchinello outside a circus tent was in the voice saying, "But my dear child, I am so embarrassed and I *do* so want to see you."

The person that went with the voice was a stranger but the voice was not a stranger's voice, it was the voice of George, it was George shouting outside a circus tent (flap) and she had known, Hermione had known, hanging on to a tiny spar that night with the crickets chirping and the heavy heavy pre-thunder drone of the tree toads, that she would find something at the end of that small wire. Bertrand had been on the porch ... but Bertrand and Minnie were at Point Pleasant and the hall was full of sunlight now. The sun was setting. It was night (that night); the hallway had been a black rose open to receive her ... "But my dear ... how odd you must think me. I couldn't come today. I do want so to see you." A voice far and far, a stranger, a voice that went with George, someone else standing with George shouting "And I know how embarrassing these things are and I *do* want to see you." Hold on, hold on Hermione to a thin spar that wavers above the sunlight slanting in sideways from above the treetops (you can't possibly tell this person you're not going to marry George) and the thin odd after-storm quality of a recrudescence of some spring bird calling now that premature hectic red streaked the first spray of red Virginia creeper. A voice far and far ... "I know it's unconventional, most, most, most unconventional but you know what my boy is like. The great lout of a boy and *engaged* actually ... and will *you*, I know it's odd but George says your people are barricaded with barbed wire. I do so understand your father's work and I hate to interrupt you and will you—come—instead—to see me?" A voice far and far, the merest bee in a flower voice (I can't possibly say that I'm not going to marry, she takes it so for granted).

A bee in a flower, there was a bee shut up inside the telephone receiver, there was a murmur of the sea, far places, ships shut up in the telephone receiver. Hermione pressed the telephone receiver to her ear as a child presses a round shell. She listened as a child may listen to the murmur of far waters. There was the sea and far places and little seaports and sunlight slanting across a Tintoretto. Somewhere the sunlight now was creeping up across the ledge of a marble basin (they were all in the same sunlight) and in Rome the fountains played and played, falling, rising, rising, falling, silver and gold into some marble or some porphyry basin. Sunlight fell and Hermione held on to a tiny spar that floated above the top of things. She held on to a tiny spar that sank with her yet held her safe. She was connected with ships, with people sitting around a table and with Christ lifting a chiselled bowl embossed with Renaissance grape leaves. George like a showman was in that odd far voice, shut up in a shell voice, bee droning in a flower voice, "I have so much to tell you."

eight

It was obvious that George's mother, that the mother of George should be saying, "Now the first time he had his hair cut," should be telling. "He went quite blatantly to the pantry and you know," should be announcing trumpet voice of mothers that "George never would be careful of his stockings."

A mother faced Hermione and the mother said none of these things, and the mother had odd red hair that waved up from a forehead, odd wax luminous quality of forehead, oddest just-not-matching one-shade-darker eyebrows. She's rather like a figure in a shop window, the sort of distinction you get from a wax figure wearing just the right clothes.

"And do you *care* for clothes, I mean designing, thinking out your own clothes?" The mother of George was asking her equal to equal if she liked designing. "I mean your own clothes," eyeing her a little askance, at the same time with patronizing approval; well it's obvious, she thought it out herself, "those wide cuffs aren't worn this year."

Hermione faced some sort of Isabel of Spain dressed up in a waxwork show, some sort of odd person who was part of the roar of George outside a circus tent saying "this is the forest primeval, the murmuring pines and the hemlocks."

"Do you like the country?" The mother of George was asking "Do you like the country?" Someone somewhere else had said that, just that, "do you like the country," but Hermione carefully mincing over a sticky little gateau couldn't remember, everywhere everyone was always saying, "do you like living in the country" or "do you like the country."

George came in then. "Bella, most Bellissima, how do you like Belinda?" singing it, chanting it as George would do and looking up to face George with hair just not matching his mother's hair and hearing her say "Ginger I hate that new name" and hearing George say "It so suits you in that bustle sort of new frock" and seeing a little image with uplifted hands on the piano, lift up strange little terra-cotta wrists toward an imaginary deity herself shout, "But that—what is *that?*" seeing the wall back of the little figure hung with heady blue flowers and twisted blue dragon as background for a tiny little figure.

The terra-cotta made that hard clear note against the water-blurr of the length of Chinese tapestry, the long embroidered panel at the back of the piano. The tiny figure on top of the piano increased, decreased like something seen remote and far at the end of a field glass, like a tiny hawk poised with two exquisite wings against a mottled blue sky. The figure drew nearer, increased in size, became huge, a sort of huge odd beautiful naked tree branch, a sort of holm oak, Chersonese oak branch, a slim heavy trunk with two branching arms … the arms of a tree, the limbs of a man … and George was saying like a showman, "Now mother—do you *get* her?"

"You're so intense, so oddly intense, dear. You're like George so intense about things. We live in an odd bustle, a crowded gaping universe," she spoke as if she had read it; little distinguished waxwork making a little speech, a little speech made up for it by someone else but taking on distinguished quality when the wax mouth pronounced the wax words written for it.

"You seem to have that odd way of—of—" she had forgotten her speech, was forgetting her speech, "of *seeing*." And Hermione just perceiving that the mother of George wasn't angry with her, had not written her down, blunt, rude, crude, said, "But you—where did you *get* it?" And the mother of George said, "Oh, it's a little thing we picked up. I don't know where we got it. Anyhow my dear it's only imitation—that boy praying—it's only a little tu'penny-ha'penny" (she *said* tu'penny-ha'penny) "imitation of a late Tanagra"

"It's not, mother, imitation of a late Tanagra. It's the boy of—praying boy of—" and George too had forgotten. So coming back to it and the bazaar or the street or the steamer they had been on or got off, they went on arguing, waxwork and showman about a Greek boy praying.

She saw it now. She saw it now. She would always be seeing what she saw now in a flash, in Saint Paul's "twinkling of an eye." Something that has been going (kaleidoscope whirl) star and whirl, frost flowers on a windowpane, rainbow prismatic frost flowers going (kaleidoscope) round and round in her tight head, became … static.

I am standing here for someone has come in, more people have come in and "Yes, I am so happy to see you" and "Yes, I knew George" giggling "when he wore lace collars" and "Yes, you are the sort of person George *would* like" (whether it was a sting or a compliment didn't in the least bit matter) and "How very kind of you dear Lillian to ask us" (how odd her name was Lillian) and "Now won't Miss Stamberg tell us about her concert" and people sitting and Miss Stamberg who was giving a concert or had given a concert or some sort of theatrical affair for some sort of committee (Hermione couldn't follow) stood beside her by the piano and said, "You play, it's so very obvious" and Hermione not taking the trouble to answer, gazed at the thing, looked at the thing, seeing the branch broken off a Chersonese holm oak, stripped of its leaves, a live thing, the praying boy with his two arms uplifted growing simply out of the grand piano.

Her looked at the praying boy of whoever it was and things whirling in her head, making coloured patterns like frost flowers on windows, became static, but static *in colour* not simply frost flower but the thing in her mind (whirling pinwheel) became fixed, became static.

"I will always remember this afternoon," and someone took up words that she had just whispered—"Is it the *first* time you've seen your finance's mother," and finance and mother became linked forever with that boy with lifted hands standing on a piano, lifting his hands, holding on his lifted hands all of the universe, slender Atlas, holding and discarding, taking from her the burden of her intellect ...

His hands seemed to be lifted toward a heaven without edge or end or side or top or boundary. Into that heaven the vultures of her chained thoughts might now fly openly ... "Vultures."

"Did you say vultures; but its not Prometheus." George was standing by her standing by the grand piano. The room was filled with skirts brushing a square of bright carpet. Sunlight fell like clotted Matisse paint along the violet edge of a rich carpet. "What colour is this carpet?" "Mother calls it petunia. She likes the word petunia." "I should imagine your mother would like the word petunia. What George do you call it?" "I call it putrid purple." "It's not, George, purple; it's certainly not putrid." Skirts, too dark-gathered in a far corner, darkened the purple carpet. Sunlight fell (now she saw it) straight out of a French picture. "Heavy clots of paint should be smeared on everything." "What, graceless hamadryad?" "Am I graceless? Am I a hamadryad? I mean I thought thought should be smeared over with paint. It's too unthinkable."

"She's pep-igrammatic," George said, striding proud showman across a strip of violet, "our Lady of Sorrows, Miss Gart here says, looking sorrowful" and he repeated her remark making it funny, imitating Hermione with stoop-forward of shoulders and a hand uplifted as if holding a stiff lily, "She says looking so sorrowful" and he repeated it again while people shouted and said "How quaint of her" and Lillian murmured above the murmur "Now Miss Stamberg, you *must* play for us."

Standing like someone out of Greek drama, her hand (on the piano-polished piano top) felt beat and live quiver of naked nerves that were the quiver and live beat of song, that were the long tones drawn from a harp. People in a circle, in a half-circle, people in a sort of splice of a bit of a circle shaped like the harp frame were (it appeared) making tired things sing, notes open and spread and tired nerves (the piano's?) respond, sing and break into little catch-in-your-throat noises, making her hand just conscious, acquisitive, making her say my hand can dip down into this very black pool (the piano-polished top of the piano) and lift up odd star-notes, and things drawn out like the nerves in the dissected frog I did for that biological treatise that I never finished, that went on kicking after he was carefully dead.

She seemed, like a frog on a wide slab of beautifully sterilized and radiantly clean glass, to be kicking, to be feeling with some set of nerves other than the set of nerves that had so carefully deadened in the processes of her becoming dead. I was dead and am alive again.

Music is a thing that makes notes of light pulse and beat and it's so odd so often such very unlikely and uninspired people can play like this one. Before Hermione, standing like some young Greek hierophant by the piano, a face emerged, emerged from the stir of notes and star-notes of notes (some sort of super-Chopin chopped up into bits, a new musician she had never heard the name of) and a curious flat glass surface emerged, two flat glass surfaces that caught light, that dispersed light, that suddenly let light through her pince-nez and showed the smallish uninspired eyes of the musician. Her name is Stamberg, Jew or German or German Jew with a figure like that and wearing eyeglasses that have a tiny chain, a little rolled gold chain that fastened now behind her ear under her rat-tail untidy lean hair and that when she stops playing will be pulled off with a jerk and will fasten to a ridiculous little hook-in thing that is hooked in to the flat part above the protruding part of her odd humped front of drab cerise shirtwaist.

She has one of those patent things for holding glasses, a chain in a sort of piano-polished pillbox sort of holder fastening on to the front of her almost-cerise shirtwaist. Miss Stamberg went on playing. Beneath nerves that went on kicking after the frog was dead, notes beamed and shot star and meteor and shooting star, reflection of star and meteor and shooting star seen in the polished top of the piano that was a black pool ... *lilies of all kinds ... lilies of all kinds* ... I am out of the *Winter's Tale*. I am Hermione.

George and this woman who is common, who is obviously

Jew or German—have a secret, a power I haven't. Why haven't I ever *done* anything?

The eyes met her eyes. There was shuffle and voices and applause and voices and shuffle and "Won't you play the *Aprés-Midi d'un Faune.*" Someone (Lillian?) speaking the sort of French George was never tired of speaking, saying *"aprés-midi d'un faune"* and there was a world she had never seen, had never entered that beat luminous and faint and far and near and nearer and luminous, that had so beat under her hand resting like the hand of some ouija-board expert on the polished top of the piano.

Their eyes met, eyes went on looking at her, praising her, "I like playing when someone listens." "Listens? Don't they all listen?" "No. George listens. But George hasn't a scrap of real music in him. I mean he listens but he is faulty. He has no possible sense of time, no quality but he has a timbre." "George has a—?" "A timbre. A sort of vibration that most people haven't."

Who were these people who talked like this? People who talk like this ought to have great luminous agate eyes like eyes set into a Mena-period or pre-pyramid-period Egyptian image with hair carefully put on, all of a piece, like a wool hat. People who say "timbre" like that, who say "vibration" like that, ought to be beautiful, how odd of her and of George to have such odd, close together inanimate eyes though sometimes the eyes of George get a flick of jade, seen through trees, like eyes seen underwater. In themselves they are nothing, these eyes look at me from behind glass, from behind conservatory glass … she has put on her glasses again, is running over a sheaf of pages she has unrolled from a rather shabby music-roll, has found something.

I would like to scream at her, "Now don't play anything" for I see suddenly she is letting things loose; music is like science, it is all made to a pattern, it is all made like frost flowers or the leaf on leaf set opposite leaf on the rather naked stem of a tall lily. The leaf set opposite a leaf that makes a geometric pattern and the veins of a dissected ox eye that made a pattern and you must be careful cutting things up, have a glass slab and clean slab, for music makes patterns like things cut up on a piece of flat glass ... music makes patterns. I am tired of things that make molecule pattern and pattern like planets rotating round the sun and planets making just so much of a slight variation in their so set circle. Everything can be predicted by everything before it and music is only another way of predicting things. God who is light, who is song, who is music, is mantic, is prophetic, that is what Helios means, a god who is prophetic ... I see the god who is prophetic held like a round globe on that boy's hands.

Scuffle, ruffle, people going, people coming. Lillian wasn't paying any attention to anyone, to anything. She was standing at the piano, standing by Hermione. Her eyes too were set too close under eyebrows that just did not match bright hair fluffed up in an exaggeratedly only just not fashionable pompadour. The hair was fluffed up just so as not to be fashionable giving Lillian a sort of distinction none of the other people in their coats and skirts and their summer material and their handbags and their shoes crossed on footstools, had.

"I like you because you're not fashionable." Was it Hermione who had said that to Lillian or Lillian to Hermione? "We must be thinking alike, thinking in a sort of pattern" (it was Lillian who had said it to Hermione) "because *I* was just thinking I like the way your hair fluffs." "Oh my *hair*—impossible." "No. Not impossible. Improbable a little." "You *are* like George." "Like *George*?" "He's always playing with words, juggling, I tell him, like a circus rider." "George is rather like a circus rider." (It was odd she should have seen it) "Now I think George has genius, George might be great yet." "George—great?" "Why, hadn't you thought about it?" Her eyes were the colour of an ox-heart daisy, the black brown center of the flower heart and her hair was the fluffed out row of odd ragged petals of a late summer oxheart daisy. Gone warm, she was the colour of a great aster, gone mellow, a velvet dahlia. The waxwork quality was overlaid like some old painting with mellow sunlight. "But that great lout of a boy. Don't let's talk about *him* … and my dear child you must take that with you."

For Hermione had said, apparently with that part of her brain that catalogued pamphlets from the Institute de France and that catalogued pamphlets from the Universities of Berlin, Bruges and Brussels, that catalogued and made little notes in a neat note book, "Now I must be going" and another part of her mind, apart from that mind, had prompted her as apart from the wings somewhere, had whispered so that she had automatically reached out a ouija-board thin hand and picked up the statue.

Lillian was saying, seeing her lift the little object and turn it, turn it, oh so carefully "And my dear child you must take that with you."

nine

She talked to this little thing. She went on talking to it. Life poised hawk-wing above a desert in her words, life poised and life above a desert said "I have wings, see, I have wings," for the hands of the boy were always lifted toward a heaven that had neither top nor side nor length nor edge nor any end whatever. Heaven, a flat lid, was pressed (in Pennsylvania) over their heads. Heaven pressed down (like Carl Gart, like Uncle Sam pressing things down in test tubes) was lifted by these frail hands. The praying hands of the praying boy sustained her.

Yet why should I be sustained, she said to herself? Eugenia is pleased now about George's great-aunt; she loves Lillian, Lillian is back and forth, they both work on underclothes, they put things in the hope chest … they seem happy about it. I will go to Europe. It's odd people getting reconciled so quickly … Carl likes Lillian … the hands of the praying boy sustained her … it's odd that Carl likes Lillian. Lillian sits tight in her shop-window wax figure and talks so prettily about things she's never heard of. Lillian met Professor van Holtz in Antwerp on a boat. She is always meeting people on boats, off boats, everyone in the world sooner or later is met by Lillian on or off a boat. Boats became one with edges of things with an initial H. G., Hermione Gart. I am Hermione Gart and will be Hermione Lowndes … it wasn't right. People are in things, things are in people. I can't be called Lowndes.

She met Lillian at the head of the stairs. "Oh my darling. I adore that colour." "Colour?" What colour was it? A colour wavered about her, automatically chosen from a row of things, new dresses, old dresses made over. The colour was (wasn't it?) green. "This green colour?" "Yes you are Undine, or better, the mermaid from Hans Andersen." "Yes, I am Undine. Or better the mermaid from Hans Andersen." Undine long ago was a mermaid, she wanted a voice or she wanted feet. "Oh I remember. You mean I have no feet to stand on?" That is what

Lillian means. Lillian is the first to find me out. Lillian has found me out. There is something about Lillian. She knows perfectly well that I don't belong, that there is no use. Eventually I will tell them that there is no use. Lillian has found out that my name is Undine.

"Well birdie, will you stand there always staring?" Hermione heard that odd note in Eugenia's voice. Her wasn't pleasing Eugenia. Something hit me on the head, Gart and the formula, how dare they go on pretending I am just like other people? For Eugenia ... I will go on pretending I am just like other people. "Hermione is getting *spoiled* by all your petting." "Petting? Do we pet her?" "George has a new vocabulary, Rossetti, Burne-Jones—odd distorted creatures. I think them odd distorted creatures." Odd distorted Hermione descended the hall steps. She moved odd, distorted like a mermaid with no feet to walk on, down the steps, sliding with mermaid gaucherie across the hall in the green chiffon gauze, that was something from last year refitted, made green and gauze-like by Mrs. Rennenstocker who came every day now and was always sewing.

"If you could stand still Miss Hermione." "Yes, Mrs. Rennenstocker." "If you could move a little till I see how this seam will hang." "Yes, Mrs. Rennenstocker." "I mean if you move graceful as if you was at a dance." Hermione stepped forward, pirouetted woodenly between humps of sewed material and lumps of discarded material and pins making pin-patterns, catching little spark and pin-glow of light as evening just dipped above the Farrand forest. "Is this what you mean, exactly?" "No. I don't mean any exaggeration—I mean as you would move if you might be at a party."

How did one move, if one might be at a party? Hermione stood frozen, stiff with terror, a studio mannequin hung with blue silk. Where now would all this lead her? Clothes made green and gauze-green and blue (for George liked her in green and blue and blue-green) runnels across the bared boards of the old nursery. The old nursery with its strip of rag carpet had been a sewing room for Mrs. Rennenstocker since the day when the sewing machine first stood where the dollhouse used to. Mrs. Rennenstocker was always at the sewing machine, the light was always just about to fall above the Farrand forest ... "Ain't you happy to be having all these nice things?" "Oh, yes, Mrs. Rennenstocker. I am awfully happy."

A man came to see about the rain pipes. The job-lot man he had with him said there was stagnating dead moss and god knows what in their well ... "Another three days and" ... Hermione went dizzy ... days ... days ... typhoid. Someone said "typhoid." They hadn't any of them typhoid. Thank God Minnie is away. She would have blamed it all on mama and quoted *House Beautiful.*

A boy was shooting in the Farrand forest and caught his leg in a trap that the Farrand coachman or caretaker had arranged there for trespassers. Hermione heard him howling, ran into the Gart woods to find him half-way down their woodpath dragging the trap on an ankle. The woodpath was splashed with raw blood almost to the Werby cross-field. She tried to unfasten the wretched iron but the Farrand coachman caught them halfway through it.

Mandy had to go south because her father died. There was a strange blowsy Irish woman who wouldn't serve Mrs. Rennenstocker her meals in their upstairs little sitting room.

Gart Grange wilted like a butterfly put under a glass case, like a leaf, suffocating ...

"Ain't this here heat too suffocating? I always say this September heat is worse than real mid-summer." "Yes, Mrs. Rennenstocker." "Did you say your mama didn't like that new Nora that you've got now?" "No. I didn't say mama didn't like Nora. I said it was hard not having Mandy." "That darkie is one of the real old southern kind. I was saying to Mrs. Trecken the other day at New Bairnsworth that Mrs. Gart was certainly most fortunate." "Yes, mama is most fortunate." "Could you stand a little this way, Miss Hermione, and move like as if you was at a party." "How does one move, Mrs. Rennenstocker, at a party?" "Don't make me laugh, Miss Hermione. After all the dresses I've turned out and made you over and for those cotillions and everything at the Farrands." "Those were different ... children." "Then nothing came of Miss Kitty and the Baron?" "I don't know. They don't write much. I only heard from Minnie, who heard from other people ... from my brother's wife." "Mrs. Bertrand don't look so peaked as last year." "No. Mrs. Bertrand don't look so peaked as last year." "People *did* think—"

The light was about to fall above the Farrand forest. The light would always be about to fall above the Farrand forest. The Farrand forest was sealed in consciousness ... in the Farrand forest was sacrifice, was redemption. "Try on this new blue, won't you?" So she tried on the new blue and decided to keep it on as it was so late and so much trouble dressing. Mrs. Rennenstocker protested with pins in mouth but relented and sewed up half a seam under the arm with the ordinary blue basting cotton.

"Your eyes, your dress, the woods and the moon are all in some conspiracy." "Yes. George. It's lovely now it's cooler." "The moon stands there, will it go on standing? How long Miss Gart does the moon stand still on just such summer evenings?" "The moon never stands still, George. The earth never stands still George. The earth and the moon revolve on a fixed orbit." "Thank you Miss Gart. Do you think I'm a reporter?" "You talk George, sometimes like one of their 'breezy bits.'"

"Gart and the formula seem in their minds to be responsible for everything. There was an earthquake in Peru—I think it was. They thought Gart formula was answerable." "Was it?" "No. We have no seismograph." "No—" "I mean we have some sort of odd barometers and meteorological appliances in the barn (what used to be the barn) but we have no seismograph."

"I have to explain the seismograph or they write up anything. They say Professor Gart and the eclipse or Gart formula and the tidal wave or Professor Gart says the north pole has moved a bit to the south or the north pole is tilting toward the north. I have to tell them really sometimes the north pole isn't exactly a—a pole at all, like telling children kings don't really wear crowns." "How many reporters have you ever told the north pole isn't a pole at all and what exactly is a—a sisma-graph?" "A seismograph, George," she went on patiently, "is a thing that records earthquakes."

Her head was in the moss. The moon shot down a shaft that caught the bronze gilt on George's harlequin head and made a sort of bronze gilt sort of upsticking clown's cap of it. His head above her, wore, now she saw it, a sort of peaked pear-shaped cap like a Phrygian, like Paris and the apple. His hair taking on strange semblance made a clown of him, made a fool of him, made him Paris with the apple. The moon made one solid block of silver and she lifted a hand, surprised to see it quietly pass through this molten metal, this heavy gauze of silver that, it seemed, must give out ripping tearing noises as her hand passed through it. She lifted her hand again. The gauze permitted her hand to pass through it. Just above her wrist, above her hand the gauze looked heavier. She flung her arm suddenly at full length upward … zzzz … Oh God it's something tearing.

Her arm emerged white from the gauze of the blue chiffon, emerged phosphorescent and white from the silver gauze of moonlight. Her arm was clothed, her body was clothed equally in silver gauze and in blue watercoloured chiffon. "Your dress tonight looked like larkspurs in water. You looked like a reflection of a tall blue flower in water." Her head was again a head on tufts that darted up like the harlequin head of Paris, like George holding a golden apple, like the fool in Lear or Touchstone saying *so this is the forest of Arden.* "This *is* the forest of Arden." It was George back at the beginning, starting where they had left off so long ago, a month ago? A year ago? "How long ago is it George since we were here last? I mean since that first day you came back from Venice?" George said, pressing her head down into tufts of soft moss, moss now with moonlight on it, "It's several volumes back, if I remember."

Her mind began working. Volumes. What were volumes? George, she remembered, several volumes back had had a mouth like a red hibiscus, had smudged her face with kisses. George like a sponge had smudged her smooth face with kisses, had somehow, now she recalled it, smudged out something. A mouth like a red hibiscus had smudged out something. George had done away with something. The back of her head was at one with the front of her head, a head fitted to a body that belonged to a head.

There had been a sort of firework explosion and Eugenia saying "But you can't possibly marry George Lowndes" and a sort of cold dynamic explosion, an explosion in a glacier that didn't show on the top of the glacier but that had been responsible for a sort of landslide in her. Carl Gart calling her "daughter" like a Middle West farmer and saying in different words that she couldn't possibly marry (or words to that effect) anybody.

There had been that and a fiery determination thwarted by Lillian … "Lillian I thought looked beautiful" and hearing her words Her saw the face of George bending over her looking somehow like Lillian.

"I think Lillian looked beautiful tonight at dinner." Her heard words praising Lillian, she saw George looking in some odd way like her. She said "Lillian is beautiful"; the back of her head and the front of her head acted together and she said again "Lillian looked beautiful." The back of her head prompted the front of her head, slid a fraction of a fraction (of a tiny measurement on a thermometer or a microscope) away from the front of her head, actually almost with a little click, separated from the front of her head like amoeba giving birth by separation to amoeba. "Some plants, some small water creatures give a sort of jellyfish sort of birth by breaking apart, by separating themselves from themselves." George's kisses stopped her. "Oh God, hamadryad, forget all that rot."

Rot? Was it all rot? Stars revolving above their heads were blotted out by moon and moon would soon be blotted out by sunlight. "I seem to remember something …" and sitting up now, straight against George's shoulder she told him of the boy screaming (it was a few mornings ago, after the last time he had come to see her) on the woodpath just here, with a horrible twisted ankle and "I couldn't help him." Her eyes wide open saw the woodpath a trickle of brown by day, a thread of velvet by night, a black irregular line like the river Meander on a Greek Xenophon map in the back of the book, running like the river Meander across the forest, through the forest. "The river Meander runs like that woodpath across the forest." Her arm was hanging limp and bare from the torn ripped dress stuff. She saw her arm hanging limp and bare in the bright metallic moonlight. "I am like a blue cornflower in water. You said I was a blue flower seen in water." "I said you were a larkspur, a sort of blue hyacinth or Canterbury bell." "But they're all different." "They are and they ain't so very. I *said* you were a larkspur." "Larkspur," she repeated, and added "Ritterspuren" recalling the Farrand's governess who had taught them the names of wild flowers and garden flowers, making two columns of them.

"Ritterspuren," she repeated to the glazed gilt that was the just perceptibly waning moonlight, "are knight's-spurs, Georgio" and saying "knight's-spurs" and remembering blue and larkspur-blue and the blue of cornflowers which George said she wasn't, she recalled the first time and *this is the forest of Arden* and how the sunlight then had made Christmas tree tinsel and matted tinsel and tinsel sprinkled carelessly like tinsel on a Christmas tree. And she remembered *I am the word Aum* and I am Tree and I shall have a new name and I am the word tree. And she remembered (saying Rittenspuren, knight's-spur) strength and granite and yellow violets against granite ... the blue that was the blue—that was the blue of ...

"I remember blue that was the blue of the dark blue of the rainbow." And George was saying, as if her mind was still one mind, not separated like amoeba giving itself another amoeba, a sort of birth, a sort of twin repeating itself, "You've found another blue then?" And the half-tender, half-taunting way he spoke reminded her of Lillian and she said, remembering Lillian and Eugenia on the stair and herself coming down and Eugenia a little half-adoring half-frowning (as mothers will do) at her, "Your mother called me Undine."

But she knew seated upright by the tree bole, remembering the seven-branched larch boughs and the boy screaming on the woodpath, that Undine was not her name, would never be her name, for Undine (or was it the Little Mermaid?) sold her sea-inheritance and Her would never, never sell this inheritance, this sea-inheritance of amoeba little jellyfish sort of living creature separating from another creature. "I am not Undine," she said, "for Undine or the Little Mermaid sold her glory for feet. Undine (or the Little Mermaid) couldn't speak after she sold her glory. I will not sell my glory."

George helped her to stand, not kissing her, saying "We must get back quickly."

ten

It seemed now Lillian and George had gone home, standing before the little image, that she had always known what she had known now always. I have always known this, she said to herself, that I can not sell my glory. Hibiscus kisses smudged me over. Yes, I did completely several times let go, give in; I may for a bit let go, give in, but it won't be forever … she heard the boy screaming and knew the woodpath was dyed red because of … because of … not Undine, not any Mermaid. The woodpath was dyed red because of … because of … *Itylus*.

She was an image standing by a crossroad. I saw her with uptilted blue eyes, set like jewels, like sapphires and I never knew her. Hibiscus kisses smudged out my memories but also left me free for … memories. The thing I saw was an image with blue eyes standing beneath an oak tree.

Eugenia said "You look better this morning." Hermione said "Yes," helping herself to butter. Eugenia said "I like Mrs.

Lowndes. She has endearing manners." Hermione said "I said, I always liked her." Eugenia said "I don't understand how people so misread George Lowndes." Hermione stopped with a bit of buttered toast halfway to her gaping mouth and said "Yes?" Eugenia said "I had no idea they had had a house on the Riviera." Hermione said "And what mama, has that got to do with anything?" Eugenia said "Hermione you are inhuman sometimes." Hermione said, biting through the crisp toast, "I am always."

Eugenia said "I don't see what has kept the postman. I hate this waiting for letters." Hermione said (going back some volumes) "I ought to go to the post office for them. I'm getting lazy," she repeated "I know I ought to go to the post office for them." Eugenia said "I think that running out before breakfast is a little—a little unwholesome. I mean running out before breakfast is a little erratic. Still it was nice to have the letters." Hermione said, "I used to do it to keep Minnie quiet morning and toward evening. She used to get so frantic. I used to be glad to get out of the house any time of morning, noon or midnight to get away from Minnie." Eugenia said, "You shouldn't Hermione talk that way about your sister."

Hermione said, "She isn't and never could be my sister," and she paused, shoved her coffeecup across the table toward Eugenia, listening to something within herself that sang a lilt from somewhere. Somewhere something within herself heard something like a ouija board that feels something, like that day standing at the piano with the ouija-board feeling running through her fingers. "I sometimes think you drink much too much coffee." "I do Eugenia." "I think it would be better if you *ate* more, didn't pick at dry toast and really *ate* something. I think it's too much coffee."

Something within her was saying something but she couldn't

comprehend the something that something in her kept repeating ... a bird dipped as from the house eaves (she saw it) and skimmed across the window. "Do you remember that awful, awful morning?" "What awful, what particular awful morning?" "I mean when it rained so awfully." "Oh when it rained. You mean when poor Carl lost his microbes." "They weren't, mama, microbes." "Well, you know what I mean, dear." "Yes, it was that morning." Something far and far within kept repeating something that had no words, to which words fitted. A sort of ouija-board sensation to which words fitted. "The birds are screaming and making the usual change of season row about things. You'd think they'd think it's summer." "It's really nearly autumn." "Yes, isn't it. Isn't it funny English people (Lillian told me) think it's funny when we call the autumn *fall*. They think it's funny." "Yes, Lillian is very well-bred." "What has well-bred got to do with English people thinking *fall* is funny?" "Well, you know what I mean, Hermione. She shows she's been about without seeming to say anything." "Is that your definition of a well-bred woman?" "It's one of my definitions."

Now, helping herself to a fresh bit of toast, ignoring the platter of bacon, helping herself to fresh toast, buttering her bit of toast, she wondered, shall I go on with this conversation or shall I stop this conversation. And she counted one I love, two I love with the strokes of the little butter knife and putting aside the knife thought of Bertrand slicing slices out of the tablecloth. "Just when is Minnie coming back then, Eugenia?" And Eugenia said, "I don't know. I'm waiting for the letters. She *said* she would let me know by Monday. This is, isn't it Wednesday?" A bird repeated its trapeze-turn across the window looking as if it were held aloft on movable wires, making just that odd mechanical curve that birds do make toward autumn. "Do birds make a certain mechanical flight toward autumn?" "What, what, Hermione?" "I was wondering about birds. Have they a special sort of flight toward autumn?"

Then as the postman rang and as they waited and as the odd somewhat dowdy Irish woman (Mandy was still in Georgia) shuffled in and dropped the bundle of ill-assorted unmatched envelopes beside Eugenia's bacon, Hermione knew what she was saying in that part of her mind that was collecting something, that was apprehending something, that was perceiving something like a dynamo vibrating with electricity from some far distance. Picking up the three or four casual envelopes Eugenia sorted out of the odd bundle for her, she saw Nellie Thorpe had come back from Bridgeport.

"People are all coming back. Now here's Nellie writing (I didn't know she was due back) with a West Philadelphia postmark." Eugenia was saying "Yes, Minnie is well. She wants to stay on a few days. She says they'll be here by Friday." And Hermione said "And Bertrand? Is Bert well?" For things dropped from her, you might as well call Bertie Bertie and call mama mama. The ouija board was sifting values for her and a voice, a thing so simply remembered but connected somehow with the bird flight and the sea and the letters on the table and the bit of dry toast and the early morning flights to the post office and Carl Gart and microbes, repeated systematically and went on repeating ... *the world's division divideth us* ... and *sister my sister* (she had said, Minnie isn't and never could be my sister) and *sister my sister O singing swallow, the way is long to the sun and the south.*

"The way is long to the sun and the south." "You read too much poetry." "Did I say anything?" "You keep saying Oh sister my sister, Oh swallow my sister. Oh swallow my sister," and Eugenia laughed an inane little laugh; "It would be far better Hermione if you would try to *swallow* this nice bacon."

And the brown bright nightingale amorous came from somewhere, came from nowhere ... *is half assuaged for Itylus* came from somewhere, came from nowhere and *to the place of the slaying of Itylus, the Thracian ships and the foreign faces, the tongueless vigil and all the pain.*

She couldn't go on with it (it beat from somewhere outside) till she found the book, till she opened the book, *O sister, my sister, O fleet sweet swallow, hast thou the heart to be glad thereof yet* ... she finished the page she leafed over the book ... *the hounds of spring are on winter's traces* ... she leafed over the book, she turned back pages,

The sound of a child's voice crying yet,
Who has remembered me, who has forgotten,
Thou hast forgotten, O summer swallow
But the world will end ... the world will end ...
the world will end ... when I forget.

"But you know I don't like your bringing books to the table." "I didn't. I mean I thought breakfast was over. I mean anyhow you were reading letters."

A bird (the same bird?) swung again its trapeze-flight across the sort of little open stage set window. The window was square and they were looking (looking at the window) at a flat screen. Things out of the window, across the window seemed to be on the window, against the window, like writing on the wall. Things, a bird skimming across a window, were a sort of writing on a wall.

"The Greeks made birdflight symbolic. I mean the Greeks said this spelt this. The sort of way the wing went against blue sky was, I suppose, a sort of pencil, a sort of stylus, engraving to the minds of augurers, signs, symbols that meant things. I see by that birdflight across an apparently black surface, that curves of wings meant actual things to Greeks, not just vague symbols but actual hieroglyphics ... hieroglyphs ..." "Bert found at the end that the canoe was leaking ..." "Yes. I said it would go. I said it wouldn't stand another summer. Minnie was no good at all. You don't *row* a canoe. At best she rowed ..." "And they have already locked up the upstairs. I don't know that it's wise. I always wish there were someone who could stay all winter ..." "Oh *mama*. Couldn't I stay there all winter?" Mad, wild against her brain like innumerable white swallows, went beat of sea surf, the heavy growl and thunder of the surf and the outgrowl growling of the sea surf. Against that spume and rise and fall of white froth what wouldn't she give ... "I'd give *anything* mama, to see a snowstorm, a real blizzard struggling with the whitecaps. I'd give anything to see snow against swirling waters ..." "My darling child. You're far too Fujiyama." "Too—too—?" "Too those sketches, you know Hokusai, whatever his name is, Japanese snowflakes, cherry trees, obvious cherry tree snow-flakes on water."

"My mother is a poet. Cherry flakes on water." She said to herself "Eugenia is a poet" and started stacking the dishes waiting for Eugenia to say "Don't touch the dishes, darling, that old thing is getting far too careless." She stacked the dishes, went on stacking dishes. Eugenia said, "My dear child don't please *touch* the dishes," sweeping from her chair, swirling her flimsy morning gown about her flat-heeled down-and-out cosy bedroom slippers. Standing with her hair done high at the back with her usual fringe, she was démodé but with the curious characteristic touch that made her tea rose, not fashionable like Lillian but with a tea rose sort of atmosphere like that poem on Whistler. "There is a poem in this book that Swinburne wrote to Whistler." She turned pages, pages, "Oh mama, I can't find it." She turned pages, "Why is it when you want something in a hurry you can never find it?" Eugenia said, "And what about your letters?"

"Yes. Oh I forgot my letters." Her turned pages, pages in the narrow volume. "Oh here—now—mama," but Eugenia had trailed out not hearing or pretending not to be hearing words that followed, "*art thou a ghost my sister, white sister there.*" Hermione went on undiscouraged, her voice making a silver pulse and dart in the wide room, "*am I a ghost who knows*" … while somewhere she heard the scuffle that preceded that awful Nora padding from the kitchen … "*my hand a fallen rose*" … I think I like the wall-of-Troy pattern better than the double-rose. Someday soon if I don't dodge Eugenia I'll be let in for mending linen … "*lies snow-white on white snows*" … Eugenia said cherry flakes on water … "*and takes no care.*"

She scraped her letters up and went into the little morning room re-sorting them like a fortune teller with a pack of cards.

Everything is in fortunes, fortunes are in everything. One I love, two I love, three I love, and shuffling the letters like a fortune teller's cards, she abstracted the one apparently most unprepossessing. "This one looks like a bill or something, all so businesslike."

Two stiff bits of blue cardboard slipped from the letter and stooping to pick them up from the worn morning room strip of potpourri-coloured carpet, she saw blue strips of tickets of some sort, two tickets someone has sent; people are always sending tickets. I hope these aren't any tiresome charity. Stooping to pick up the blue tickets, she saw they were very blue tickets and the morning room strip of brown worn carpet looked the more brown, almost earth-brown brown (she saw it) of the little woodpath that trickled like the river Meander. I wonder if George actually ever studied anything. He is so frightfully clever. And she remembered blue and hyacinth blue and George saying Canterbury bell blue. And stooping to pick up the bits of two tickets she saw they were plain cardboard with a name, with an address and across them, written across them in this same rather businesslike writing a name, "Compliments of" and a name, she saw as she slanted them toward the wide morning room window across which the Virginia creeper had now finally flung its red, almost a spring red, soft rose.

Looking closer at the name written in the unfamiliar writing Her read "Compliments of Fayne Rabb" and wondering at the oddness of the name Fayne with Rabb so hard and casual, rather nice; there was that Mrs. de Raub at the University, I think they were originally Dutch, this is sort of the same kind of a name. She glanced at the letter that went with the tickets reading, "I am sorry you never told me your name. You asked me to come to see you but you never actually *told* me how to get to the horrid little station you said was your horrid little Werby. I looked up Werby on several maps at my uncle's. You said you were a little slant off the Main Line if I remember and perhaps that is why I never found your Werby. Then Nellie turned up a day or two ago and gave me this name, this address, is it possible that your name *is* Hermione? These are for a sort of ridiculous concert sort of thing with a play to go with it that I am to act in. Will you come to it?"

Things making parallelograms came straight suddenly.

Vibrations beating in the air outside her, stopped beating suddenly. Hermione saw the Virginia creeper, its curled edges; leaves curled brown toward the wall where the hot sun caught them. You'd think the Virginia creeper would think that it was summer but no, it turned mechanically obeying something, seasons, things out of Hesiod. The Pleiades, the Hyades, the sun and the moon, the rising of the sun and the moon and the Dipper turning around and around the north star on its handle. Names are in people, people are in names. I don't believe anything in the world can convince me that the creature with odd eyes slanting rain blue, dark blue at the corners is called anything. Hermione said "Fayne, Fayne" to herself, repeating it. Parallelograms came almost with a click straight and she saw straight. Then she is only a most ordinary (after all) person that I met at Nellie's.

eleven

She said, "Yes, Oh yes Nellie," she said, "No, Oh no, Nellie," she said, "Nellie do you think so?" A voice that was Nellie, Anglo-saccharine backwash of Bryn Mawr repeated the oft-repeated, "Oh I am so glad. I know you will be happy." And Hermione went on, "Yes, he wants me to go to Europe. Yes I will shortly go to Europe," and Nellie coming back with her "now the last time we were in Florence, no the time before that" like a rubber ball on an elastic that a child drops from a painted wand, from a sort of jumping-jack. Conversation went on like that, Hermione holding the rod, Hermione really working the thing, the stick that made the jumping-jack (Nellie) jump; jumping-jack ball on a bright elastic cord, ball on the end of a rod, drop it, let it bounce automatically back. Hermione held the rod by right of courtesy of her announced engagement (who had announced it? it was in all the papers). Nellie said, "I saw it in the papers," this jumping-jack sort of wand, of stick with ball on an elastic that held Nellie at the end of an elastic string, bouncing, bouncing. Drop Nellie with "Did you have a happy summer?" Know what she would say, stop her in the middle "And your sister?" drag her back to the little painted stick and push her off with a little "It was hot here" and watch her superiority in bouncing "We had so much dancing. I am quite exhausted" and go on with it "People are coming back now. And you will be so busy," watch Nellie take it up with "I'm on that awful dramatic arts committee. That's what really brought me back now. They are giving a play, a sort of modern thing, an awfully modern sort of thing. I mean Shaw *is* so modern." "Yes, yes Shaw is modern" and "They made me one of the committee because of scenery, decor, all that because I had that experience in Europe." "Yes, decor and all that" and "Is it possible that you are coming to it?"

Well Nellie must know that she was coming to it, because the girl had said, because Fayne had said, "Nellie gave me this name, this address, is it possible your name *is* Hermione?" and immediately and for the first time in consciousness Fayne became part of life, part of the clock ticking away on the little upstairs sitting room mantelpiece (there were some odd unassorted people downstairs with Eugenia) and part of the curtains that were rose-grey, that were meant to be rose that were getting potpourri-coloured like everything else in this house of little oddly assorted rooms leading into other rooms and rooms that ought to have been linen cupboards and butlers' pantries, crowded out with tanks and aquariums or shelves of things in bottles.

Fayne with a click for the first time in consciousness became part of these things, part of Nellie sitting so prim, so upright with her little finger crooked out from a Dresden china cup. There were only two of those Dresden china cups, two and a half really if you count the leftover saucer that Hermione herself after getting Nellie's message this afternoon had spread with a tiny doily to hide the saucer circle and piled the minute sandwiches in a little Tower of Babylon upon it. Fayne, for some inconceivable reason, became real at just that second, became part of things just as the clock hand was making that almost perceptible little forward jerk, that cricket-leg jerk that little old clocks do make, toward (was it?) the xi that preceded the xii, that meant that some hour was near (v? vi?) and that Nellie would soon be pretentiously making her departure.

Nellie was a little ill at ease, insisting "This is so much nicer," really wanting to see the people downstairs. "They are so horribly dull," Hermione had said for she couldn't bear breaking herself up again into a thousand pieces, one set of words for Mrs. de Raub, another for old Miss Horton, another for Eugenia, another still for Nellie. Nellie broke through Nellie, saying "This *is* so much nicer" for she didn't really think that. Nellie wanted to be downstairs; like Minnie, she wanted to watch, to catch up little servant-girl ends and tags of gossip to quote "Oh Mrs. de Raub, the American School at Rome you know, such charming people."

"This *is* so much nicer. Of course people will chatter so. You must get tired of all this sort of thing, people coming, people going." "Oh there's been no one at all this summer. But people are coming back now. People like to come to Gart now before it gets cold. We don't see many people. Only Eugenia has her afternoons in October. She has always had her afternoons in October. Of course George says—George says it's so *suburban*."

There was no reason for Nellie to have asked about the con-

Well you know—she always was Pauline. Paulet, her mother called her, Paulet or Paulette. Her uncle used to call her Paulette. Her uncle is responsible—" "Responsible?" "I mean Mrs. Rabb should have married again. She is really quite a young woman. I mean she looks young with her face and her hair—" "Her face and her hair?" "Her face I mean doesn't go with her hair or should I say perhaps that her hair doesn't go with her face?" "How, does or doesn't it go exactly?" "Her hair is too white, you know what I mean exactly. People who have such white hair always look a little—odd. I mean her hair is so white that it looks artificial, she looks artificial and with her odd colour, most unnatural, almost as if she made up." "Does Paulet make up?" "Paulet?" "You said they called her Paulet. I mean the girl Fayne—" "No. I don't mean Paul. I mean her mother. Her mother looks as if she made up." "Oh." "I mean a woman of her age—she's really quite young—but you know what I mean. She goes about too much with Paul, with Paul's friends. She's always around with Pauline and her friends." "Is she—is she, I mean married?" "Pauline? Oh, Oh, Oh, Oh dear no. Why should you think that Pauline was married?" "I didn't. I didn't think that Pauline was married. I meant was her mother—" "*Married?* Oh, Oh, Oh, Oh Hermione you are a quaint thing." Nellie went off into high shrieks of pseudo-sophisticated laughter. "How you do *get* things. I mean how you do, do *get* things," and she went on laughing. "You mean she isn't?" "Oh my dear what a witty question. She is—of course, she is. The idea of asking if Mrs. Rabb is married. She's so—she's so *respectable.*"

"I thought you just said she wasn't respectable. At least you went on saying that she was too young for her clothes or for her face or something." Things emerged, people emerged. A branched at either of her elbows, to run up half the width to the floor above them. Across, a little above, cut off by the half of old gold gilt rail was a sort of mammoth sort of Perseus with wings as big as an albatross fastened to either plump heel. Perseus brandished something and the upper half of a maiden showed leering teutonically and half-clothed across at Perseus. Things are funny, pictures are funny ... "It's all so awfully funny. Don't you think George it's all so awfully funny?" But George struck an attitude, elbows jerked out at black sides, a sort of wooden elbow jerked out with its sleek black sleeve and George was shaking hands with somebody who had been to London, who hadn't been to London, "No I've come from Paris" and someone else (a stranger) was saying "Delacroix. That's our 1870 Philadelphia Delacroix." She heard someone to her left say "1870 Philadelphia Delacroix" and a voice appreciatively gasp "God, Delacroix" and "More likely Courbet. But Courbet was too moss-green" and that is how people should talk thought Hermione. People who know bring things into proportion with 1870 Delacroix, they bring that Perseus with goose feathers at heels funny into proportion. George puts everything out of focus. Those two men with their voices make it right, 1870 Delacroix and that makes it all right. If you say 1870, goose wings become at once impressive. Why can't George get things in proportion? "No" said Hermione, disrespectfully to George, "I *like* this old Academy."

Things are in people, people are in things and they were being propelled by arms, by legs, by shoulders, down a corridor and there were those odd early Sargents, a sort of odd leftover of an exhibition and George tugging her at her elbow, "Don't look at those things" and if this is what Europe does to people, Hermione thought, I don't want Europe and she was being propelled forward listening to voices, a rich rare sort of mellow feeling of being pushed forward into a lace shawl that was fastened across a shoulder with a cluster of lilies-of-the-valley. Something familiar in that breadth of shoulder. "*Lil*-lian."

"Oh my dear, dear child. Everybody's turned up. I *am* so glad." "But George so frightfully hates it." "Oh George. Ginger. Don't pay any attention to our Ginger. He's sour because he never was able to do anything at art school." "*Was* he at an art school?" "Sh-hhh—don't tell him that I told you."

People, things. Lillian pushed forward and somewhere a crash and long thunder, something drawn-out; thunder, something familiar, unmistakable "You can't mistake Aïda Stamberg's method even when she herself exploits it." And Lillian said to someone who said that "Yes. It's Aïda there already. We must hurry."

George jerked her (harlequin odd gesture) forward and propelled her outward. The odd queer and distorted feeling of being jerked out of the mellow width of space, out of the length and breadth of people, out of black trouser legs and that nice voice understanding that Perseus is funny and the faint sweet perfume of Lillian's lily-valleys. "Where does your mother get lilies at this season?"

Away to the left, muffled now by a space of wall between them came the reverberation and the thunder of Aïda Stamberg playing—Brahms, she supposed it must be. Hermione glanced at the programme dangling with a dance card by a blue string. She had fastened the dance card with the programme by the string to her arm, had forgotten all about it, now felt George tugging at it. "Well, I've come here to dance and to dance and to dance after this damn show's over" and she rescued the dance card saying "George this mark here and this mark here and this mark and this cross that you've smudged in sideways don't any of them count for dances."

Lifting her head, tugging at her dance card on a blue string, she saw a woman standing on a sea shell. At the far end of the now absolutely empty outer corridor where she and George were sitting (George had propelled her toward a wide red-plush bench built into the wall) there was a picture of a naked woman standing on a sea shell. At the far end of the room she saw with ironic precision, the upstanding rather dumpy form of the upstanding dumpy woman who was too white, like cheap mother-of-pearl handles to little showy cheap knives, like the mother-of-pearl top to a workbox Mandy had, that Mandy loved—that sort of thing's all right for Mandy; "Well, I do see," she found herself exclaiming, "that sort of woman standing on a sea shell sort of art is simply negroid."

She had said that "that sort of woman standing on a sea shell sort of art is simply negroid" and she was waiting for George to acclaim her, to say, bravissimo Bellissima or words to some such purpose when she heard the music stammer to some sort of odd castanet climax on the piano, climax silence, silence, climax and then people clapping. She had heard clap, clap, clap, clap. "They clap so solemnly, so steadily, it's like castanets" and she felt somehow, something in her taking shape, being solemnly slapped so to speak into shape by the solemn precise well-bred clap clap clap that still continued. "They clap clap at something. They're not really thinking, just all clap clap, a sort of group clap clap."

George laughed like a goat, a chortle that turned to a fit of coughing affectedly persisting across the clap and the clap and the clap-clap. "Something in me's taking some shape somehow." And she remembered the ouija-board feeling that Miss

Stamberg always gave her, "Such a common little woman. I mean isn't she ordinary." And she recalled the throb and pulse under her fingers that first day at Lillian's and the boy who lifted a weight from her tired head. There was it appeared no weight to her tired head; it was full of steady rhythmic clap clap clap. "Oh now they *must* stop" but they went on clapping. Something takes shape in me with those people clapping. Ouija-board sort of things having nothing to do with clapping ... is it the "1870 Delacroix of Philadelphia" pronouncement on the stairway that has given me the clue to these things? "All this, all this," she found herself saying to George like someone in a play "is of *supreme* importance." And George was answering her, not having deigned to applaud her somewhat striking (to herself) epigram about the too-pearl-pink and too-pearl-white woman standing on an unconvincing wax shell at the end of the long corridor, George was saying "You mean Sargent, all those people painting, showing here" and she saw that George hadn't got her point; it wasn't because Carnation Lily Lily Rose (Damn Silly Silly Pose George—not originally—called it) was there, hanging there, that she had seen little lights and cross effects of lanterns among roses and recognized some mellow humane super-European consciousness playing here with sunlight, some hand, mellow and humane—making pictures here in Philadelphia, it was something else, something greater that went with planets swirling. George had said, "Don't talk such rot Hermione."

Stars had been swirling in the Gart woods and a boy had shrieked and spilt his boy-blood across the Gart path and something had happened in the Gart woods when a spray of moonlight had caught her and she had remembered blue on blue on blue and George had not known what game she had been playing when she had said rainbow blue and when she had said that hyacinth blue and Canterbury bell blue were not at all the same thing. The woman at the end of the hall was negroid art. That was negroid art and once one sees a thing and it goes click into place, it becomes by the very act of its so falling with its click into its right perspective, great. Everything is great seen in its right perspective, but George will never see that. George had said "Oh rot, what rot is this you're talking" when for a moment she had realized her head—the bit here, the bit there, the way it fitted bit to bit—was two convex mirrors placed back to back. The two convex mirrors placed back to back became one mirror ... as Fayne Rabb entered.

They waited for the music to stop or the music to begin and they didn't know where to go. The group of actors had to wait, for there was rustling and it seemed that Miss Stamberg was going to begin and they drew their robes and they drew their tunics self-consciously about them. "Oh Gawd—now *that* thing" George was saying "Pygmalion in Philadelphia. Poor damn Shaw would be delighted" and Hermione hated George with his affectation of familiarity with crowned (so to speak) heads and saw that Fayne Rabb was Pygmalion. That could be no other than Fayne Rabb because ouija-board perceptions saw Pygmalion, saw a stretch of sea coast, saw a boy in a tunic who was Fayne Rabb, who was Pygmalion. George was squinting at a programme held slanting to his left eye. "I've forgot my gig-lamps. When *is* the dance beginning?" And Hermione said, as if Fayne Rabb had not crossed her vision, as if a girl in a Greek tunic had not stood for one ironic moment before the negroid sort of art-picture of a woman on a sea shell, "Oh when this thing's over. When this play they call Pygmalion is finished."

Click. Those really sophisticated two men on the wide stair

before the show began had brought things together (things out of focus), had been perceptive toward the really awful Perseus, had seen the Perseus as not so awful, bringing what he stood for into some sort of affectionate realm of recognition with their "Philadelphia Delacroix," with their "Courbet and his moss-green." Affection brought things with a click right, brought odd distorted images, Perseus with great halcyon wings (great white turkey wings, goose wings) on his wide sandals, sandals on his plump heel into perspective. Click … George couldn't play this game, not really play this game, for art was what science wasn't. Art was the discriminating and selecting and bringing odd distorted images into right perspective. There was good art, there was bad art, there was Carnation Lily Lily Rose which might be good or bad with lanterns hanging in a garden and that was no nearer, no further than … Pygmalion.

"I'm glad I waited in this corridor." "Oh—then you recognize me?" "*Recognize* you? But I always knew you." And George was shoving her in. "Who are these wretched dramatists, these highbrow art sort of college girls?"

"I don't know who they are. I mean I only know who one is. I mean that girl I spoke to is Pygmalion. I met her at a party. A sort of hot day when the dust was so hot … it's so much, isn't it, cooler … it's quite isn't it cool?" And she knew being pushed into an end seat, with George pushed in a seat behind her (they were late, hadn't got their own seats, had to take leftover seats) that she would always say to George now and to all the Georges "The dust was so hot … it's so much isn't it cooler … it's quite isn't it cool?" hearing an overture on a violin and seeing a form step forward …

PART TWO

I

one

"Sea beat up and wind fell hesitating..." "Go on..." "It's rotten rather just here." "You read so beautifully." "I don't want you to think I'm reading. It's things back of me. It's things back of me. You draw things out of me like some sort of... some sort of..." "Go on." "I mean you draw things out of me." Fayne Rabb was sitting on the sofa. The remains of the tea things scarred the floor beside her. "I mean the tea things look wrong here. Like setting teacups down on some pre-fifth-century Attic boulder. I mean to see teacups now in this small sitting room, to see you now in this small sitting room makes the sitting room ... I mean it makes the sitting room seem like a gauze curtain." "How exactly gauze? And how exactly curtain?" "I mean the curtains, the potpourri-coloured curtains..." "The— *what* exactly?" "I call the curtains potpourri-coloured. I mean everything in this house is potpourri-coloured. You make everything in the world seem shabby."

She stuck out her head like a bird; seeing everything, Fayne Rabb saw nothing. She saw like a bird that sees a tree not as heap of leaf, haymow stack of leaf on leaf, a heap of green making a curve or a cushion or a feathery sort of blurr on a horizon. Fayne Rabb saw not the potpourri-coloured curtains, not the figure drawn a little apart, drawn just too far, just too near that made a voice ring and resound and colours jab and dart against the dark faded rose of the faded-coloured curtains.

Fayne Rabb saw as a bird, seeing nothing of importance. "All the things that make the world important ... all the things, I mean mama thinks important ... you don't ... you don't ... recognize. I mean you don't see the things. It isn't as if you were destructive. Nellie said you were odd and so destructive. You just don't *see* them."

"I just don't see what? This is interesting." "I mean there is George. Now you would, I think, like George. I don't want you to see George *as* George—" "Is it likely?" "No. It isn't at all, not in the very least bit likely. But I have talked so much, so much about George—" "Are you still infatuated?" "In-*fat*-uated? That is just what all this time I've been telling you I wasn't." "Little, oh Miss Gart." "No. Fayne. I'm not. I'm not so very little." "You're as little as a bird that has no wings, no beak, no feathers. You are the sort of thing a caterpillar would be before it were born, if all the time a caterpillar before it were born kept its own fur—fur-*i*-ness (is that what I mean exactly?), you are like a caterpillar just the minute it changes to a phoenix." "A caterpillar doesn't—I mean it doesn't change into a phoenix." "Who told you that little Miss Her Gart? A caterpillar I say does change into a phoenix." Chin thrust out, days are getting darker, days are getting longer; Hermione said, "Now when I look into your face I think the most ordinary things. Now just now looking into your face I just thought the days are getting longer." "Why looking into my face, shouldn't you say the days are getting longer? Ordinary words aren't always ordinary. Anyway I am—" "Am?" "Are" "Are what exactly?" "Ordinary." "Fayne. Fayne. Fayne. Fayne. Fayne." "You sound like a prophetess shrieking before Olympus." "Not Olympus. It's Delphi." "It's Olympus." "You don't really know the difference." "Now little blasphemer—"

A hand thrust out. A hand swift, heavy; small, heavy swift

hand. A hand thrust out and the hand (as it were) was thrust from behind a curtain. "All this room, I've been saying is like a curtain." The words were (as it were) dragged out of her long throat by a small hand, by a tight hand, by a hard dynamic forceful vibrant hand. The hand of Fayne Rabb dragged words out of the throat of Her Gart. "The whole thing comes right perfectly. I mean it is true that man is a shadow (what is that Greek tag?) I mean man being a shadow or a spirit or a bit of fire or something holding together a corpse. You are, aren't you?"

The hand let go dynamically. "Am—what, Hermione?" "You are—you make me see the transience in everything. You are conscious aren't you that Fayne Rabb is nothing?" "I am, little blasphemer, conscious of none of any such thing. I am of *great* importance." "You are and you just aren't; don't joke about all this. I mean I see (through you) the meaning of—of—" "Eternity?" "No-oo—not that exactly." "Maternity?" "Oh horrible—" "Paternity?" "Fayne—are you really still there?"

"I am, Miss Her Gart. And I am not. I mean looking at Miss Her Gart, I see a green lane. There is some twist to it, a long lane winding among birch trees." "No-oo—not birch trees." "Yes. I say they *are*. I say they are birch trees. We are and we aren't together ... we go on and we don't go on together ... there is fear and disaster but Fayne and Hermione don't go on together. I see a lane and the sea. The sea sweeps up and washes the steps of a sea wall. I mean the steps run down from the top of the wall and are half covered by the sea tide. There is wash forward, wash backward, there is wash of amber-specked weeds beneath the water. I don't know where this is. I can see you are and you aren't here. You are here and you aren't here. I hate all these things that blunt you. You aren't firm enough. You are transient like water seen through birch trees. You are like the sparkle of water over white stones. Something in you were her new possession. Her Gart had found her new possession. You put things, people under, so to speak, the lenses of the eyes of Fayne Rabb and people, things come right in geometric contour. "You must see George Lowndes."

For George Lowndes pirouetting like a harlequin must be got right. Hermione must (before discarding George Lowndes) get George right. "I'm seeing him tomorrow."

two

"This woman's not good for you and I don't want to see her." George tossed back a tuft of upstanding harlequin thick hair. Through upstanding harlequin thick hair the odd Swiss chalet and the little boy and girl painted in one side (to the corner) came straight. Seen through harlequin tuft of the upstanding hair of George Lowndes, it seemed charming and quaint suddenly that Eugenia should have done that. Fayne Rabb had said "How charming and Victorian of your mother to have done that" and the picture, the odd green on green that was the green on green daub of a picture by Eugenia, a picture that Eugenia had done when she wore a dart across fluffed-out Hellenistic hair and a row of ruffles tied round her waist to puff out at the back, became perceptible.

"I saw that picture when I was a very little girl, when I said to mama, 'I want to paint a picture,' and I saw that picture when I was a young grown-up big girl just finished school, and wanted to have all the old things put up in the attic, and I saw that picture a third time when Fayne Rabb said yesterday, 'How charming and Victorian of your mother to have done that.'" Hermione said words from somewhere, from nowhere but harlequin upstanding hair of George waved like a jungle tuft of rank grass; it was brushed upward again volcanically by George who hadn't heard a word she had been saying. Harlequin fingers jabbed upward and the high forehead and the thick beautifully modelled upper bones of the face, the cheeks and the heavy modelling of the forehead were revealed as George leant back. George ran his hands again through jungle tuft of rank hair and uttered. "Who helped you do this thing, Hermione?"

A picture was cut off by the shoulders that squared across it. At either edge of the shoulders a bit projected, oozed, so to speak, out, thick, thick green put on thick thick green. The little boy and girl daubed in carefully showed to the right of the squared shoulders of George Lowndes. On the other side, the stream that started high up on the hill ran away into the gold frame. The thick gold frame projected, outjutting beyond the squared-in shoulder of George Lowndes. "What thing do you mean George? Who helped me do what thing?"

"Well I'm ballyhoo damned if I'm going to help you with your bally writing." "What's ballyhoo George?" "I am. Damned. I won't." "Won't what George?" "Did or didn't we call a sort of truce just this instant?" "What instant?" "Did or did we not say we'd make a bargain?" "We did say George that we'd try to make a bargain." "Hell. It will take some trying."

Pages fluttered in the hands of George Lowndes. His hands fluttered white pages. What George holds in his hands is my life's beginning. What George flutters is my life's ending. Mama should have given me watercolours. I would rather paint. I wish I could have painted. "Mama should have let me play the violin like Fayne Rabb." "What's that you're gurgling?" "I was saying I wish mother had let me play the violin like Fayne Rabb's mother. I was thinking I wish I could have painted like Eugenia."

"Painted? You call that painted?" George following the di-

rection of eyes through his jungle tufts of violently upstanding bright hair, had bent his head over the back of the chair
and was looking upside down at Eugenia's old oil picture.
"Well. Yes. I mean think of the fun she had putting that pine
tree by that pine tree until way up at the top of the mountain
the last pine tree is just one speck of colour." "You don't call
that thing colour." "No. But you must see what I mean exactly.
You must see how she loved it." "Love doesn't make good art,
Hermione." George Lowndes bounced forward like someone
who has had a tooth out. "I tell you *this is writing*."

Hermione faced George Lowndes across a forest jungle.
Writing. Love is writing. "It's like—like—Theocritus." "Yes."
"It's like an epilogue, you know." "Bucolic?" "No. The other
things. *Not* Tityrus tu titulae ... it's like the choriambics of a
forgotten Melic"

three

Choriambics of a forgotten Melic. Choriambics of a forgotten Melic beat rhythm and rhythm through the alert avid
out-watching mind of Her Gart. "Choriambics," she repeated
valiantly swaying with the jerk and sway of the trolley. "Choriambics," she said to herself, sustained against the bulk of
a huge negress who pushed through and through her, who
pushed Her aside with a lumbering basket, who cried in
harsh bull-bellow to the conductor, "I done said 22nd Street,
I done tol' you when I paid you." "Choriambics of a forgotten
Melic" sustained Hermione against a broad-shouldered sort
of butcher who jolted her knees as she swayed forward pushed
by the bulk of the negress. "Choriambics," she said, "Choriambics, this part of town is dreadful" and sustained and pushed
and pushed and sustained and pushed finally into a corner,

she was somehow made conscious by numbers on houses, by trams passing trams, by huge lumberings of vans and furniture vans and the odd cross-traffic of Market Street that she was getting near her destination, 36th Street. West Philadelphia. "As Nellie says 'West Philadelphia sustains our mediocrities.'"

"Melic mediocrity," said Her Gart as she slipped to a cobbled pavement, picked her way across rough cobbles and rough stones, turned a corner; turning a corner, she darted down a long funnel off a side street where little houses all bore little numbers. "The address, as Nellie said, sustains modernity or was it mediocrity? Anyhow it's melic." Her Gart turned into Greenway Avenue. Greenway Avenue spread its length like an unfolded toy street. Greenway Avenue unfolded before her avid vision as if she herself had cut out all the little roofs, placed little house by little house, run them together. Greenway Avenue looked as if it would fold in triangular pattern if you picked it up, if you unspread it to put it back in its toy box or flat toy envelope. "Greenway Avenue is the oddest avenue. It doesn't seem to be here."

Her Gart stood at the head of the slightly down-tilting narrow long street. Houses and houses and houses all just like this, all with West Philadelphia for a postmark. Fayne had said "Oh yes, we live in West Philadelphia," and Her had seen a house with wide-opening great doors and a little tree set somewhere. Her Gart reading Greenway Avenue had visualized a little tree, magnolia perhaps blossoming toward summer or a little almond in bloom against a side wall. The street ran on and on and on, a study in perspective, stage street going on, not there, getting nowhere. "This street is only in the imagination. It's not anywhere."

"I suppose you are surprised to see us, find us just here?" "Surprised?" Hermione sustained a manner, sustained herself with a teacup handle, waited for the pause to grow, to spread, waited till the pause had worn itself out and was vibrating behind walls, behind doors, was beating and vibrating. Her waited till the silence wore itself out (it must have been all of twenty seconds) and caught herself back as if from sudden drowning, mind black and dark. "My mind has been so avid" she said to herself in the fraction of a second before her voice shook out callous and casual into that lurid strange air, "Oh—surprised?" and thought, turning, revolving her teacup casually in her stiff fingers, "My hand is like a wax doll in a toy shop. I seem to have been set here like a doll in a window, set upright with a wax hand curved on its wax-wrist joint around a doll teacup." She thought of herself as a doll in a window and of Mrs. Rabb as of thousands and thousands of eyes outside, child eyes, greedy eyes, poor child eyes, rich child eyes, people-with-no-dolls' eyes, people-with-too-many-dolls-wondering-if-they-wanted-another-doll's eyes, people who stared at dolls in windows, not knowing whether they wanted the doll in the window or not, stared at her in the eyes of Fayne Rabb's mother. "Why, why should I be surprised Mrs. Rabb to find you—to find you just here?"

"I don't know." Mrs. Rabb did know. Mrs. Rabb knew everything. Mrs. Rabb was too old. Mrs. Rabb was too young. Nellie was right. Nellie had given Her a picture. It was not this picture but something in Nellie had seen something here. "I mean Mrs. Rabb why should I be surprised? It's a very pretty part of Philadelphia."

Her mind jabbed and beat and clicked against a metallic part of herself that had no meaning. Melic mediocrity. Melic or choriambic and Her Gart was caught in the lurid sort of strange silence that Mrs. Rabb punctured from time to time by her caustic sort of sarcastic sort of belittlings till *Fayne Rabb will never come* was the one sound, the sound her heart made. Fayne will never come, and she clattered the teacup against the saucer like some sort of miniature castanets, like tiny cymbals, was shocked and frightened, I might break this cup, said "What a pretty cup" and waited for Mrs. Rabb to follow it up with some further tyrannical outbreak, the sort of thing that made you say, against all your better judgment, "But this is such a lovely part of Philadelphia."

Heart beat against herself, her heart beat against itself, her heart beat; Fayne will never come, Fayne will never, never, never, never come here. It was incredible anyway. It was impossible that Fayne ever could have come here. Eyes staring were not part of heart beating. The heart and the body were one, they beat one tired eurythmic rhythm, they beat she isn't coming and she can't possibly ever come here. The heart beat in a nightmare but the eyes stared steadily. All of Her except the eyes of Her were in a nightmare. "But my dear, you stare so. I suppose you find our poor little wretched things amusing."

Now she was at it again. Mrs. Rabb was at it again; our wretched things, our dreary street, us and us and our always with that sniff of her nose in the air, all the time saying we, we, we are so insuperably above you. No, said Her to herself, no Mrs. Rabb isn't any better than Eugenia. No. No. No. And then she said no again. People needn't act that way. What *is* the matter with her? "I was adoring that odd portrait."

"Oh that—" with an uplifted voice, with an uplifted face, with eyes uplifted, "Oh that—that little thing." A shrug and "that little thing" meant "Go on admiring it, we may be poor, but we have our pride, we have our caste, we have our heirlooms."

How was I to know she would act this way? Fayne asked me

to come, Nellie was right. Her face doesn't go with her hair or her manner doesn't go with her face, there is something wrong, disjointed, all this is too preposterous. Her wanted to shake Mrs. Rabb, say don't be such a damn fool, we're both intelligent. I am intelligent. I don't have to sit here making a wax doll of myself anyhow. I came to see Fayne. Who are you anyway?

"I came to see Fayne." "Oh—my dear, my dear. Don't remind me of how bored you are talking to Fayne's old mother." "Oh this is impossible. But you're not—you're so heavenly—so young. Why the first time I even heard about you, I said (it was to Nellie Thorpe) is she a sort of cloud, is Mrs. Rabb a sort of cloud." "All cotton-y?" "No. Oh my dear Mrs. Rabb, no. I said you sounded like some whisp of cloud on a summer day. I saw a cloud against the very bluest—the very most, most blue of summer-blue skies." "My dear child—" "I did. I did. You can ask Nellie Thorpe. She simply *raved* about you."

The teacup handle may come off the teacup, then where will I be, thought Hermione.

"Bickering?" A voice from nowhere, a voice from somewhere, a voice somehow in the nightmare, somehow out of the nightmare, the voice of Fayne that seemed incredibly not the voice of Fayne, repeated "bickering?" and Fayne all dramatic, made dramatic entry. Oh if Fayne is like this, Fayne is like this. She wasn't at Gart like this, not at Gart Grange. If Fayne is like this in Greenway Avenue, I do wish I hadn't tried it, I do wish I'd kept her. Fayne is incredible.

"Pauline." "Mama?" "Do sit down. I expect you're tired, my Paulet." Now this was all wrong. I expect you're tired Paulet meant, I don't like this intrusion, I don't like this thing you asked here. I do hate your asking people here, do you think I like wasting my time serving tea to your friends? Something said all this and Her stood. Well, well, I won't intrude here. Let them stick together with their pride and their filthy little gimcracks, that Wedgwood that's cracked and those chairs. I suppose they're Chippendale. I don't know what Chippendale is but it's the sort of thing people who act like Mrs. Rabb have. Chippendale—Chip *in* the dale. I wish I'd never come. I wish I'd never come here. I do wish I never had come. "I think I'd best be going." Oh, hell. I came in here, all this jolt and noise with my mind avid and I landed in a nightmare. I came in here all alive and my mind was pulsing and I was going to read my poetry. I wrote (George said) choriambics like some forgotten Melic. Well, I will stay forgotten. "I'm so sorry Mrs. Rabb that I disturbed you."

"Oh mama, mama, what *have* you done to Her Gart? Oh mama you've upset her." There was voice that might be the voice of Fayne. A voice far and far that might be the voice of Fayne. A voice that had said "Hermione you're like an un-born phoenix." A voice that had said "Hermione is a gull's name. Were you an albatross, Hermione?" A voice that had said against potpourri-coloured curtains, "You have eyes like Illyrian nights. How many stars in your eyes?" Fayne had drawn her close against blotted-out potpourri colour, against the blurred-out curtains of the upstairs little sitting room and Fayne had said "You are made of this and this—listen. Your eyes are the eyes that made Poppaea furious. If I were a Roman empress, I would put out your eyes."

Someone had put out her eyes. Someone had put out the eyes of Her. Her Gart saw a very shabby room furnished in excruciating taste with about three outstanding features to exonerate the horsehair sofa, the crayon portrait, the heavy frame that held the picture of Fayne looking out over a basket of artificial roses. Fayne in the photograph had a fringe, hair frizzed over hidden ears, sleeves over-ornate, the whole thing out of keeping. Fayne in the picture was not Fayne. Fayne is not Fayne. "I think I'd best be going."

"Mama." A voice rasped, cut through Chippendale, cracked Wedgwood, across the heavy ornate frame of a shiny photograph of a child with embroidered wide sleeves. "Mama." Ma-aaa-ma bleated out it a,a,a, its maaaa-a-ma like some wild thing, like some goat on a hillcrest.

Fayne had liked the picture of the hillcrest of paint on green paint. The picture was awful, of paint on green paint. Her had known the picture was awful when she was a little grown-up big girl just out of school. All the things people gather about them hold people. The picture was not awful. Fayne had liked the picture. I came here ready to like Mrs. Rabb, to love Mrs. Rabb. Her face is too red now, the colour of turkey gills, turkeys puff up that way. The face does not go with the hair, the hair does not go with the face. Fayne does not go with Mrs. Rabb, not my Fayne. The voice that rasped, that cut, that bleated like a wild thing on a hillcrest was Fayne. Fayne was in the voice that rasped, that bleated. "Now Pauline. Now, none of this Pauline." The face that did not go with the hair was an angry face, it spurted out "Miss Gart's insulting to me." "Oh mama. Oh mama." The voice that was the voice of Fayne was the voice of a hurt little hill thing, a wild little goat, a small thing cooped up in a cage. The voice was a frightened cooped-up voice. Because of the voice, Her answered "Yes. It must be awful for you. Teaching all day and then having people like me—like me—" The voice that was a small goat voice said from somewhere "Oh mama, can't you *see* her?"

"Your friends, Pauline. They come—your friends, Pauline."

"Mama they're *your* friends." "Oh Mrs. Rabb if only you would be, let me be your friend." Words from nowhere impelled Her Gart forward. She would have fallen at the knees of Mrs. Rabb, would have wound long arms around knees, would have made a goddess of her. "Why Mrs. Rabb from the very first moment that I heard about you, you were a sort of goddess to me. Nellie Thorpe said you had such a young, young face and such a rare—such a rare, such a sweet way of talking. Nellie told me you were so rare." Words impelled Her forward; make her see, blind her, gag her, throttle her with flattery. People stare at dolls in windows wanting to break windows, to break dolls. What *is* the matter with her? "Mama, you do *see* Her Gart?"

"Pauline. I see Miss Gart. I see that you have put Miss Gart against me. She has had the attitude all afternoon of—of protecting you against me. Against M E. I say all afternoon." "Yes. I know mama. It's only that she's just—just—Her Gart. She's like that."

Crouched in the corner of the slippery horsehair sofa Her would have been taken for a disjointed, broken, utterly useless doll now if Mrs. Rabb had seen her. Now the day had gone away, the autumn day had left Greenway Avenue and day leaving Greenway Avenue brought clamour, the clang clang somewhere of a distant fire-engine, the shuffle of innumerable children dragging innumerable toys along the asphalt pavement. "I suppose, I should be going." Children outside dragged squeaky toys and a crowd of boys stamped the length of the pavement, following (one surmised) a shabby football; ball kicked here, kicked there, finally would be kicked into some empty meadow, some dump heap of a meadow down the street, down the street, away away the boys' voices were dispersed, were deadened and finally there were no boys' voices, just the dreary up and down, up and down of some child with some silly toy, some drab duck probably dragged listlessly, dragged lifelessly, might as well drag a duck said the wheels of the little toy, I might as well be dragged said the toy duck, staring hopelessly with hopeless duck eyes down Greenway Avenue.

"All these children—" "Yes. Isn't it terrible?" "Oh is it? I don't think it's terrible." "Oh you do, you do think it's terrible." "No I don't. I mean it's rather—rather—tragic." "It's all rather tragic. *I* am rather tragic." A voice that was the voice that went with the potpourri-coloured curtains said "*I* am rather tragic." It said it again, it repeated it, a sort of utterance that went on mechanically like the squeak squeak of the hopeless little drab duck that stared down Greenway Avenue, that stared up Greenway Avenue, that was turned on its miserable little wheels just once too often to stare up, to stare down. Like a little drab toy that stared, the voice spoke. "You see we have each other."

"Yes, yes. I see you have each other." "You see I never knew—I never knew my father." "Yes. It must be terrible. Never to know a father." "You see people wanted to marry mama. Several people. One had a pony. He said I could ride the pony. His name was Langstreeth. He had a farm. Mama said he wasn't a gentleman. You know what I mean. He was rather common." "Yes. People who have farms sometimes are but sometimes people who have farms are—are gentlemen. I mean a sort of gentleman farmer. He might have been a gentleman farmer." "He was. I mean he was a gentleman. He said one day if mama wouldn't marry him, he would wait for me to grow up and he would marry *me*. Then mama struck me. I mean it was so funny." "Yes it must have been funny." "You see there was something wrong—I mean mama won't let anyone come near me. I mean she never did let anyone come near me. Then I had to go to school because of the—the board of whatever it is you know. I met Nellie at High School." "Oh Nellie." "You may think Nellie is too awful but she was the only thing I had there. There were rows and rows of girls—rows and rows of girls. I got a sort of scholarship to study." "To study?" "Drawing. I got so far. Then mama said I was ill. That the girls at the academy were bad for me. She made me ill." "Yes." "Then nursed me." "Yes." "She would make me ill and then nurse me. I used to think and think and think until I saw things. That's why somedays I see things. You make me see things."

Things now crowding out of corners, out of the corner by the dark square of window, across the window did not frighten Her Gart. Things did not frighten Her Gart, noises did not annoy her. *Agace.* George should see Fayne. Things are not *agaçant* now I know her. I know her. Her. I am Her. She is Her. Knowing her, I know Her. She is some amplification of myself like amoeba giving birth, by breaking off, to amoeba. I am a sort of mother, a sort of sister to Her. "*O sister my sister O fleet sweet swallow.*" "Oh Her, Her what are you saying now in all this cloudy darkness?" "*The way is long to the sun and the south.*" "I'm glad the noise has stopped now. It's as if your voice so far and so sweet had stopped it, charmed it quite out, a voice like waters rippling." "Sursurring, George would call it." "Sursurring. Yes. George can call it. George, if George calls it sursurring, can't be so very dreadful." "He's not, he's not so very dreadful."

George now standing by a woodpath, George now with his upstanding hair might be of some use. "You must come to see him." "I would like to see him." A voice spoke from the depth of the horsehair sofa, a broken voice, a thwarted stricken voice, "I would like to see him. You see it's so, so difficult ever to see anybody." "Yes. I do see." "*The sound of a child's voice crying yet, who has remembered me, who has forgotten.*" "Can't you start and say it all off?" "I've forgotten—*thou hast forgotten, O summer swallow, but the world will end,* the world will end, the world will end *when I forget.*"

"Won't Miss Gart then stay for supper?" Light sprang from somewhere, sudden and violent. It showed the frame, ornate and heavy and the overdressed child staring out shining like a mirror. The surface of the photograph was glazed, gave back light, the ornate frame gave back light, edges and ridges of things gave back light. The rim of the gas jet, the edge of an ash tray, the gilt clasp of some sort of huge old-fashioned album. Things sprang metallic and violent, shining with violent surface. "I *am* sorry." "Oh don't apologize. Do, do stay with us for supper." The voice now was soft, it saw its mistake, it had hated to be seen seeing its mistake. It strode out fearless. The voice of Mrs. Rabb strode out fearlessly; it said, I know no wrong. I love Paulet. It said I love Paulet in glittering surface, it rammed I love Pauline at you like the surface (hard and glazed) that hid Paulet in the showy old-fashioned photograph. The voice dressed up Paulet like the Paulet in the picture. The voice rasped I am a mother, I am her mother. I am mother, mother, mother. The voice said rather tenderly, "But we must not make your mother anxious."

Down the street, down, down, down the street. The street runs and I run with it. The street is running like a spiral staircase that runs up and up and up. The street is moving but in order to get there quicker I will move too. I need not move for the street is a thing that clicks with little metallic click as it moves forward. I will turn the corner. I will run here. Here is where the boys turned off and here is where the fire engine made that hideous clanging. All this street is a sort of stage street, an experiment in perspective. The street as a street is quite magnificent. The little toy duck spoiled it.

Things spoil things. Mrs. Rabb spoiled her effect by being nice at the last, the very latest minute. Fayne spoiled her effect by bleating at her mother. Fayne made herself out some sort of Pythian priestess who has visions, who sees, who can prophesy. She frightened me against the upstairs curtains. In her own room, she was negated. The album negated her, the window negated her. Mrs. Rabb negated Fayne Rabb. Pauline and Paulet negated Fayne Rabb. Her negated Her and all the poems I slaved over, copied out and out and out were no use. Were all the poems no use? Some poems are useful one way, some poems another (she ran to catch the trolley) and I used one poem. "*Thou hast forgotten,*" she chanted in an undertone as she slid into a side seat, "*O summer swallow*" and I'm glad it's empty this time. "Do not spit on the floor" she read and "Wear Washable Whalebone" and "Extra, Extra, Extra" a boy shouted and "All about the big fire" above the rumbling wheels. I'll be late. Eugenia will be furious. "*Thou hast forgotten O summer swallow but the world will end when I forget.*"

four

"*They* are watching him breathless." "Yes, Fayne." "They see and wonder. Steel flashes and there is some sort of long— long—I mean there is that same green lane and the sea step coming down from the sea wall." "Yes, Fayne." "*You* are not of him being pure, apart. You are the cold ice, the radiant stream head, the very waters of Castilla." "Yes, Fayne." "*He* is beneath you, below you. He has part and parcel of some other fortune.

He is not for you." "Yes, yes Fayne." Eyes glared across space, across chasms, across valleys and hills. Eyes stared at Her Gart and eyes caught eyes that lifted mist-blue above frozen waters. Waters were frozen in Her Gart. She was bored with what Fayne was saying. I want to take her hand, press it against my eyes. She will say the moment I let go, get away from this thing, "You are just like *people*. You are like everybody. You can't follow me."

Her Gart lifted eyes and by some dynamic power of readjustment made mist-blue eyes go steel-grey. She felt concentration hold, her head go hard, she would follow Fayne into the space beyond space. "You can't *see* what I see." "No, Fayne. I don't pretend to." "Why do you baffle me, escape me?" "I don't altogether mean to. I don't exactly want to." "You *seem* to see. And then you quite escape me." Light flung upward, fell on the carpet and Her Gart sitting on the carpet was sitting in light reflected from cold paths, from stripped orchard branches, from box trees static and green, more green but cold against autumn branches. Light cast up from beneath was reminiscent of last spring, was prophetic of next winter. Eyes met eyes and the storm held, storm of ice, some storm in an ice crater. "Yes, Fayne."

"But you don't, you don't care. You have so many interests." "I have you, only you Fayne." "And this—this *other*—"

"Other? Do you mean my writing?" "No. Your writing is nothing really. It is the pulsing of a willow, the faint note of some Sicilian shepherd. Your writing is the thin flute holding you to eternity. Take away your flute and you remain, lost in a world of unreality." "It's not—I mean—*all*." "It is all—*all* unreal. You accept false, superimposed standards ... all these people." "But I'm trying to escape them." "You turn back. Like Lot's wife you are a frozen pillar." "I'm not a frozen pillar. I'm

not anything like Lot's wife. I'm not—not anybody's wife."
"You jeer at me, make fun of my poor pretences. But there is
one grain in me will vanquish, conquer every one of you; one
grain, certainly atomic, minute, but very core and center of
pure truth. I am pure truth when I *am*." "You so often, Fayne,
aren't." "Now little blasphemer—"

This was better. This was real and funny. The hand thrust
out made its habitual movement. "But you haven't told me yet
if you like George?"

"I don't like George. I don't *care* for him." Words, dynamic
twist of a rare mouth. The empress mouth made its down-
twist, made its up-twist that scarred the line of the face, that
made the face regal. *Curled lips long since half kissed away.* "Wh-
aa-at, Her?" "I said *long ere they coined in Roman gold, your face,
Faustine.*"

A face drew back, luminous and intense. A head was set on
space of blue serge, shoulders rising beneath schoolgirl sort
of blue serge one-piece dress, made sort of pedestal for the
column that rose above it. The throat rose from squared-in
space of shoulders, as if someone had come in, said this thing
needs furbishing up, needs sandpapering (what do they do
to statues?), needs cleaning, had wondered how to move it,
had turned it about, found it was too heavy and finally flung
a length of dark cloth on it. Someone had thrown a length of
blue dark cloth over marble. The blue cloth was flung across
marble nakedness but nakedness remained unclothed, remained pure beneath it. Beneath schoolgirl blue serge a marble from some place (Heliopolis? Persepolis?) far and far and
far. "I don't feel now that at all I want to go to Europe." "Oh—
Europe." Fayne spoke, a society debutante, wearied by sugges-
tion of trunk, of box, of maid, of tickets, of orchids. Fayne put
into her low voice the sort of scorn that went with *curled lips*

long since half kissed away. "I suppose *some* day we'll get there."

"Get where Fayne?" "To Europe, little stupid. Don't you ever listen to what anyone is ever saying?" "George says not." "Oh *George*." *Curled lips long since half kissed away* came right in the white face. The mouth was straight now, the mouth of a boy hunter. The mouth was a mouth that had hallooed across stones towards some escaping quarry. Across the shoulders there was a strap holding arrows. Marble lifted from marble and showed a boy. "You might have been a huntress." "I'm no good—no good at anything." Fayne said "I'm no good at anything" as if one had asked her to play in a tennis tournament or join a bridge club. "I don't mean huntress like that—like that. I don't mean country clubs—not things like that. I mean a boy standing on bare rocks and stooping to take a stone from his strapped sandal. I mean you might wear sandals or else boots laced crossways." "You mean?" "I mean you were so exactly right in that stage tunic. You were so exactly right as that Pygmalion." Her bent forward, face bent toward Her. A face bends towards me and a curtain opens. There is swish and swirl as of heavy parting curtains. Almost along the floor with its strip of carpet, almost across me I feel the fringe of some fantastic wine-coloured parting curtains. Curtains part as I look into the eyes of Fayne Rabb. "And I—I'll make you breathe, my breathless statue." "Statue? You—*you* are the statue." Curtains fell, curtains parted, curtains filled the air with heavy swooping purple. Lips long since half kissed away. Curled lips long since half kissed away. In Roman gold. Long ere they coined in Roman gold your face—your face—your face—your face—your face—Faustine.

Seated in cold steel light, drawn back again, away from that blue-white face, face too-white (eyes too-blue, eyes set in mar-

ble, black-glass eyes like eyes set in pre-pyramid Egyptian effigy) Her Gart saw rings and circles, the rings and circles that
were the eyes of Fayne Rabb. Rings and circles made concentric curve toward a ceiling that was, as it were, the bottom of
a deep pool. Her and Fayne Rabb were flung into a concentric
intimacy, rings on rings that made a geometric circle toward a
ceiling, that curved over them like ripples on a pond surface.
Her and Fayne were flung, as it were, to the bottom of some
strange element and looming up … there were rings on rings
of circles as if they had fallen into a deep well and were looking up … "long since half kissed away."

"Isn't Swinburne decadent?" "In what sense exactly decadent, Fayne?" "Oh innocence, holy and untouched and most
immoral. Innocence like thine is totally indecent." "Innocence? Indecent? What's the meaning of 'innocence is indecent?'" "I'm being cryptic, pepigrammatic as George says."
"Did George say you were—pep-igrammatic?" "Why yes. Why
shouldn't George?" Circles making pool-ripple came close,
came close, they were not any more circles, they were a blank
pool surface, the rings on rings were not. "I mean what made
George exactly say it?"

"George. George. Is there nothing Miss Her Gart for you to
talk about but George, but Georgio?" "Do you call him Georgio?" "Why—doesn't everybody?" "No. I did. His mother calls
him Ginger." "Oh, his mother. He insisted on her coming to
see madre." "To see?" "Mama. His mother is—eccentric." "Eccentric? I thought she was most proper." "That's what I mean
exactly." "Why is it eccentric for Lillian to be proper?" "Do
you call her Lillian?" "Her name is—" "*Your* name is—" "Is?"
"Lily. White out of darkness. You are so simply perfect." "Perfect?" "In your—your idiocy, I mean perfect." "Idiocy?" "Oh do
let up Her Gart. You are so simply childish."

electric odd emotions. George got me loose, lifted, as it were, a tangle; mama knotted to Minnie and Gart to Gart. The web of Gart on Gart and Minnie (though the summer is always worse in any family) were lifted by George but she had been too tired to run and shout. She hadn't cared to, simply. She had run and shouted at the sight of Fayne ... had run to far hills, and found foothold on odd continents. Stones were pulsing beneath thin sandal soles and her feet were shod in purple. "Sometimes exaltation makes a curtain open." "What's all this, Hermione?" George had dropped her wrist. He had turned to the piano. "Why don't you ever any more play anything?"

There was that about George. He liked her playing. There was that odd thing about George (Miss Stamberg had called it a vibration) that made him not care about mistakes here and there. Mistakes that tore the fabric for Her, to George were simply vaguely pleasant dissonance, meaning nothing as long as the fabric of the sonata or the fugue or prelude stayed secure. "I'd rather hear you run and sursur that way with your fingers than to hear anyone (save our divine grotesque Aïda) play me anything." Her ran and ran arpeggios. "I never practice. I gave all that up." George was George on a divan, with the half of a lamp making a half-orange circle on his shoulders. Her saw him remote with little beginning of a pointed faun moustache and with hair that was brushed back but that showed hair pulsing as if a helmet had been pressed down and now was lifted from it. George was Georgio out of Venetian pictures, out of the renaissance section of the two great volumes open on the floor, out of the quattrocento and Giants of Painting selection that came under Florence. Water ran off her fingers. "It's horrible not really being able to make music."

"You do, Hermione. Your melic chorosos aren't half so bad as simply rather rotten." George sat secure, legs crossed, head pressed against a black square of pillow satin. His face came up white, came up red. His mouth was too red. "Your mouth is too red." The mouth twisted suddenly, a thin serpent twist of thin red mouth. His mouth in his face was beautiful. "Your mouth is very beautiful."

"Na-aow" (he was being Uncle Sam, he hadn't been for a long time, she thought he had forgotten) "Little Miss Her Gart. I aoin't goin' to take any of this here fulsome flattery. I said your pomes were rotten." "I heard you say my pomes, my *poems* were rotten." Water ran off fingers. "Just how now are they rotten?"

Under her fingers water ran. Water was running under her fingers. "Mama is out and father is out and Bert and Minnie." "Oh Minnie-ha-ha." "Yes Minnie-ha-ha." She achieved a burlesque of George being funny. I can be funny too, she thought, running water through her water fingers. I can be as funny as Georgio being funny. Sometimes exultations make one feel quite funny. "Gart and Gart and the Gart formula. They've all gone out to dinner." "Oh 'ave they?" "Yus." Gart and Gart and the Gart formula. I really should have played things. Science is to music what music is to—what music is to—"Science is to music as music is to what, Georg?" She called him Georg suddenly, hard nice sound; Georg in the bright room, Georg in the shadows in the bright room, Georg like a stone thrown into a well. Georg fell heavy like a stone in a well. George sitting there looked Polish or something, the count of something out of a shocking novel. They were out of a shocking novel. Mandy standing in the doorway (how long had she been standing?) waiting for Her to stop running and sursurring water music was out of a bad novel. They were out of a bad play or a bad novel for it was evident there was no reality. George was right. They should have been burnt for witchcraft. Crouching forward against the keyboard, she thought, I won't see Mandy. Mandy likes to listen. I won't let Mandy see I know that dinner's ready.

Now more than ever she thought "we are out of a bad novel." Room was set square but it wasn't the usual room. Emptiness made it different and George made it different. The table was different, the cloth and the china and the glasses and the knives and forks. Everything was different. "George do they really eat like that in London?" George was dangling knife and fork, crisscross chopstick of knife and fork; George was dangling a knife and fork, symmetrically like a drummer. George worried at his cutlet, let the knife and fork fall with a clatter, said to Mandy "Please some water." "George you shouldn't ask Mandy for things." (Mandy had gone for water). "It confuses her. If you ask her for something and she is supposed to be doing something else, she looks at me to know if she is to do what she is supposed to be doing or if she is to break off and do what you ask her to do. If you ask me for water then I will tell Mandy." "That's the longest speech I ever heard from you Hermione." They were in a play and it was easy to make a speech out of a play. The reality of concentric circles had slashed like a knife so that she talked volubly, talked and chattered and talked and George said "I think Hermione that you are going to be a tyrant." "A—a—?" "Tyrant. I don't think that, after all, I want you." "Want me?" "We are, aren't we, supposed to be getting married?"

A jingle as of harness and bells and the slide that might be sleigh runnels over hard snow. Mandy was clearing things, was padding to the kitchen. Words made jingle like sleigh bells, for he might as well say "We are going to get married" as say anything. Everything he said was out of a bad novel, out of a play anyhow. You might as well go on helping him with his part of the play. Her sleeve caught in the silver basket. "Mandy is so funny. When any one comes she drags out this old silver."

"Why don't we take the fruit in the other room and have it with our coffee?" "All right." She managed an exit that started being stately but she forgot and came back for the little fruit-knives. George had strutted forth holding the silver basket of oranges before him.

"Now it's winter" said Her, sitting on the rug before the open fire space, "oranges make it winter." She held an orange in her hand not wanting to cut it with the fruitknife and George said "You are so damned decorative." "I know." She said "I know" (not having heard George) "oranges are so decorative" and George said "You, you, you, little Miss So-Stupid" and she said, "Have coffee" and she said "But you can't have more than three lumps" and she said "I don't smoke very often but I should so much like to" and he said "You'll have to smoke when you're my wife, Hermione."

And she said "Why will I have to?" and he said "Because it's company." And she said, hearing her own laugh peal and break and shake against the roof, against the roof of the room upstairs, against the eaves of the attic and then out and out and out to waiting starlight, "But I won't ever—ever be your wife, my Georgio." And he said "You're being very funny." And she said "You just said you didn't want me." And he said "I always say that in case I never get you." And she said "Anyhow I love—I love Her, only Her, Her, Her." And he said "Narcissus in the reeds. Narcissa. Are you a water lily?" And she said "No, no, no—George have another orange?"

So sparring against coffee clatter and George having too many little cups and too many lumps of sugar and Mandy

taking the things out, she realized a thing that had caught
her oddly by the hem of her skirt, that was tugging her somewhere like someone enchanted in a Tale of the Black Forest.
Trees made water music, the lamp might be some great autumn branch casting its orange shadow. Trees caught her, a
small birch tree might burst suddenly at any moment into
violent green flame of first flame, birch leaves of early spring.
For something had Her by the hem of her skirt, had her for a
moment by the throat. She achieved a note, a song note that
brought her back to a body that was vibrating, that was static
yet vibrating here and there. Why should one go to Europe?
Fire and water made rhythm in Her and she caught a note in
her throat and she hurtled it forth, achieving by some miracle
the key, pitched too high (could she sustain it?)—*Du meine
Herzen, du mein Ruhe.* She wished George wouldn't try to join
in, he had no voice whatever, neither tenor, baritone nor hon-
est-to-god deep bass. He hadn't a voice really. It was George
with his volumes who was wordless, who was inarticulate; not
Her Gart sitting on a hearth rug with *Du bist mein Grab* going
now too deep down into her insides. "I wish I were green fire.
I would run along a birch tree. I would run along a pear tree. I
would make our pear tree by the corner of the barn burst into
flower this moment. *Du meine Herzen, du mein Ruhe.* Do stop
chucking orange peel on the fire George. It's smoking."

Odd fumes bit into her nostrils. Orange peel burning created scented warmth, created no Her-mood in the wide room,
created something not of her (it was George's doing) in the
space between the piano and the table, in the black pool that
lay behind the piano between it and the window that in summer stood wide open. The window was closed now, curtains
drawn across it. Anything might exist on the other side of
the window if one had (as Fayne hinted) bodies beyond these

bodies and these bodies were just nothing, minds beyond these minds and these minds were just nothing. "Fayne says we are underdeveloped, are all of us racially babies in development or sort of moles. We have, she says, only mole eyes that see in the dark, that we are in the dark. She herself *sees*—we don't see." "Oh *that* girl." A thing not of Her's creating, not of George's had entered the room. It stood heavy in the corner, a hand lifted to adjust a headband. "She's so—so classic." George with his affectation pretended to have hysterics. "Oh, Oh, Oh," he chortled between painful convulsions, "Hermione, you *are* funny." "Funny?" "She's out of a tu'penny ha'penny" (he said tu'penny ha'penny) "bad playlet. She isn't in a real play." "Wh-aa-at Georgio?" "She is so darn theatric." "Not theatric, not theatrical—dramatic in the best sense." Again George had convulsions. "My dear, she's simply shoddy."

A green flame ran and she realized that George would never make a pear tree burst into blossom, would never raise out of marshes the heads of almost-winter violets. Yellow violets might flower against granite and stone and stones remain for feet to tread on. George languished in Elizabethan doublet in galleries, he was painted upon ceilings. He did not run with a stream's running, he had not throaty sounds in a long throat that rose from a bath of Tusculum. "George you've been everywhere." He mustn't see what Hermione was thinking. He had been to Tunis, to Bulgaria. George and Lillian had been everywhere. "George, I am so unlettered." She used the word advisedly wondering if he could possibly not know she was thinking of the lettered hyacinth. "You are simply witchcraft." This was the thing that caught her; "Hermione, you and she should have been burnt as witches."

Now George rising from the divan, drawing nearer became luminous with some sort of phosphorescence. It was phosphorescence a fish gives out, a glowworm or a wood-branch. The thing in him was nebulous, was the edges of things, was the Renaissance, burning with reflected glory. He wanted Her, but he wanted a Her that he called decorative. George wanted a Her out of the volumes on the floor, out of the two great volumes. He wanted Her from about the middle, the glorious flaming middle, the Great Painters (that came under Florence) section. George, regarding Her, was saying "You are so decorative." There was something stripped of decoration, something of somewhat-painful angles that he would not recognize. George saying "Choriambics of a forgotten Melic" was flattering her, tribute such as some courtier might pay to a queen who played at classicism; he did not proffer her the bare branch that was the strip of wild naked olive or the tenuous oleander. George saw Her at best as some Florentine page or some Florentine girl dressed for a pageant as the Queen Diana. To George, Her was Dian or Diana, never Artemis. To George, she was the Queen of Love, never white Aphrodite. People are in things. I am in Her. George never understood me. Rising to her feet, knowing that he would not understand Her, she was drifted toward the divan. George with a twist and deft knee movement had thrown her on the low couch. So lying she regarded the ceiling; thought "How high, like a palace ceiling; it looks low sometimes." Thrown on the wide couch, she had no thought but "The flames leap higher and do odd pointed things, make points like a harlequin's cap, like the Phrygian cap of Paris" … Now George had put the lamp out.

six

Now more than ever she knew they were out of some bad novel. Sound of chiffon ripping and the twist and turn of Hermione under the stalwart thin young torso of George Lowndes. Now more than ever thought made spiral, made concentric circle toward a darkened ceiling. The ceiling came down, down. The ceiling became black, in a moment it would crush down, crushing Her and George Lowndes under a black metallic shutter. The ceiling was a sort of movable shutter like some horrible torture thing out of Poe's tales, the wall that came close out of Poe's tales was coming close, the wall was coming close. Doors were no more in walls, the curtains were no more curtains. Walls were coming close to suffocate, to crush her … "You've torn this chiffon sleeve thing horribly."

A twist, a turn. Men are not strong. Women are stronger. I am stronger. I turn and twist out of those iron arms because if he had held me, I would have been crushed by iron. Iron is in walls. She said "Please put the light on."

Room sprang into being. Firelight pulsed lower, was nebulous, was faint in the sudden glare of lamplight. "Why did you come so near" was the sound her heart made, was her accusation, or "Having come so near" was her accusation, "why didn't you come nearer?" There is something awkward in the whole proceeding. Now why does he stay staring?

A face was staring at Her. It was not the face of George Lowndes. Mandy has gone to bed. It will be queer if I call. Her slid to feet that pulsed under Her, would drop away like toadstools, like feet of water. Her limbs were water. The limbs of Her were water. Could she stand on water limbs? She swam (found use for limbs in water) toward the piano. The piano was a rock, a raft. She remembered suddenly from nowhere a boy standing on a piano. There was a boy on a piano standing against a mist of blue embroidery. The blue had been cloud, had been mist, had been larkspurs seen in water. Wide eyes stared at a face that was not the face of George

Lowndes staring, a masque set incongruously on somewhat London shoulders. The shoulders of George were London shoulders, George had looked like a count or something. The face of George looked a wolf, was a wolf, it was a wolf mask on a man's body...

Standing by the piano with incongruous light making too-heady fall and flow of orange, crimson and orange, she saw George Lowndes. What is he? What am I? *What am I?* Shadows were not in corners, the whole thing was too luminous. Light was beating on Her from some great arena. In a moment (her thought went) he will pounce, he will bound forward. His movement will be gracious, swift, an Orlando sort of movement. He will crouch and leap but he won't—he won't be anything. Things can't happen that aren't meant to happen. She said "I wish I had a gramophone. It's a bore not being able to play better."

So coming closer they looked through some sort of water layer, the blur of water was before eyes that saw George now gone paler, gone slacker, gone not so white with that white-wolf mask clapped upon his face above somewhat London shoulders. Her saw George through a blur, water fell and rose and her body pressed against the raft, against the piano that was a sort of raft, she must hold on to this great rock; a house on a rock, I will build my house, she said, on a rock. For she remembered a boy with hands lifted toward a heaven that had neither breadth nor width nor edge nor line nor any end whatever. Some sort of heaven out of the Revelations had been revealed to Her in a flash, in Saint Paul's twinkling of an eye that day at Lillian's. Yes, Lillian had helped Her. Now Her recalled Lillian and recalled Lillian having helped Her. Straight and strong like some girl athlete from Laconian hill slopes, straight and brave like the maiden Artemis, she felt

water-knees break and water-ankles let her feel how very in-
secure her marble feet were. Two people. I am Her. I am the
word AUM. I am Her. She said "Em, Hem, Um" clearing her
throat, making a little choking noise in her throat and saw
George standing like young Orlando. George put two hands
under the armpits of a statue that was falling…

"I didn't mean Hermione to hurt you." "You didn't—
didn't—" Her teeth were chattering. George had dragged a
shawl from somewhere. How did he find that old carriage rug?
We never use it. An old rug she had used to tuck about her feet
in the days before the barn was turned into a laboratory, was
tucked around ankles that now were frankly broken.

"It's funny with me. I'm so strong. I feel so strong, so right.
Nothing can ever hurt me. Then—" Humiliation choked Her.
Tears choked and humiliated Her. And George had turned the
lamp down a little as the flick and flare of the light had burnt
against Her. Now she said "I'm too strong and I'm nothing and
I'm frightened." She achieved a very ugly voice that blubbered
unbecomingly from somewhere, saying it over and over like
a prayer wheel. "I am frightened. I am the word Aum, I am
Her. I am Her." Her blubbered in a child voice against the
somewhat London shoulders of a George Lowndes, "I am—
so—very—frightened."

seven

"I think George is right. I don't think that girl is good for
you. Don't let her come here any more, Hermione." "Yes
mama." "I have been talking to Lillian. I think the whole thing
is wrong, a strain on us all. You ought to marry George Lowndes." "Yes, mama." "This girl—she's all wrong. Lillian thinks

her most—*most* unwholesome." "Yes, mama." "Lillian and I were saying—" "Yes, mama." Yes, yes and no, no. Yes and no. No and yes. I will say yes, I will say no. I will say yes Lillian, I will say no mama. I will throw yes and no and no and yes like the shafts of a Pythian goddess. I will slay and kill and burn and break and slay and kill and burn. I will and I won't be taken in by all their vile antics. They know so simply nothing. "Yes, mama. I do think that George is looking better."

"I don't mean that he looks ill exactly though he's not what you would call robust exactly. I don't mean that. He looks more—more—normal. He looks much less eccentric. "Yes, mama. I do know what you do mean." "Now Lillian was saying that you have been so good for him—that she is so pleased." "Yes, mama." Keep Parthian quiver strapped to a stalwart marble shoulder, don't let any go. Don't let any single shaft escape you. Wily and divine, keep it all, keep it all. Save yourself and offer them a sort of water creature. Keep marble for yourself and keep marble for marble. Keep a marble self for a marble self, Her for Her, Her for Fayne exactly.

Hermione watching Eugenia across a patch of vivid winter sunlight thought, "normal, unwholesome, their vocabulary gets more meagre. I understand Fayne bleating that day at her mother."

eight

"Bodies beyond these bodies and these bodies are just nothing; minds beyond these minds." "Yes Fayne." "But you don't care. You live in everyday things, like a snowdrop under an evergreen. You are a snowdrop, parasitic, you have no real life." "Yes Fayne." "Why do you say yes Fayne, why do you say, no Fayne? Have you no reality, no voice, no articulate self?" "George says—" "Oh George, George. I thought we had crossed George out, made a clean (so to speak) slate of this Lowndes person." "I thought you'd come to like him." "I? Oh—I—he interests me. I consider it my right, even my duty to flow toward that from which I may take wisdom. Remember always Hermione that the thing I have is minute, a very atom of a grain of a thing but it is pure." "Truth, I know Fayne." "The thing in you is not so small. It has reason, being, dimension. It has in fact reality. It *is* beauty." The room shrank and quivered. Pythian to Pythian, prophetess to prophetess, the mood was on them. "Ye-e-ees, Fayne."

Teeth might chatter in a head bent backward and Her Gart might quiver with suppressed emotion and with curious, terrible, intense terror, terror of the things that Fayne saw clearly, terror of the world that Her sensed piecemeal, that was to Fayne (Fayne said) the one reality. Her head bent back into almost-evening of the small room upstairs, saw Fayne and Fayne and Fayne. "Why is it Hermione, your mother so dislikes me?"

Terror might throttle and choke Her Gart but something more than terror held Her. Her was held by insatiable curiosity; the desire to turn, so to speak, the little wheel that brought psychic states clear and into focus. "Eugenia. Oh, I don't know—we'll talk about that later. What—wh-aa-aat do you mean by beauty?"

"George calls me a psychic charlatan, you heard him say it." "Noo-o. I mean yes he did say something." "George is lie upon lie upon lie. He is a tatter and a ragbag. George, not so many lives back, was—" "Was?" "Was some wandering student, his own Provençal sort of thing carried to its logical conclusion. George is lie upon lie upon lie. George interests me because I try out on George the thing that is in me. The thing that is me." "Truth, pure truth exactly." "Truth pure truth, that atomic center of me, draws George to me, separates George from George like some deep distilling acid. The thing in me, pure upon pure truth, disintegrates George and I watch the disintegration, matching element to element, saying this *is* George, this *was* George. The George that is to be—" "Yes Fayne—" "Is something I can't follow." Fayne Rabb fell back in the low divan like a professional crystal gazer whose half-hour consultation is now over.

Her Gart rising on her lean shanks, rising from the floor, stepped forward. Greater than the mind, greater than the spirit, certainly greater than the body, is our curiosity. She felt fibre tighten and sinew harden. She turned, so to speak, a little wheel, adjusted, so to speak, her psychic vision. "You must tell me what is beauty?"

"Beauty, said jesting Pilate—" "No that was truth, Fayne. 'What is truth' is what you mean. You know what truth is as you are pure truth, but what, just what is beauty?" Fayne Rabb lifted a necromancer's slim hand and motioned toward the curtains. "I am so tired, I wish you'd read, Hermione."

There was only one thing to read to Fayne; she had read and she would re-read it. *"O sister my sister …"* Fayne fell back into the divan recess, Fayne was a prophetess receding to her cavern. "You are, you know, Itylus." "Itylus?" "This thing that I must always quote you because the day your letter came—" "The day my letter came?" "I was reading it. But I've told you this so often." "Tell it again Hermione." Fayne Rabb spoke like a sick child. She lay back in the cavernous divan. "You go so peaked and wan so suddenly." "It's trying to see, trying to understand things. Your voice is drug to me. I never know what you're saying to me." "I'm not saying anything. I only said *O sister my sister O singing swallow, the world's division divideth us.* And then that afternoon I was sure that your name was Itylus." Her Gart spoke and read, read and spoke, her words made rhythm to the poem, the poem made rhythm suitable to her swift words. Words came from nowhere, tumbled head-long somewhere ... "and mama doesn't hate you. She is in another world. She and Lillian are Eleusinian. Life to them means simply more life. They have justified themselves in having children. They think it right that George and I should marry ..." "Oh George—and—you." The voice spoke like a child in a delirium "Oh you—and—George." The voice was drawn up, up out of a deep well, a prophet's voice.

"Oh I know. I won't. I promise you I won't ever marry George, my swallow."

Hands pressed against the swallow-blue that were now the swallow-black great-pupiled eyes of Fayne Rabb, were the long cold hands of Her Gart. Her Gart dropped book, dropped af-fectation of sanity, sank down to the floor, through the floor, above the earth, was on the earth, rock of earth-rock simply. Prophetess to prophetess on some Delphic headland, Her Gart pressed cold hands against the eyelids of Fayne Rabb. "Your hands are healing. They have dynamic white power." "Sleep, sleep my Itylus." "Your hands are white stars. Your hands are snowdrops. Tell me what does George Lowndes say about me. Tell me, Hermione."

"He says you are—he says you are—" gallantly Her Gart tried to drag out some little gesture, something that might be rightly interpreted to mean something. "Oh it isn't what George *says* exactly." "You mean?" Fire and electric white spark pulsed in thin wrists. "It isn't what he says, it's the—the way he says it." "He thinks I'm—I'm beautiful?" "Oh he doesn't exactly *say* it. He thinks you very striking. It isn't the thing George says as the thing behind it." Fayne Rabb lay passive, hypnotized by white hands.

O sister my sister O fleet sweet swallow ran rhythm of her head and *hast thou the heart to be glad thereof yet* beat rhythm of a heart that beat and beat against the ragged edge of the pot-pourri-coloured old shawl (it had been grandmama's) flung over the upstairs sitting room little sofa. A sofa. What is a sofa? A sofa is that horrible thing in Fayne's house that you slide off of. A sofa, rightly speaking is slippery. You slide off. It's better her coming here ... up in this room, alone in this room. Heart beat against the old shawl whose paisley pattern faded out in the onrush of winter darkness, darkness out of a temple. Her heart beat like an owl in the darkness ... *hast thou the heart to be glad thereof yet ... thou has forgotten, O summer swallow ... but the world will end ... the world will end ... the world will end ... when I forget.*

Heart might beat its rhythm; it would not beat out thought. Her with hands stretched like some suppliant across the dead body of its child or slain young lover, though my heart beats and beats it won't drown thought. Thought goes on, I am a sort of cavity for thought. My head is a sort of cold stone hollow bowl and thought is caught in my child head. Her hands lay stretched, crossed on the white marble covered with blue serge. Her hands lay where they had fallen when finally she had felt under hypnotizing fingers the temples in that other head cease their terrible pummeling and pounding and the eyelids (under hypnotizing long fingers) flutter and fall, swallow wings fall and flutter and stay silent. The heart under the long hand of Her Gart went on beating. It's as if she just hadn't died. What is so terrible about it? She seems to get away, get across into some other world. Her eyes burn like blue stones with fire back of them, blue stones with no fire in them. Her eyes go black suddenly like the black wings of a swallow. Her eyes go shut, are shut. Will they ever open? Her seemed to be dragging beat on beat out of that heart by her very static willpower. I will not have her hurt. I will not have Her hurt. She is Her. I am Her. Her is Fayne. Fayne is Her. I will not let them hurt HER.

Resolution, beating its valour into early winter darkness, was overtaken by a host of enemies. Sitting alert her thought was, "Oh they will wake her, they will wake HER. Her must not be wakened." Her was sleeping after tussle and pummeling of veins in a taut forehead. One day at Lillian's a boy had lifted a heavy weight from her own forehead, had showed Heaven without edge or width or line or any edge whatever. Heaven without any edge whatever, became a room ceiling, became a ceiling cut in the corner by the triangle of light that fell across from the lamp at the edge of the driveway. Tim lights the lamp early these nights. Carriage lamp at the driveway threw triangle ...

"Aren't you having any dinner?" cried blasphemy across circles of temple light. Should she answer? It was Minnie. Her answered, "Oh tell them that I don't—Fayne's here—I'll come later." Feet followed voice and went out. Feet went out finally like a snuffed candle. Feet had padded down the corridor. Thought from below stairs now would creep up. Her could hear them talking; "But hasn't that Rabb girl gone yet?" Her could hear them discussing Fayne. Minnie and mama at least would be joined in this instance. There would be nothing left ... nothing left ... her heart pressed back again against the rough edge of the sofa, against the old soft paisley stuff of the old shawl. Fayne hadn't heard them, mercifully under hypnotizing white hand a heart went on ... went on ... I will keep her heart beating. I will keep Her asleep. Her is asleep here out of some cavern. Her lies asleep like Juliet, like some slain young warrior. Her lies in state like a prince who is dead, like a king. Her is asleep ... Her must stay there sleeping.

"Hermione, unlock the door. This is—this is—" Oh heart don't wake up, don't move Her, don't move. Stay sleeping. Her rose and tiptoed backward toward the door, pushed herself to some raw reality against it, caught at the little fastener. "But it isn't locked Eugenia." Her turned around the door, slid around it as around some upstanding marble pillar, closed it, stood against it. "The door's not locked Eugenia." A face regarded Her. It was Eugenia. "But—but—" Eugenia was choking. She looks ugly. Her face came up wrinkled about the eyes, furrowed in the chin. The chin was furrowed. Her face was angry. Her eyes were innocent and looked like violets. The face was a sort of face looking out of tea leaves in a trick fortuneteller's outfit. A face out of a gipsy-teller's fortune looked at her. It was marred with tea leaves. The eyes were violets.

"Mama. She's—she's—sleeping." "*Sleep*ing." "Yes mama." "Sleeping?" "Yes Eugenia." "But how—how can she be sleeping?" Innocence regarded Her out of violets. The eyes were violets. It was horrible. I am a second-rate necromancer. Part of Eugenia appears and that's what makes it terrible. If I stare and stare with the utmost concentration, will the rest of her evolve out of nothingness? The face is going round, the eyes are violets, the nose is a nose from an Eleusinian frieze above an altar. The head is set right. But the whole thing's marred with tea leaves.

"You're all blurred out with tea leaves." Eugenia snatched at a handkerchief, scrubbed violently; "It *can't* be tea leaves." And something deep in Her rose and tossed rags and tatters and yet could not think it funny. "Now if I were George I would go off into fits of affected laughter." "Did you say that George is here, too?" "No, I said 'If I were George I would laugh at what upset you.' Fayne's alone. I don't want to wake her." "But you must—must—why it's almost eight. It's terrible. Dinner is really over." "Mama, I can't wake her."

Now the corridor and the lamp at the turn of the stairs and the shadows of the banister railings and the little low stool set in the window ledge at the hall-end and the window at the hall-end showing blue-black and a bare tree branch across it like a picture hung there and the carpet with the two edges of dark polished floor and the pattern on the carpet not quite symmetrical where feet had passed to and fro to the bathroom and the door half open that was Minnie's door left half open made a scene, made a drop curtain for Eugenia.

All these things and the marks on the carpet made a swing between worlds so that she knew herself the heart of a king buried in a sepulchre (in the land of his love) while the body of the king is elsewhere. My heart lies buried in there like Coeur de Lion (or whoever it was) who had his heart buried at Havre (or wherever it was) and the rest of him somewhere else properly at home. My body standing here staring at Eugenia is properly at home, my heart ripped out, all very neat and perfect, the thing's so perfect. I will say that for the thing, "The thing is perfect." "Wha-aa-at, Hermione?" "I said," her voice repeated, "the thing is perfect." "I see nothing perfect. Everything turned upside-down by this girl and ever since she's come here, things have been different." "How different?" "Meals. You never used to miss out lunch *and* dinner." "I didn't." "You have done. You are taking things too—too—nonchalantly. You don't seem to realize you're being married." "I'm not." "No-oot?" "No, mama."

Eugenia was in the light that was the yellow somewhat corn-coloured light the lamp at the turn of the stairs made even here at the end of the long corridor. The mellow light persisted and Eugenia went on, "*She's* done it." "Done what, mama?" "Made you hate him." "I don't hate—as you say—George Lowndes." Things that had been spoken were re-spoken. The things Eugenia had said Hermione now uttered like young oracle taking dying spark from a deserted old one. Eugenia always had been right really about Georgio. "I don't love him." "Since when—this intricate nonsense?" "Don't go on, Eugenia. Minnie is sure to be—to be—listening." "But—but—*Lillian*—" "Am I to marry George because of Lillian?" "Things—people—people are always talking." "Well, they talked before I took up as they say George, before George took as they say me up. They will go on serenely talking." Light cast from the lamp made such static shadow. The whole place ought to be whirling like a tenement fire. The whole thing is like a tenement blazing. And don't feel it.

"But she can't go on there—sleeping." "She won't. She'll wake up." "But she can't go on there sleeping." Eugenia would repeat this, would repeat this, would repeat this. Hermione made her elaborate gesture. "Come in, mama. Perhaps now she's already wakened." The door flung, showed darkness and Eugenia fleeing, as before an upraised Gorgon head, this thing called Fayne Rabb. What is it Fayne Rabb does to everybody?

No. Not everybody. Again, a suppliant at the door of some ancient altar, Her gasped out "What is it, what is it Fayne Rabb does to people?"

A voice like a voice from a tomb, like a voice at the other end of a telephone wire answered her, "I always do. I have done always." A tired voice but a voice as of someone who is dead "that Greek tag, a little soul for a little?" "*A little soul for a little holds up this corpse that is man.*" "Yes. But why go on, why go *on* with this thing?" "What thing, swallow?" "This going on and *on* with this thing." Her could not see the hand she apprehended. She knew a hand was lifted, was sketching its hieroglyph toward an imaginary heaven. Birds across windows spelt things. Her had realized that birds made a pattern, made a hieroglyphic for people, wise men, augurers. Fayne was a bird, that swallow, flown here simply. People would not see her or, seeing her, regarded her bitterly, as an outcast. Fayne was a swallow making pattern across a window.

"I wanted to get away ... get away ... then George said that I was merely human, that I wanted love. George said that I wasn't so odd really, he was so inexpressibly tactful with poor mama. I sometimes think mama is mad. I know I am." "Go on, Fayne."

Suddenly in the region of that hollow space that was or (she thought) should be the place a heart should be, a heart was. A heart (not the thing she had laid in a white vase) beat and made its answer. The heart in a white urn froze and bound Her so that she could not run away from the other, the unfamiliar beat and whirr her heart made at the name of George. George Lowndes in a moment, in Saint Paul's twinkling of an eye became George Lowndes. "I ought to have thought sooner. Of course, I should have known that. I might have been quite happy."

nine

Now playing with an éclair under a pink lampshade, the thing became more difficult. Now facing George across a white small cloth with cream sort of inserted edges and squares and

triangles on the cloth and an inset little dolphin, ramping in
its little square of insertion, it was the more difficult. The hat
made it difficult which George said would be too big on anybody else and that made a flap of broad brim over one eye so
that she could crouch, so to speak, under the hat waiting for
the right moment to come when she should raise wide eyes,
accusation making fire and spark to wither George and defi-
ance making George quiver beneath spark and fire of accusation. This was somehow not the moment. George said, "We
will do this sort of thing everywhere. There are little tables all
along the lagoons and little tables set properly at Florian's."
"Florian's?" "Venice. Fancy anyone not knowing Florian's. I'm
going to get the kick of my life showing you Florian's and the
Prado; little tables at Madrith." "Ma—?" "—drith." "Oh." Her
realized (she ought to have remembered) that when George
said Cadiz, it sounded like what he was saying when apparently (by the same logic) he was meaning Madrid. "Oh Spain.
I don't know that I'd like it." "No." George leaning back, con-
templatively sipping something in a long glass that (to Her)
was nameless, said, "No-oo, you're awfully *late* Italian." "But
no one ever said that." "I don't mean it in that sense; I mean
mid-earlyish. The sort of thing that happens in Tuscany.
You know. That vague half-sensed aura of antiquity—" "My
aura of antiquity is, wholly sensed, quite blatant." "Then you
shouldn't wear such hats."

She knew the hat was wrong, had sensed from the beginning that the hat was badly chosen. Something underneath
me, that isn't me, wanted George all the same to like me. I am
playing not false to George, not false to Fayne. I am playing
false to Her, to Her precisely. Her became an external objec-
tified self, a thin vibrant and intensely sincere young sort of

unsexed warrior. The Hermione that sat there, thought pa-
tronizingly of that Her as from an endless distance. The Hermione that faced George, that had really wanted George to
like her, drooping with pseudo-sophisticated languor under
the extravagantly and fantastically brimmed hat said "That
last act was so boring." "The thing was monstrous. I never
should have asked you." Now she contradicted herself with
false bright show of affectation, "Oh no. I really loved it."
George motioned for a waitress who presented a menu like a
dance card. Her said, "But I don't want—anything."

"We can't sit here forever." "Can't we pretend it's dinner and
wait and then go and dance" (the menu gave her this idea) "or
something?" "Why—Hermione—" "It's so late anyhow."

George danced badly but some rhythm took her, held Her
so that George through no fault of his own was moved into
some rhythm not of his own making. "You're the only female
I could ever dance with." "Why female at this moment?" "You
aren't are you, exactly masculine?" "Oh-oo?" "I mean are you?"
Far and far-seen as at the end of a telescope, a young thing
with stiff muscles of slender forearms was fastening an arrow.
Somewhere else the same kind of a person, only a fraction
more robust, was beating through underbrush of Chersonese
oak boughs. The person beating against impassable barrier of
underbrush was alone—beating; I can't desert Her. Her said
"What do you think now of this Rabb?" The moment was chosen out of many moments. Moment under a pink lampshade
was too obvious, moment to fill conversation waiting for a
cab while he wrapped her fur about her was not the moment.
Moment in the cab too obviously just right for some such outbreak was not the moment. Moment on moment on moment
filling long evening in this slightly shoddy dance place, one by

one had been discarded by something far and near, something
in her that was Her, something of her that was no creature in
a broad flapping hat but was HER precisely. Her spoke out of
the cobweb Her had wound about Her. Her spoke out of the
moments on moments she had carefully used for this minor
motive, using all moments but this moment as web to catch
Georg, Georgio and George Lowndes. Beneath the web on
web (Her was so beautifully now hidden) Her raised its white
head. A head rose out of the mesh on mesh, a silver spider rose
with venom. George did not see the spider. Arachne. Pallas. I
weave and weave and George has not seen the spider. Moment
in the cab was nearest when George had said, "But all this is
so unlike you." What was you and what was you and what was
you? What was like Her and what was unlike Her? George
had no inkling.

She sank back toward the broad bench where she had left
her hat. This was not the sort of place Lillian would approve
of. No one in fact would ever. She sank back on the long bench
and lifted her hat and examined it critically. "Hermione."
"Georgio?" "This place isn't—" "One—just one more—"

Music went on, went on. Her said "I mean do you still like
her?" "Like?" "The Rabb creature." Moment after moment
had been discarded for this moment. This moment hung,
shaping an eternity, shaping the whole of Her. This moment
was a small bridge, a book with a map, a path running through
a forest; no, it wasn't Xenophon who crossed that river, "it was
Caesar." "Caesar?" "Is it this moment." "I don't precisely follow." Her balanced the broad light brim of the extravagantly
picturesque hat. "One can wear this sort of chiffon lined thing
winter *and* summer." "It's the least bit obvious." "Yes, isn't it?"
The flower at the side fastened with the narrow velvet was

a lily in a black pool. *Lilies of all kinds, the fleur de lys being
one.* "The fleur de lys—" "It *is* rather a white iris. They grow
on banks and in small clusters under olives. I mean the small
humming-bird-blue-dart iris." "Iris? Where my George?"
"In Corfu. That's Greece really. I'll take you to Corfu." "Yes
George." "The hat is atrocious really." "Yes isn't it?"

A fall of dress stuff fell back from her thin wrist. Her wrist
emerged apart from herself, a sort of wax wrist in a milliner's
window supporting a hat with a white-gold flower set at a
slight angle, with a flower that went white-silver in the lamplight. "Put a lamp in the window, pull down the shades you
might sell this hat for new." "No-oot exactly. The edge is frayed
out here." There was that about George, he could always play
these games. "Then I must get a new one." "I always wanted to
buy wide hats for people. Lillian wears such small ones. Set too
far back like some 1880 (I tell her) Belinda person." "I remember you called Lillian Belinda." "It appears my father bought
a hat once." "Your—?" "Father." "You know I never saw him."

An arrested moment, a moment with a white wrist, a moment that was balancing a hat on its hand, might last forever.
One moment sets the pace for all, all moments and one moment trembled in a white wrist balancing a too-wide black
floppy hat brim. The moment sank, rose. The moment swayed
with dancing. The moment was fluid, it was "Yes, you are Undine. Or. better the mermaid from Hans Andersen." The moment was fluid, the moment answered the moment; "Yes. I am
Undine. Or better the mermaid from Hans Andersen." Her in
her detachment so answered the set moment. The moment
said, you are consciousless, a reed in a river. Fayne called you
a reed, one reed pipe with a single motive. One reed pipe, a
slight singing like some Dresden shepherd's, modified to this

room, to this lamplit boudoir corner. A singing was in a slight reed. "I mean you said you liked her."

Now he was protesting in the cab that the woman was mad. "She's insane." "What did you *do* to her?" Accusation now spoke blatantly, a black hat was crushed across knees, fur wrapped tight like an Acropolian aegis, fur wrapped close about panting flat breast beneath which a heart beat and beat, die or get it right, die or get it clear while George protested violently that he had never liked the woman. "Why do you then *love* her?" "I—never—" "She said she wanted happiness, sort of escape, that you made her feel free." "I tried to—to help her." "Then why did you lie to me?" Rumbling of wheels and Her knew more than ever they were out of some bad novel. One didn't say "Why did you lie to me?" It was too crude, to blatant, everything was too blatantly crude. Her feet were cold. "Aren't we nearly at the station?" Her feet were frozen, the whole day had been disaster. Why didn't I just go on with it under a pink lampshade, all of life to be tread to music under a pink lampshade? If I had let it go, just let today drift me along, I would have drifted to Venice, to Vesuvius. I would have drifted to Vienna, to Versailles.

"Why did I go on with it?" "With what? … pull yourself together, don't *don't* be hysterical." Her feet were cold, her head was hot. "Why did I go on with it?" "On with what?" "With you—with you—can't you see? Can't you see you've tampered with me like an ill-bred child with a delicate mechanical instrument? You have no respect for science." "I thought that was the thing you wanted to be rescued from. It was you who did the screaming." "I did want to be rescued—I do, I do."

Words formed in the air, beat against the low peaked roof of the old-fashioned cab, beat and suffocated Her in the narrow funnel-like peaked-in little carriage. "What are you screaming after? The moon precisely?" "Yes. I mean I must understand this—" "There's nothing to understand. I tell you I went at your own instigation." "That's true, George. I blame myself." "Where's the blame?" "She was delirious at my house." "Delirious? She can throw herself into those sub-normal hysterical states at a moment's notice." "It wasn't hysterical. It was real." "Wha-aat happened?" "Oh the usual thing. Row on row on row. I had to stave off mama on one hand and Mrs. Rabb on the other." "Mrs. *Rabb?*" "She telephoned and telephoned *and* telephoned. Then appeared with the milk for breakfast. She had on rubbers—that's all that I remember—her rubbers." Her felt tight gasps of pain drawn out from narrow flat chest. "It was so incred-ibly fu-uu-nny. I can't tell you how incredibly it was funny. It was awfully funny."

The low roof of the cab became static. They were in a little box, shut in a little box, the box had been put away quiet on a shelf, the box was quiet. "It was terribly, at breakfast, fu-uu-nny." The lid or the side or the floor of the little box was prodded open. A face peered in, a face out of a jack-in-the-box, the wrong face, everything would come alive suddenly, faces of dolls, cups and saucers. The things in little boxes would come alive. The teapot from the dollhouse tea set box of tea things would have a long nose. "It was so awfully fu-uuny." The box that held the jack-in-the-box would be a mutilated empty box, not good for anything if the jack-in-the-box didn't step back. The head poked and prodded forward, moved like the jack-in-the-box head on its cylinder of springs. The cylinder of springs would rest on the floor and he would soon drop side-ways. He seemed to be dropping sideways or he had upset the box they were in.

"Hermione. Hermione." A voice called Her Hermione.

"My name's Her. I am Her. She is Her. I am not Hermione out of Shakespeare. Hermione out of Shakespeare was more or less one person like the person who went with Orlando. Have you noticed in Shakespeare everybody goes with someone? Almost everybody. Not fools—and—*lilies of all kinds.*"
"Her-mione." The person beside her who was George out of a Punch and Judy show, that Punchinello with harlequin's tight painted-on striped trousers was now shaking Her. "Come. Come. We can't have all this nonsense." Her was standing on the pavement with the harlequin who was Georgio. He was looking at Her. Georgio was looking at Her.

"I don't understand this nonsense." Wheels were rumbling under Her. "Is there anything so cosy as a train that's moving? Now we might be going to Venice or Versailles." The train made stable growl like back-drawn Atlantic breakers. Her throat was warm, a hot hand and open fingers seemed to scald her throat that had been so cold. Her throat had risen to December like *lilies of all kinds ... the fleur de lys being one.* I am Hermione out of Shakespeare. I am the word AUM. She said Em, Hem, Um, clearing her throat and her breath made a runnel in her throat like an icicle on a hot stove. Breath became red hot and melted an ice throat. Words made runnels in the throat, different shapes like frost on nursery windows. I never saw frost on any other window. Stars of frost were incrusted on her long throat. The fur was inadequate, did not keep the cold out. The fur was too hot, a mass of prickly little sticking out bristles, the sort of badger's collar that a dog wears.
"I am tired of this fur." George was at her, speaking to her "Don't always talk such nonsense. *What* did the woman tell you?" George was white under the slight sway and sway of the light in the long corridor. They sat facing a polished door

at the end of a long corridor. Walls rumbled like breakers drawing backward. "It wasn't what she said. It was the way she said it." People in Shakespeare go in pairs, but not fools. I am a fool. "It wasn't exactly what she said ... it was the thing back of the thing she said ... that mattered." "Wh-aat was the thing back of the thing that mattered?" A wolf face; a wolfs face was looking at Her. "You must get me in quick George, not loiter on the driveway." "Am I likely?" "There's something wrong here"—she caught at a straw that sank, and sinking, whirled Her into obliteration with it. "I've got a—sore throat or something ..."

II

one

Banality that was a sore throat made Her answer Minnie. "I do wish Minnie you would answer the telephone. It's so difficult." Her sat on a rug just inside the sitting room door. A green on green that was pine trees climbing heavenward was the wide gilt-framed picture. The tiny children painted in were merest smudges of colour; a dab of red—somebody's jacket, a dab of cobalt—that was somebody's wide wee skirt. Skirt like a paper doll, it was such fun dressing paper dolls only mama should have lent me that old paint box. The box was in the attic and brushes were stiff and there was a smell of turpentine.

Minnie said he must see Her. "He says he's waiting. He says he'll just wait." "Well, go hang up the receiver." "He says when it's hung up, he'll start ringing." "Well go to the kitchen, ask Mandy for the meat ax, smash it." "He'll come then right out." Minnie was interested. Minnie scented romance. "Oh Minnie, I wish you'd do something for me." Her never asked anything of Minnie. She seemed suddenly sunk to Minnie's level. What after all, did poor old Minnie matter? After all, it was darned dull for Minnie. Who would want to marry Bertrand? Minnie had married Bertie thinking she was going up in the world, she never thought she'd be stuck in a barn of a place with people with hushed voices. Her wished she had some chewing gum to offer Minnie. "Minnie do you know, I think chewing gum would be good for my throat." Minnie was looking at Her. "You look sick." "I think I am. Will you tell George." Minnie went obediently back to the telephone, playing a major role for a change. Oh let Minnie be leading lady in this show. Her hair is against her, her hair ought to be beautiful. Do you know, given the right environment, Minnie might have been right. It's this dreadful beauty of abstraction that's done us all in. What is the darn use of coping with the gracile suavity of (say) a fern, of (say) that sort of sperm-pod of moss propagating seen under the microscope. Minnie never understood the deprivation of pure beauty. She ought to have scent. It would make her happy. "Minnie do you ever use scent?" Minnie was standing by Her. "He says he'll ring up later." Minnie was redheaded, such a common creature. She said, "You look sick."

It might have been February. It might have been August. Heat pulsed and burnt but the flowers were wrong. There were great king-carnations, maroon, the colour of paper on chocolate—that thick colour; mama should have let me have the paint box. Why when people don't want things, do they keep them? Mama should have let me have that paint box, should have given away that paint box, so I should give away Her but I keep Her out of some outworn sense of odd association. Paints worn thin with holes in the middle. I don't want Her. I am tired of Her ... It might have been May with flowers drooping from a branch. Someone had sent white lilac. "What month is it?"

Someone said "Sh-ssh" and she turned over on a pillow. Someone said from somewhere "People keep sending flowers. There are too many in here." Someone said "Sit up. Now hold her shoulders"; someone said "I'll call you if there is any alteration," someone said "Under your tongue. Now, *don't* try to swallow it," someone said "No, no, no. It's serious," someone went on and went on and it went on through days, through years, through many years for the lilac bloomed again and this time it was purple. "Mrs. Lowndes keeps sending lilac. I do wish she hadn't broken her engagement."

Minnie hissed sibilantly over all this "She looks so sick." Minnie burnt, a zinnia in the darkness. Aren't common people after all, the right ones? What is achievement? What has it brought me? Then she dreamt she was waiting for examinations and had forgotten logarithm. Logarithms. Something binomial and something conic that was a section. She went on breaking test tubes and the hydrochloric acid was spilt and someone said "She needn't take it. There's no use forcing these things" and a friend of someone who knew Minnie sat on the bed and said "But you aren't sick. Now listen. Elijah arose at the voice of the Lord and walked. Now he was old and you are young. You aren't sick. You can walk." But when she got up someone called and Minnie called and Minnie and Mrs. Banes (it was Mrs. Banes) went out whispering "There was no harm *trying* it."

It was quite obvious to Her that there was no pain. That life was not. That material had no existence. She did not need that thing proved. Someone said "These Christian Scientists do more harm than good. Now I remember a woman who had a growth—" It was odd how many voices could crowd into a room filled with pulse of August heat and filled with winter lilac. The white lilac flowered again and then lilac stopped, altogether, coming. "They've gone. They left this message." Someone read something on a card, and Her asked for it. A face looked astonished at Her. "Then you're—you're—*better?*" "Oh, I'm all right." A feeble voice came from a hollow but it left no runnels as of a red-hot iron on a hollow ice tube. There were no runnels where her throat was. "But don't put your arm out of the blanket," and someone was reading to Her, "So sorry not to see you. They wouldn't let me come in. Lillian."

Then the voice explained disapprovingly that there was another card but it was too difficult to make out that scraggy
writing and Her said "I must see it."

It made pattern on her tired brain. It brought back summer
long ago, so long ago, a summer before white lilac, before purple, before white again and then lilac had stopped coming. A
summer long ago before there was a Fayne, before there was a
Her. There was no Her sitting in a dining room that lifted and
sank and lifted a faded bowl of mountain wild azalea. "Someone should send azalea." "What Miss Gart?" Her looked at a
strange face but it was not a strange face. It was a face that had
been there for eternity through white lilac and then purple
and then white. "You've been here then three summers?" "Oh
my dear—just rest back." "No. I mean it. You've been here just
three summers."

A summer before these three summers (Tim grubbed up
one bush, there was one by the old hedge with the wild cherry)
there had been upheaval; Eugenia saying "But you can't marry
George Lowndes" and "That George person" that was Fayne
before she saw George. There was something in everything
and three summers are a long time. "I've had a long time." "Yes
it's been a long siege. Started before Christmas." Christmas.
What was Christmas? A bird had done a trapeze-turn across a
window like a bird on a string hung on the Christmas tree and
I am the word Aum and I am Tree. I am Tree exactly. George
never would love a tree, she had known from the beginning.
If you follow your instinct from the first you will be right. I
knew George could never love a tree properly.

Now she saw Tree and I am Tree and I am the word Aum
and I am Her exactly. For the writing was what had started
things and the writing was the same writing. She had read

"I am coming back to Gawd's own god-damn country" and she had read "Go straight to the telephone ... to see a girl I want you to see." She had read that and the other while she had suffocated and she had flung herself before a window in a low sewing chair (in which she never sewed) and it was still suffocating. "It's so—so ho-*ot*." Minnie had said "None of you realize how this heat affects me" and perhaps Minnie was right. "None of you realize how this heat affects me" Her said, for she was a fool out of Shakespeare and if she went on and on saying the same thing perhaps in time people would realize that the thing back of the thing was the thing that mattered. "Then take this woollen coat off." The woman who was the strange woman who went with winter lilac took off her woollen jacket. "I don't mean hot in that sense." The woman treated Her as if Her were incapable of knowing what Her was. I am the word AUM. I am Her. The word was with God. I am a fool in Shakespeare. There's no use getting anything right ever for George had written "I am coming back to Gawd's own god-damn country" like a harlequin. Now he was writing that he was leaving Gawd's own god-damn country. Why didn't he stay put somewhere?

It was obvious that people should think before they call a place Sylvania. People are in things. Things are in people and people should think before they call a place Sylvania. I am the word AUM. The word was with God, the place was Pennsylvania. Pennsylvania was some sort of Lilliput or Gargantua, things like that, places like that, nowhere was Pennsylvania.

"Nurse, what state do you come from?" "Oh, I'm from Pennsylvania." There was no use. Nurse Dennon was tying up odds and ends and bits and bits and odds and ends. It was astonishing the amount of work she could make out of nothing. There was something in that. "Nurse." "Yes, Miss Gart?" "Do you think I'm too old to take up nursing?" Nurse Dennon went on winding up bits and odds and ends and odds and ends and bits. "Oh-o. I don't know." She was mumbling over pins, was making something, had forgotten Her. Nurse Dennon (I suppose she is Miss Dennon) is from Pennsylvania. Then she is out of the same sort of thing. I won't get any change out of her, for people are in names and names are in people. "People should think before they call a place Sylvania." "What Miss Gart?" Miss Dennon condescended to look up, "I don't know the place. Is it perhaps in Russia?" "No. It's a place I read about. It was mostly trees. It was settled by—by some sort of sect, people who believed in silence, in God in silence." "Like Quakers?" "Yes. Like Quakers. It was settled by people like Quakers. It was called (I don't know why) Sylvania." "It sounds Russian." "Yes. It sounds Russian like Lithuania. Is Lithuania Russian? I think some of them were Polish, some of the settlers. It was heavy with trees, a sort of paradise of trees, trees, trees, trees; dogwood, liriodendron, you know, the tulip tree." "Yes, Miss Gart." Miss Dennon went on politely listening. "People, I always feel are in things and things I always feel are in people." "Yes, Miss Gart." "You know, nurse, my name's Hermione."

The person who was Nurse Dennon dropped her sewing. Rather she put it carefully in the corner of the armchair, her substitute for dropping. She came and stood by the bedside. Her apron was starched and her skirt was starched and she seemed altogether set in a cone, a sort of cone, a sort of thing like the jack-in-the-box that ought to fall over when it was pulled out of its box but Miss Dennon stood on her own feet like Ham, Shem and Japheth. Miss Dennon, it was obvious, stood on her own feet. "Are you a little tired of talking?" "No. I'm tired of not talking. It seems I have never talked. I want to talk and talk forever." "Then don't you want to see your— your—mother?" "No. I don't want to see my mother. She isn't."

"I wish Miss Gart now you are getting better you would tell me what's upset you." The figure spoke as Ham, Shem and Japheth might speak if Ham, Shem and Japheth could speak. It made it interesting. "I don't know. I do know. It would take too long to explain it." "Well, won't you try to?" Miss Dennon made a motion backwards as if to draw up her chair and drag up her bag of sewing. "Oh, I'll try to."

"What is your name Miss Dennon?" "Amy." "May I call you Amy?" "Please do Miss Gart." "My name's Hermione." "Please do—Her—Hermione. It seems quite too beautiful a name to be used in conversation." "Yes isn't it? They call me Her. I am called Her." "That seems a little—I mean a little too short." "Yes. That's my way. I am too—too remote you know and too—too silly. I am both." "I didn't say Her was silly. I said it was—short." "Well, didn't you mean silly?" "No. I can't say that I did." Amy spoke like Ham, Shem and Japheth. There was that about her. "It's this way Amy..." (You call your doll or your toy dog by a name and it becomes *your* dog, your toy doll. Nurse Dennon became by the same token her very own Ham, Shem and Japheth. It was some sort of figure set in a frigid temple, where people would come and offer prayers and where people would tear their hearts out and it would never listen. Yet if you happened to know its name was Ham, Shem and Japheth it would do anything for you. You had only to address it by its name and it would do anything. Remove mountains. Its outer or world name is Amy Dennon. Its inner or occult name is Hamshem.) Hamshem went on sewing.

"I can't say that there was anything special. You see I was to marry George Lowndes." "The gentleman who sent carnations?" "Did he? They seemed wrong somehow. He never could love a tree properly. You see he couldn't love Her. I mean he couldn't." "No, no of course he couldn't."

Hamshem was running a seam, did not look up, answered (there was that about her) automatically. It was like putting a penny in the slot and knowing what will come out. It was interesting that nothing came out that you did not expect to come out. It was the greatest comfort. "I went on afterwards for a little. Of course Fayne wrote me letters. They were terrible. She accused me of having plotted with him to upset her. How was I to know that?" "How indeed were you to know that?" "Her mother came out one morning in a pair of rubbers." "Was it raining?" "Yes. It had been raining a sort of slushy snow-rain. She came out in her rubbers." "People should wear rubbers when it's raining." "I don't know what upset me. I laughed and laughed. My mother used to say when I laughed like that, 'It's what your grandmother used to say when I laughed like that,' (so she must have laughed like that), *there's a black rose growing in your garden.'*"

Carnation Lily Lily Rose. "Things had been going on like that for a long time. I mean we had some tickets sent us. They were from Fayne. Nellie came out, was interested, then was frigid. It was Nellie asked me in to meet her. Nellie was away during the summer. They go to Bridgeport." "Bridgeport's pretty. I had a patient there once." "They came back." "People don't stay longer than September. That's what made it so nice." "I wanted more than anything to see snow against white breakers." "There was a line of breakwater and my how it did froth sometimes." "That's what I mean. But I wanted to go to Point Pleasant. Minnie had the cottage." "Cottage life I always think most pleasant." "Yes. We had a cottage. It wasn't altogether the actual surf. But we took the canoe up the salt creeks, further than anybody. My brother used to take me in vacations. Then he married." "I know. Having a brother married—" "Not that I *minded* Minnie—" "One never does mind. My sister-in-law is Bessie." "Well you know what I mean." "Yes. She always wanted everything different. She insisted on moving the hall things into the back parlor and she insisted on breaking up our little conservatory where mother had begonias." "Yes. Isn't it funny? Minnie wanted the front garden beds grubbed up to be used for a sun parlour. We had quite enough light anyway. She insisted she was delicate." "They do." "Minnie did. But you know sometimes I'm so sorry for poor Minnie." "It was that way with Bessie. My how she did adore Frank. My brother you know, Frank Dennon. He had flour mills." "Oh mills. How interesting." "Yes. We used to run about (in my father's day) and get covered with flour dust. But of course, then Frank (he was most progressive) had new bins and great improvements. They're well off." "Oh. I'm glad they're well off. You see with Bertrand (my brother Bertrand) it was science. You see science doesn't lead one anywhere." "Now I wouldn't say that. Look at the doctors." "Oh doctors. Of course with doctors. But that's making things fit somehow. I mean abstractions are so frightening."

"Don't you think you've talked yourself out, Miss Gart?" "My name's Her." "Don't you?" "I have only just begun. I mean about Fayne. Her uncle is a doctor." "Yes? Where does he practice?" "I don't know. Somewhere vaguely in North Philadelphia." "Oh *North* Philadelphia—" "Yes. Isn't it funny the way we all feel about North Philadelphia. I mean I think there was some trouble. He was very advanced. Fayne read a lot of books, wanted to lend me some books, psychoanalysis, German books." "Of course the German books are very solid." "That's what I think. I've forgotten all my German ..." Now

German came clear and ritterspuren and hummingbird blue and Her said "Yes, I think I want the light out."

two

Now with the light out, eyes turned inward, words formed, made gigantic pattern, German that ran on and on and the translations read odd, didn't mean the same thing. German had caught one in a mesh, it was inferiority complex if you translated it. Fayne's uncle was translating it; it was mother and father and Oedipus complex and it made pattern on a brain that rose from a black mesh. A white spider rose from a black mesh; there were people who loved ... differently. There were people with suppressions; if George had let himself love, had let herself love, if George had not kissed Fayne, if George had really kissed Fayne ran its ornate pattern, made Gothic pattern. I am not Gothic. George Lowndes is Gothic. I can't see the trees for the forest. I can't see the forest for the trees. Could he have caught Her?

Light made intricate pattern on a black sky. Light heaved and blazed, made pattern like white wisteria brushing in a storm across a dark wire netting. The screen door wouldn't fasten and white lilac (it was white lilac) makes a pattern. Minnie said Bertrand had disgraced her. Bertrand had disgraced *her*. Bertrand cut knife patterns into a damask cloth. Mama said Minnie was her sister. *O sister my sister, O fleet swallow, the world's division divideth us.* Yes. Because there was no use, the trolley was already empty, people got out at the end of the line, a transfer please conductor and Nellie said you could trade the yellow ticket for a blue one. Things were in people, people were in things. "Hamshem."

"Did you call me, Miss Gart?" "I can't sleep. Would you

mind turning the light up now. Up, up, up. She went upstairs with the telephone book under her arm. I couldn't find the number."

"What Miss Gart?" "I thought we said my name's Hermione." "Yes. We did, I mean yes Miss Hermione." "I don't mean Miss Hermione like Mandy and Tim. Only Mandy and Tim call me Miss. They call me Miss. I am a miss. I have been a Miss. Hit or Miss." "Yes, Miss—yes, yes, Hermione." "I mean haven't I? Now look at me. I mean I had a birthday. The fireweed has a sort of vermillion centre. Some people call it paintbrush. It grows in the swamps with the butterfly weed. Why weed? Lilies of all kinds, the fleur de lys being a sort of lily, a weed. I am Hermione out of Shakespeare." "Yes, Miss—yes, yes, Hermione." "You know, I would rather that you pulled your chair up, that you went on sewing. The clock will tick so loudly." "Yes, yes, Miss—yes, yes, Hermione." "No. I don't want anything. I don't want to take it. No. No. *If* you *will* listen." "Yes, yes, Miss—Hermione." "Miss. I am a miss, a miss, a miss. I am as good as a mile. Now don't you see it's funny? A miss is as good as a—" "Yes. Yes. I see the thing is very funny." "I would feel much better if you'd go on sewing." "I will do, Miss—Hermione."

"A miss is as good as a mile. Hit or miss. I am as good as a mile. I have missed everything." "Oh I wouldn't say *that* exactly." "Now there it goes, there it will go, there it will go forever, ting, ting, ting. It crawls its little cricket jerk forward and that is why they put the little old clock upstairs. Up, up, upstairs. And that is why they put the little old clock upstairs. They put the little old clock in the little old potpourri-coloured room upstairs." "Yes, yes, Hermione." "It was nobody's room. It was a study when Bertrand was at school, it was a tiny little storeroom and then mama said the sunlight was all wasted. Mama has the little glass room downstairs." "Yes, Miss—Hermione." "I mean the vermillion leaf slashed like starfish purple. Starfish if you leave them on the rocks cook dry. I never left starfish on a rock to cook dry. I scraped them off and made the Stewards angry." "The—?" "Horrid boys. They were not friends of Bertrand's. I mean they ran after us, howling and I loathed them. Afterward the people ran and the people ran." "Yes, Miss Hermione." "Don't call me Miss Hermione. I am as good as a mile. George never could love anything quite simply. It ran and ran, made the Xenophon pattern though I don't know much Greek. The little room upstairs (I said) will be my room. I was going to work and I was going to work and I was going to work. George called them forgotten lyrics of a lost Melic or iambics of a forgotten Melic. I have forgotten. I am the lost iambics of a forgotten Melic. Melos is an island. The Venus de."

"The—? I admit I don't quite follow." "The Venus de Milo is standing in the Louvre now. She is the face of the—that face of—she is the forgotten Melics of a lost iambic. I don't like the Venus de Milo. But George said taken at a certain angle squinting sideways, she comes up like the moon crescent. She is meant to be seen at the end of corridors, not in these cheap photographs. You know what I mean, nurse. The Venus de Milo … it's not a good thing really. I mean if it were good it would come up better. Like the coloured Tanagra praying boy of … but I can't remember. George said it wasn't. Lillian said it was. Lillian sent me the purple lilac—that was better." "Better?" "I mean. Carnations. What do they *mean* anyway?"

"Germans, I mean, doing things in layers. A top to a thing, a bottom to a thing, things going on and on and on, oneself the Her-part of one holding the whole thing like a pinwheel."

"Fourth of July?" "No. Yes. I mean Uncle Sam, a sort of Carl Gart person is too much for us—too much for us—I mean for us. And who is us? There is a sort of us that holds the Carl Gart Uncle Sam sort of thing together. The whole thing is vibrating, not that, whirring and seething like the heart of a planet before it's cast out. We're incandescent and it doesn't seem fair." "Fair?" "I mean too much comes to some of us, not enough to all the rest of us. So few of us to do the thinking. I mean so few of us have to be so incandescent. There is me and Fayne for instance—brightness—burning—" "The light on?" "No. Yes. Sit there and go on sewing. I should have had a night nurse. At night I need a nurse. Day time, things stand static. At night I need a night nurse. I need a night at night nurse. You see the thing is inchoate, incontrovertible. There is always, isn't there, in the heart of a new world that is forming, just that center, that pinpoint of incandescence that holds the thing together? There is a pinpoint of incandescence. George wasn't." "George the gentleman who sent you the carnations?" "Understanding but not of it. A sort of three circles beyond; three circles is near when almost everyone else, when almost everything else is some ten or twelve or twenty circles off. You know. Like concentric circles when you throw a stone in. White water lilies are of all kinds, the Her-de-lys being one …"

… "You see the white thing being broken, the whole world falls to pieces. White lightning scarred that across an irate heaven. Hold on, hold on Her Gart. Hold on, hold on Her Gart. And don't ask why you are holding on so incandescent. Why don't I go up like a rocket, a sort of decoration that goes off in sizzles? George would have made me a sort of decoration that goes off in sizzles. Fayne understood this. But Fayne's incandescence was not conscious. I mean she turned it on and off apparently at random. The thing seething and beating like a dynamo beating in thin air ... to just nothing, vibrating like the propeller of a boat out of water, attached to nothing, making everything seem useless but herself creating nothing. I thought Fayne would understand, get this. She said I was Hecate, a daemon. So I am. I suppose I am that. Sometimes when gull wings beat across the counterpane, I know she loved me. Take a gull. It's a lonely creature. It is the incandescence of the water. Cast up with eyes made of agate, onyx, those words if you attack them blatantly mean nothing. She said I was deciduous, but that word is cottony. Mrs. Rabb said, 'You mean cotton-y?' Cotton is most words; frizzle, sizzle those thoughts that go up like newspapers in a bonfire. Go on and on, thought going up in wet flap of newspapers in an old lot. Boys running down a little avenue chasing a shabby football ..."

"... so that things unhinged from nowhere. Nowhere was right here. Here was nowhere. Being here one was nowhere, in time and space there was no such thing as anywhere. Upstairs in my little room (we finally called it Hermione's little workroom) snow beat and great Hokusai waves woke from gigantic cyclones. They rose, *for art thou a rose my sister white sister there* and a ghost rose is growing in your garden. Her mother said 'A ghost rose is growing in your garden for if you start laughing that way there is nothing to stop you.' Laughter. You know. Opens doors. They turn on hinges. There is no use striving against nothing ... for nothing is nowhere. Fayne said *'Art thou a ghost my sister white sister there?'* Her hair was done high at the back and whisps never would stay right somehow and we bought a beret; we called it a buret but the stones dropped out (they were only rhinestones) and the thing was trampled underfoot. Two springs later we found the broken buret in the vegetable garden for the mauve sweetpeas and the lavender *pois-de-senteur* told one one never could cope with weeding out the garden. Plantinum spoils Gart lawn. The grass crept up from the smothered molehill. Stamp on the molehill and the trap had iron spikes. The tiny almost unborn moles had soft down like an unhatched gosling's ... my sister there. Remember always that Swinburne being decadent, there's no use arguing ..."

"Vermillion slashed across wet windows. That was Virginia creeper. Again there was a burnt ember, a common thing, the heart of Minnie Hurloe. Minnie married Gart. My sister has red hair, yellow or red mixed make a sort of zinnia colour ... *art thou a ghost my sister?* Looking in a glass I saw that Hermione looked sideways. The glass fell breaking Hermione. One I love, two I love, three I love. George said '*art thou a ghost my sister?* Narcissa, are you a water lily?' A red hibiscus smouldered through all the grey and silver. George was a red hibiscus. His carnations are really scentless. Across the red of red hibiscus-red there burnt this common zinnia ... mama of course being always summer violets. Mama of course being always winter violets. Mama of course being violets under a glass frame and violets in little pottery jugs and violets placed in corners. Follow a corner to its logical conclusion and you will find mama in a broken flower pot spilling indigo ... mama had indigo in a paint box. Red, read. Read Over Your Greek Book In Vacation. Red you see, Orange you see, Yellow and Green. Read over your Greek book in vacation makes the rainbow colour. Mama said 'Read over your Greek book in vacation' ..."

"I think you'd better take this, Miss Her." "Yes nurse?" "I said I think you'd better take this Miss Her." "Why nurse?"

George never could love anything … nor any tree … I am the word tree, I am AUM exactly. Fayne being me, I was her. Fayne being Her I was Fayne. Fayne being Her was HER so that Her saw Fayne; there was no use trying to hide under a midnight black hat rim for out of the black hat Her saw everything. Her was Fayne, Fayne was Her so that saying to George did you love, one I love, meant nothing. I knew George saw Her, saw George, saw Fayne. Out of nothing triangles shaped like Buster Brown being hit on the head sidestepping. He saw stars triangles. I saw triangles stars and the beat, beat that was the in-growl, that was the out-growl of Atlantic breakers. The flower called paintbrush weed made deep scars across the lips of George Lowndes. He sat on the couch, his lips were a paintbrush weed colour across New Jersey meadows. Hibiscus flowering in a salt marsh. Take the canoe up and take the canoe up for Minnie never could understand a canoe wasn't a tugboat. Gulls sweep and hoot … Hermione is a gull's name, Fayne said and you have the eyes that made Poppaea furious. Dealing with terms of antiquity became a sort of ritual. It was all out of reality. I mean reality was out of it precisely. The very centre of spark of the divinity was in a Greek boy praying … *which art in Heaven* … which had no side nor edge nor top nor any end whatever. Which went on for some time. Then crowds filled vacancy. People kept on coming … everybody said Oh this, Oh that and did you make Poppaea furious? Of course I did do. She was furious. She came out, sidled across the lawn in floppy rubbers, sidled across the tiles before the outer gateway and sidled like some broken image into our house. She sat in the hall under Pius Wood and harangued everybody. We had taken, we had seduced her daughter. Art thou a ghost my sister? I had finally to range myself with everyone, with mama more exactly for the things she said were

vibrous. Vicious is what the things she said were. Vibrant vi-
cissitudes but she needn't do it. We broke everything having
the screendoor mended."

"Take this now, Miss Her—Hermione."

three

"I suppose this you've given me is a replica of something
out of antiquity." "You seem quieter." "I am much quieter." "If
you slept for only a little while, Hermione, you'd feel much
better." "If I sleep now, Amy, I will sleep forever." "No. Miss
Gart. The crisis passed last night." "I don't mean sleep in that
sense. I don't mean to sleep, to die, to dream, ah there's the rub.
I don't mean any meandering really. I see clearly." "I said you
looked much better." "If you open the window ever so little,
just enough so that I may hear the sun rise." "Hear?" "That odd
infallible sliding-like-crystal air on water that means day's left
dawn for morning."

"That's the sort of thing I mean, a poem exactly. George
said you are a poem though your poem's naught. Browning. I
skipped the lawyers in *The Ring and the Book*. But somewhere
not here, somewhere else, exactly sensed, exactly seen, Fayne
was. I mean this thing you've given me, is like white lilac across
my head and everything is exactly right. The radiator in the
corner and its drip drip winter nights and sometimes the little
hard shriek of a whistle it gives as the steam comes up toward
morning. The light cuts a triangle on your stiff apron and you
are encased in your apron, perfectly right, encased in a sort of
hollow pillar, exactly seen there. You are white in a pillar and
I should like, now that this white lilac has etherealized my
senses, to do something."

"You might yet take up nursing." "Something. Something. My grandmother, it appears, left money for my trousseau. I could use it for nursing. People say my hands help. Vibrant, something comes out through my fingers. Fayne said *hypnos,* she murmured *hypnos.* That sleep and that forgetting may be, is part and parcel of reality."

"Really you'd better lie now flat, Hermione."

"I don't want to, nurse, this time. I want to sit here sensing this moment that is dawn and morning. A moment and an infinitesimal fraction of a moment and dawn slides into morning like starlight into water. There is a quivering, a slightest infinitesimal shivering. The thing that was is not."

She heard (sensing moments) realities, intentions, the footstep that trod silent and fateful toward the open window. She heard by that fraction of a second that separates sleep from waking, the window closing and she knew in that fraction of a second that divides thought from dreaming that the window was now shut fast. She sensed her head, felt it fall heavy, no valiant effort could hold her to her vast desire. A project had formed in her head, a project and a determination. I will tell someone. When I have told someone it will fall from my forehead, heavily and visibly like the very scriptural millstone.

The thing she realized in that moment, that fraction of waiting, was lost. Nothing could bring the thing back, no words could make the thing solid and visible and therefore to be coped with. Solid and visible form was what she had been seeking. I will put this into visible language, Amy Dennon will say this or this. Amy Dennon will say you were harassed, disintegrated and disassociated by preliminary erotic longings, wakened as it were in sleep, sleeping in a dream as in a dream we sleep and in a dream we are awakened, perceiving the dream (in the dream) to be only a dream and in the dream saying, the dream (in a dream) was the wildest of stark foreboding. In a dream, there had been a dream and it was the very valiant avid mind of Her that had started valiantly like some young Lacadaemonian alone across trackless pathways to entrap it.

The dream in the dream should be put into stark language. Birds in traps, enemies in pitfalls, the Athenians in the pit at Syracuse. So valiant, she had stalked across an untracked Laconian desert, hill rose, hill fell, valley and hill. At times she started into some trance, the dream was broken and a heavier state retook it. The trance caught Her and she said correctly and with perfect sophistication "You are not Olympian, Fayne, but Delphic."

Delphi, Olympus were states as different, as exact and as exactly to be predicted as the words, the reactions of a Frenchman, of an Italian, of a South American. Olympus and Delphi and Dodona were states of mind, exactly to be predicted ... but there was no one, as if a wire were beating with some message, tick, tick, dot, dot, tick dot and dot tick and she, avid and eager, beat her dot and tick into an empty area.

The dot, tick had found in Fayne Rabb another station, another receiver for messages, transferred to Her from Dodona, from Herculaea. Dot tick, we are here, always and always, we fall, we wallow in mire and filth of war time, we are stressed in unhappy circumstance, human and dark browed, our very sweat remains witness to our fidelity ... I have been faithful said Her Gart, feeling the moment was about to pass into all moments, the great majority of moments that are dead moments. Her felt her head sink into the cushion, felt; Amy Dennon has given me some sort of dope. She has cheated me of my discovery ... lilac had made exact pattern, the thing inhaled into her nostrils clarified, simplified so that the triangle of heavy starched surfaces and the corresponding triangle of darkly underlined shadow in the stiff front of Amy Hamshem's apron, meant triangle and perfect surface of some Delphic portico ... It *was* important to remember the steam and hiss of the radiator that had kept on wakening Her. It was also important to recall the exact swirl of a leaf that made Ionian columns ornate ... Corinthian. The name, the word would cut its way like a snow plough, ploughing extraneous matter to this side, sweeping it to that side. Through great drifts of impassable obstruction such things cut like ploughshares ... that was why it was necessary to remember ... to remember ... Amy had cheated Her. This was the moment that should have been prolonged to eternity ... forgotten.

Yet coming through the moment there were memories, red hyacinths in snow, red cyclamen seen through avid blighting lava. On the slopes of Vesuvius such memories burn, are cyclamen, are hyacinths. "Hermione is a gull name ... you read beautifully" cut up and across the heavy thing that she now saw was destined to entrap Her.

I will be caught finally, I will be broken. Not broken, walled in, incarcerated. Her will be incarcerated in Her. One morning I will wake, perhaps tomorrow ... in my waking I will say this was a dream, and the hot early-morning fumes of amber tea will envelope me, will blot across the surface of my frozen features and make a cloud, amber and soft fumes of early-morning tea will cloud out all this ... and I will say waking (perhaps tomorrow) the whole thing was some odd dream.

I will say, going back and back, remembering with the surface, the lava Her-surface that is sure to get me, I will say with the incarcerating part of Her Gart, all that was vague, we only

imagine such things. Fayne Rabb will become part of yesterday. I hold Fayne now for one last moment ... I will say wakening, perhaps tomorrow, where is Eugenia? I have been delirious. I will take Eugenia's hand, forget, remembering ... I will
recall exact, and specific instance, say "Mama, I was worried
really but George has left now. No ... not any more George ...
but others. I will make new friends." Exactly and precisely I
will drag Her across Her like the eyelids of some saurian. Out
of the distance there will be no more faces ... things creeping
to say lava can't keep down ... anemones.

For the moment holding to the moment, I know this. I was
a wire, connecting me with such things in my incandescence
... wire flared out. Hermione will say all that was some dream.
I want to take up nursing. All the days will go on like all
the days going on. Time will cut furrows, here there, people
will die sometimes. Valiantly I will keep Her under. I will in-
carcerate Her. Her won't anymore be. A white butterfly that
hesitates a moment finds frost to break the wavering tenuous
antennae. I put, so to speak, antennae out too early. I felt letting Her so delicately protrude prenatal antennae from the
husk of the thing called Her, frost nip the delicate fibre of the
starfish edges of the thing I clung to. I, Her clung to the most
tenuous of antennae. Mama, Eugenia that is, Carl Gart and
Lillian were so many leaves wrapped around the unborn butterfly. Outside a force wakened, drew Her out of Her. Call the
thing Fayne Rabb. I clung to some sort of branch that wavered
in the wind, something between Lillian and Eugenia, a sort of
precise character, George Lowndes. Wavering by instinct toward George I found George Lowndes inadequate. He would
have pulled back quivering antennae.
Tomorrow Amy Dennon will bring me invalid-weak tea.

She will say "You look much better." I will look at the tea fumes, sniff that acrid tonic tea scent, sniff that acrid tonic warmth and draw a woollen bedjacket across somewhat thinning collar bones.

Then in a moment, in an infinitesimal second, the moment that divides day from dawn, that other moment that divides dawn from morning, perhaps that moment that divides early morning from exact morning, will intercede. A moment will stand in a starched apron and the moment will save Her's being. I will draw back tenuous antennae of delirium ... Her will be quite sane. Tomorrow and tomorrow and tomorrow creeps on its petty pace from day to day and all our yesterdays and all our yesterdays ...

"Your eyes are the eyes that made Poppaea furious." "What do you know then Fayne?" "I know nothing, knowing everything. In your hands I am limpid, modest. In the hands of the universe I am a force not to be gainsaid, not to be struggled with. Mama and I are poor. Sometimes mama and I are hungry. Do you know *why* I was late Her Gart? I had to do the washing."

"But that, dear little Fayne, is needless. Waste. Why can't your mother." "Why can't mama get a cook in? Why can't mama keep a cook, a laundress, a housemaid? Oh my darling, your ideas are so autocratic." "I don't mean twenty butlers." "Little little little littlest Miss Gart. You are so superhuman. Then sliding from the over-layer, that Überwelt dear Uncle Mark's books show us, you are you, extraordinary and so common." "Common?" "Well there *is* somewhere, something common in you. This way you have of talking about dances." "I didn't. It was only because you unearthed that bundle of old dance cards." "Wasn't it a little—common so to keep them?" "I suppose so. I don't know. George taught me to see Whistler's jokes were funny, I don't know. I don't think George did." "Did, Miss Her Gart?" "Know. He talked blatantly. Knew nothing. Said that Chelsea bridge with mist was a sort of drug, a dope, an anodyne. Said that London was soporific and so restful." "And you?" "Would rather stay on here with you, Fayne Rabb."

"Then you didn't know that Polish uncle that you bragged of?" "Not Polish. Lithuanian or Bavarian, one of those people." "You can't be Lithuanian *or* Bavarian. There is a world of difference." "We are, aren't we?" "Lithuanian?" "I mean Russian. We aren't are we European? I mean we aren't, we Uncle Sam forest primeval people, European? We think more like Russians. We are nearer Russia. What Russia is to Europe on one side, we are on the other." "Dostoevski?" "No. I don't mean that. I mean our genius has claustrophobia, then has agoraphobia. We flee the waste on one side. The Middle West is our Siberia." "Witty?" "Not meaning to be. We are held here to the thin slope of the Atlantic seaboard like the warriors of Leonidas. We hold, holding to our intellectual standards a sort of mountain. We are so few really." "Who exactly Her Gart?" "I mean you and me and other people like you and me here in the Etats Unis, growing up, not growing up, part of the nebula, maybe in Alabama, maybe in Georgia, maybe in Oklahoma. There must be others like us for the climate makes us … we are deracinated Europeans holding valiant intellectual standards … caught here on the narrow strip of the Atlantic seaboard, caught in subtilized European standards, holding them like the warriors of Leonidas … against … Lithuania. I mean holding something against something. Someone will name the something. Germans name it. A sort of weltgeist that has a vibrant phosphorescent heart, the so few of us, the so very few of us *Americans*. The Siberia of our valiant little stronghold ... I mean the Siberia to our sort of holding on to something ... I'll never make it clear ... make it clear ... you are the sort of wire, the sort of dynamo that makes it clear. Cerebralism burning at its incandescent white heat beats into the air. Images form, we can't talk in mere words. There are bright mountains. A sort of tiny porthole and I look out on mountains. Onyx, amethyst like the apocryphal mountains. Holding on to something ...

"Yes. I love him. Understand this, Hermione. I love him. If I say I love George, it isn't this flimsy thing you call love. You loved him, if you loved him, superficially. You never saw the bright sort of aura that he wore. About George there was that bright cuirass of beauty. You didn't know, couldn't know what love is ... perhaps you thought you loved him. I suffered, watching. My suffering was a sort of burning banner. I carried it, waved it. Did you think I was happy that day, any day, ever when you were with me? Your beauty lacerated me and I said there is no use Fayne Rabb. I stood beside you, I dared to stand beside you and say I loved him."

"Well then speaking man to man, Fayne, why don't you take him?" "You would be cruel, but I am beyond your cruelty." "I wasn't." "Re-eeely?" "A little. Yes. I was a little cruel. I—" "You draw away. You are in love with George Lowndes." "One I love, two I love. I am in love with ... *nothing*." "You are as George says heartless."

Heartless means without a heart. Less a heart. Hermione. Less-a-heart. I am heartless Hermione, Hermione Less-a-heart. What is Hermione Less-a-heart? Hermione heartless is this thing. Tossed like a winter branch on a snow bed. I am

Hermione stripped of blossoms. Flowers drifted here, there, incandescent flower. Snowdrop under a cedar. You are a parasite, drifted here and there to perch a moment parasitically on George Lowndes. Branch flowers dipped parasitic feelers down and down into the live bark of somewhat common tree branch. George could love no parasite, could love no flower as I am. Burst up, up said George Lowndes, dance under a pink lampshade. You are essentially feminine, said George Lowndes, dance and dance for you make me feel a devil.

I was not what George wanted. He wanted fire to answer his fire and it was the tall sapling, the cold Laconian birch tree, the runner and the fearless explorer (my mind was) that drew spark from him. It was to disguise himself that George would so disguise me ... under a winter bonfire. Flowers creeping out from winter leaves and anemones mistaken for the fallen snowflake ... run on and on, run on and on Hermione. You are doomed Hermione for the message you carry is in forgotten metres ... run, stripped across snowbanks, fly downward with pulse beating and pummelling veins at either side of a burning forehead; beating, beating, run, run Hermione. Pheidippides run, run. You have a message but you are doomed Hermione. Run, run across the stones and let your sandal strap break and stoop to fasten nothing ... run, run Hermione. You have in your hands a message and a token. At the end of a valley seething with snow-tipped fir trees, there is a smallish temple. Run and run and run and run Hermione. Runners wait at each station to carry on the message. No god asks too much ... humanity is in a god's touch. You know running and running and running that the messenger will take (lampadephoros) your message in its fervour and you will sink down exhausted ... run, run Hermione. For the message-bearer next in line has turned against you ... dead, dead or forgotten. Hecate at crossroads, a destruction ... you have a double burden ... run, run Hermione, run for yourself and Fayne Rabb.

Fayne will not reach out, will not accept her greatness. You must bear a double sword, a double burden. We are an octopus (North and South Dakota) we are a creature even now seething with life cells, phosphorescent cells; will Fayne Rabb desert me. Run, run little blood corpuscle, tell the whole inchoate mass (Dakota, Oklahoma) that we are all together. Feelers, Siberia, run, run your way, blood corpuscle, there are others.

There are others in Georgia, in Alabama, run, run, keep life living in this formless monster ... run, run Hermione. Tell the Lacadaemonians ... that ... we ... lie ... here ... tell the Lacadaemonians that we lie here ... tell the Lacadaemonians that we lie here ...

... Obeying their orders. Whose orders? I have been almost faithful. In order to be faithful I will forego faith, I will creep back into the shell in order to emerge full fledged, a bird, a phoenix. I will creep back now in order to creep out later ... tell the Lacadaemonians that we lie here obeying their orders.

I have been faithful, said Her Gart, feeling that the moment was about to pass into all moments, the great majority of moments that are dead moments.

four

Now standing on her feet, she realized that she liked her feet. I have been wandering, she thought, too long in some intermediate world and Miss Dennon was nice about the nursing. Certainly, I must be doing something. She thought of feet wandering in long corridors, of grateful patients, of some stalwart youth (saved by Her miraculously from some romantic death) who would have a cottage on an island, somewhere off Florida, and, thinking Florida, red hibiscus in her memory made no deep scar, made no flame and burnt no scar across her consciousness.

All about her peace said snow falls and petals fall, and the fury in Her had been appeased and things had happened as she had foreseen, as she had hoped standing that black night upstairs looking out on Gart terrace. Lawn had been black and heat lightning had scarred an irate heaven, but now earth lay flat and was spread with white on white. Everything had been erased, would be written on presently. White spread across an earth, purified for its fulfillment ... "Three months is a long time. I have almost missed winter."

Snow wafted and fell. It was the white against white she had wanted ... *art thou a ghost my sister* ... it was the froth against breakers, it was the annihilation and the fulfillment. Snow caught against eyelashes, made a delicate runnel against outthrust chin and hollowed cheekbone. Snow scratched softly, made the most distant of delicate sound falling. Snow stupefied Her, cleansed Her, breathing an anesthetic. Thought was wiped out, annihilated. Thought did no good, had done none. "I think I won't think, ever."

"I think I won't think, ever" dropped a sort of casque, a sort of double armour. Her was wound in Her, in some sort of acceptance ... Things about the house were interesting. Mandy was getting married. Tim had bought crocus bulbs this year from the other flower farm. The violets, the Farrand's gardener had under glass, were frozen. Mrs. Banes' daughter had a baby. Minnie had gone to stay with Mrs. Banes while her daughter had the baby. Mrs. de Raub came out often. She had gone out in her moleskin wrap with Her to watch Tim open up the trench for celery. She watched Tim pile on loam and dried leaves and they had gone indoors. Mrs. de Raub liked Mandy's way of drying their own apples, liked the smell of dried mint in the attic and liked being shown Carl Gart's bottles and zinc tanks in the cellar.

Her trailed people from the barn to the vegetable garden and back, saying "But we love having people. We are so cut off here." People liked coming (Eugenia was endearing); they liked the trip out, made excuses, kept on coming. George had called Eugenia's Thursdays so suburban. Eugenia repeated her October Thursdays. Her accepted the people, the Thursdays, had forgotten red hibiscus. But now thinking in the snowy forest of some stalwart young male patient and of Florida, inevitable word reaction brought hibiscus and hibiscus made no scar, brought no resentment, no crippling impotence. In a moment, I am free of George, there is something so thrilling about thinking of something that might happen about someone that you never have seen. A form followed her, dogged Her through winter birches. It followed her feet, it stopped when she stopped. He would have wide shoulders, his eyes would be blue. Her thought went on and on stupidly like a nursemaid.

Her head had been alert, her head had been stupid. Her head that had split open one day didn't now much matter. People were kind. People are, if you just don't go against them. People had been kind all winter. Her feet went on making the path. Her feet were pencils tracing a path through a forest. The world had been razed, had been made clear for this thing. The whole world had been made clear like that blackboard last summer. Last summer Gart lawn had been a blackboard but not quite clear. Now Gart lawn and Gart forest and the Werby meadow and the Farrand forest were swept clear.

They were virginal for one purpose, for one Creator. Last summer the Creator had been white lightning brandished against blackness. Now the creator was Her's feet, narrow black crayon across the winter whiteness. *Art thou a ghost my sister white sister there, art thou a ghost who knows* ... the stones by the Werby meadow were getting too loose. Someone will fall one day and get a stone on his leg. She stepped carefully through an opening in the stone wall. The meadow lay flat and whiter than the forest. Across the meadow the rails ran on their little up-built terrace. The terrace and the rails cut the Werby meadow from the forest. "Hepaticas always come out first in the Farrand forest." She trailed feet across a space of immaculate clarity, leaving her wavering hieroglyph as upon white parchment. When Her got to the little declivity that supported the railroad, she looked back. Her track was uneven and one footprint seemed always to trail unsteadily. She climbed the embankment and again looked down. The meadow lay like a piece of outspread parchment partially curled under. The embankment made the roll from which more parchment might be shaken. The other side of the embankment dipped more sharply. She fell rather than ran into the Farrand Forest.

Now her feet seemed to be filled with memories and the soles of her swift feet. Here I found once an escaped narcissus and escaped narcissus brought back "Narcissa" and "Are you a water lily?" Inevitable word-reaction followed her least thought but reaction was under everything, had really been erased like last year's violets from the winter meadow. Snow had fallen, anesthetic obliterating landmarks. You might as well be happy as not be. George was wrong always. George was a red hibiscus in a globe of water lilies. We would have been wrong always. Her thought went on and began formulating its set purpose. I could have really written but it's better really to give in to people, be quite ordinary and quite happy like all people.

Now she stopped at a runnel that was frozen. Her toe hammered at the space of frozen surface. Then she stamped heavily with her heel. The heel made a sharp dent in the frosted ice. She stood with both feet on it. The opposite bank was shadowed with a tangle of old creeper. No snow covered the tiny beach under the cave space opposite. There might conceivably be just the beginnings of things, common chickweed or arbutus bud under that protective mat of creepers. She stamped further and found foothold. As Her swayed forward, the ice dipped. She heard faint reverberation, the frail thing breaking. It never does freeze properly. There's always water running. She stood wondering whether it would be better to step back or to leap and risk the breakage. The ice stood solid, did not dip further.

The ice cracked as she made tentative slipping movement. The sound it gave out suggested something beneath hammering the undersurface. The slight jar brought Her to tension. She stood tense and silent, if she moved forward it would break now certainly. The bank opposite rose sheer up above the tangle. She wanted to touch the narrow black strip under the bank, was sure of finding something growing. Every year all my life, I have discovered something really in the winter. She remembered all the years, the first year she had actually found violets in December. Violets in December, part of last year? Part of next year? She stood part of next year, part of last year, not totally of either. The crack widened, actually snapped suddenly. The ice she stood on still held, did not dip further toward the tiny upward jet of running water. Reverberation

cut like a white string, cut like a silver string. Winter branches
etched above her head caught reverberation of ice breaking.
Reverberation of the break seemed to be prolonged, would
be till it touched stars. The stars are shining all of them, but I
can't see any. She felt like a star invisible in daylight. Then her
thought widened and the tension snapped as swiftly. It's like
a violin string. It's like Fayne exactly.

When she said Fayne a white hand took Her. Her was held
like a star invisible in daylight that suddenly by some shift
adjustment of phosphorescent values comes quite clear. Her
saw Her as a star shining white against winter daylight.

Her feet were held, frozen to the cracked ice surface. Her
heart was frozen, held to her cracked, somewhat injured body.
I am glad I was ill. Her, though remembering illness, recalled
the suffocation of steam heat, the fragrance of hothouse lilac. White lilac wafted ineffable remembrance. Like the su-
per note on the violin string, the thing in Her reverberated
slightly. She shifted her frozen feet, moved back, slid backward till her heels felt the frozen grass edge of the little river.
Then she clambered self-consciously alert back toward the
scrubby pathway. Oak saplings tore at skirt and rough coat.
Her hands pushed into the wide blue pockets, clenched tight
in her fur-lined old gloves. Her head bent back, saw trees
etched here in the inner wood, more casually. One branch cut
above a mass of tangled branches and made a straight heavy
smudge across the dazzling whiteness. Heavy trunks showed
furrows and now she heard a squeak almost under her feet;
some squirrel in a tree bole or some burrowing rabbit. "Coons,
squirrels, once a red fox. But he must have got away from people hunting by Broadstairs."

Her feet were very cold. She ran for a space, leaping over a

fallen log, turning out of her way to avoid some autumn rub-
bish that the Farrand men must have forgotten to burn or had
left there for some purpose. The eaves of the Farrand stable
were visible through a break in the branches. She turned into
the lower driveway, skirting the wide lawn, dodging under
the bushes of their outer driveway. The bushes held definite
image, brought clear association. "Their spice-shrub always
did better than ours and their magnolia." Her dodged under a
tent of cedar. Great branches made a tent and the outer sweep
of them were held fast, frozen in a little ridge of ice-snow. Her
pulled at the branches, held there like trapped hands. Snow
fell over her, loosened from the flat branch. The place smelt of
cones and the little underlayer of needles (she brushed back
the half-frozen upper surface) felt (she pulled off her loose
glove) warm. "This must be one of those sort of Norwegian
pines old Mr. Farrand used to talk so much of."

The great tree in itself was a world; Olympian. Her under it,
looked up and up like a child in some tale of the Black Forest.
Scent of snow (has snow a scent? It stings the nostrils, is an anesthetic), scent of needles, different sorts of wood smells. She
recalled a red hibiscus with a sort of vicarious shudder. Red
hibiscus seemed like a tissue-paper rose in some Nice carnival. Europe as she pronounced it in her consciousness seemed
like that. Head bent back tried to recall paintings, pictures
upon ceilings. "Old paint, paint peeling off," she said aloud
to the down-sweeping branches, "What's that to this thing?"
Her hands uncurled and she caught at the great tree. George
never could love anything quite properly.

"Her." "Yes?" "I saw you dodge across the lawn. Won't you
come inside?" Her lifted the forehead of a Dodonian neophyte
from the great pure tree trunk. Her eyes caught eyes, the

eyes of Jimmie Farrand. "Oh Jimmie." "Come in, won't you? They said you were quite ill, were you?" "Yes." "What?" "Sort of—of—" "Never mind. Come on in, Her." "Yes." The eyes of Dodona looked at Jimmie Farrand and saw Jimmie Farrand as part of the whole scheme of things. "If once you let go, give in to everybody, things come right." "What, Her?" "I was saying things come right." "Yes, Her. Ought you to be here? Do they know you are here?" "Oh yes. I've been going out some time. I was really all right, weeks back." "I know—but you look—you look—Oh *do* come." Jimmie Farrand saw Her as "quaint," poor Her, those incredible Garts, "What is it?" "Oh nothing. I mean, I was out walking. I mean, I wanted to be alone to—to—see things." "Well you can see things indoors. We won't hurt you."

If Jimmie was part of things and Her having accepted things was part of things, then Her was part of Jimmie. Her argued logically, I am part of things, people are kind if you don't just go against them and Jimmie is like that. Her looked at Jimmie, recalled a house party, boys home from college, some tangle of favours and a red Columbine costume she had once worn. The Columbine costume was part of favours, was part of paper roses, was part of things that were not. Jimmie had finished college. "I didn't know you were here." "Well, I'm not. Not strictly speaking." He held the branch back like a curtain. The curtain keeps me in here. Here I am safe but I must walk out to people. People won't hurt you if you try to understand them.

"People won't hurt you if you try to understand them." She had said that tentatively stooping to the outer branches and Jimmie had caught it up, repeated it, went on with it. "No. I had such a row with them. They said the boy had cheated." "Cheated?" "Yes. It's this beastly idea people have of rightness. He, I suppose had cheated. I mean they found the papers." "Papers?" "Little rolls. All rather neat. He had all the chemical formulas and his math was a miracle. Tiny rolls of Japanese rice paper, almost invisible. He worked hours to make them. He said if he had the cribs in his pocket it gave him confidence. The funny part was he had never used them." "Circumstantial evidence." "Something like that. He's here."

Jimmie Farrand stamped snow from his house shoes. "You should have put on rubbers," and word reaction brought black rose. Why do I think black rose when I think rubbers? Then Her remembered Fayne and Mrs. Rabb. "It was like that." "Like—?" "I mean I had a friend—I had—a—friend."

Jimmie was edging Her toward the little room they used to call (before Mr. Farrand died) "the boy's room." "Do you still call this the boy's room?" Her bent her head going down the little stairway. Two lacrosse rackets were perched (as they always had been) above the mantel. Logs were (as they always had been) roaring. "This room was always more like a boathouse or some sort of clubroom." "Mother had the place put right after the Jetsons left it." "Yes. We missed you. I suppose though your mother didn't like coming back after—after—" "No. She and Kitty were away always. That was before Kitty married. Mim's abroad now on her own." "Yes. I always liked your mother." "She sent me on here to look over things—we're going to sell it." "Sell Farrand?" "Well what use? I can't afford to keep it. Kitty's married. Mim never is here. Yes, sell Farrand."

Sell a Columbine costume, sell a rice paper rose, sell favours twisted in favours and someone standing on a chair while the boys (home from college) blew out her lighted candle. "Do you remember the cotillions?" "Yes. We never dance now." "No, I hardly ever dance now." "What are *you* doing, Her?" "Oh I—I plod along. I mean I was—I was engaged." "Yes Mim or Kitty wrote me." "It didn't come to anything." "It never does do." "I mean I had a—a friend."

"A—a friend" brought a pulse or beat but it wasn't her heart. A heart was put away in an ivory box, in a marble urn like Coeur de Lion or whoever it was who had his heart buried at Havre or wherever it was. It wasn't a heart that beat under a woollen pull-on sort of jumper, under a blue coat. Her pulled at bone buttons on a blue coat. "Oh, take your things off." "But I can't stay." "Why can't you?" "Well I must get back." "It's a pity Mim isn't here or Kitty. Won't you have tea?" "Tea?" "There's old Mrs. Maer (do you remember?) in the kitchen." "Oh—that old thing that used to tie Kitty's hair ribbons?" "Yes. She's still here." "Yes. I think I remember someone saying (Minnie or Mandy) that your people had kept on someone." "She stayed on with the Jetsons. She didn't like it." "How could she? I suppose mama and I ought to have seen more of them." "More of?" "The Jetsons. They always seemed so busy." "They were a noisy crowd. I never liked them. We won't sell to them." Her heart had left off pounding. Someone was selling something to someone. She ought to take some interest. After all these people that were coming here would be her neighbors. "These people who are coming, I suppose, will be my neighbors." "Why—why Her?" "I mean they will be won't they?"

The old lady Her had remembered tying Kitty's ribbons stopped on the small stair, said "Did you ring?" Jimmie Farrand said "Yes, I wish you'd bring in tea. You know, like Kitty liked it." The old lady who had tied Kitty's ribbons stooped sideways through the narrow doorway. She came back presently with tea things. Her said "It's nice of you to do this."

The old lady who had tied Kitty Farrand's ribbons didn't know whether Her meant it nice of her or nice of Jimmie, so she waited. She said "I do miss old times." Her pulled herself up, remembered a boy with ribbons tangled about him for a harness driving four girls, said "It was a pretty cotillion." "The cotillions? We never now have dances." "You always had such nice ones." The old lady looked as if she would stand there forever, but Jimmie asked for more hot water. "I don't think Miss Her likes tea so strong."

"Oh please, I like it this way, don't take the trouble." The old lady said "It's no trouble" and got herself out of the little doorway, a crab turned sideways. "Did you tell me you had friends here?" "I? No. I mean, do you mean Grim?"

Grim like someone in a play came in then. He wore glasses. "Grim, this is Her Gart." Her Gart put out a stiff long hand. Grim took it, dropped it. "We're having tea here." "Yes, it looks darned cosy." "Won't you have some?" "Me? Tea? Never." Grim sat down stuffing a bulbous brier pipe. "Do you mind my smoking?" "Me? Oh no." Grim offered his flat tobacco pouch to Jimmie Farrand who refused it.

Jimmie Farrand picked up the fallen poker and banged at a log. The log smouldered, gave out sooty flame, gave spark and flame in smoke as Jimmie heaved the poker underneath it. "These things are too wet. They should have put them in the other outhouse. The old shed back of the stable's leaking. The whole place is, somehow." The log gave up spurt of volcanic red flame bringing out ridges on the young furrowed face of Grim (it seemed his name was Harold). "What are you going to do Mr. Grim now?" and Her recalled people jabbing at Her, "What are you doing, what are you doing, what are you taking up?" The Grim boy seemed used to it, didn't seem to mind it. "Old Jimmie told you? Oh, I mean—they found me with rice paper. Miss Gart you must never be so foolish." "I failed mine," she was glad and comforted, "without rice paper." "Oh? Where?" "Bryn Mawr. I flunked the whole lot."

"Oh Bryn Mawr. I knew a girl at Bryn Mawr. It must have been before your time. Bessie Hollock." "Oh no. She was very clever. She was Oberon in *Midsummer Night's Dream*. She was very pretty." "Yes. Funny the way girls give up though. She wears pince-nez and is teaching." "I might have worn pince-nez and be teaching," her thought caught jagged memories of tables and desks and morning chapel. There was a cherry tree in blossom against a pseudo-old grey turret. "They tried to be so English." "Yes. That was the trouble with Bryn Mawr. Your dean tried to make English gentlemen of her girls. Did you know Nellie Thorpe?"

"Oh, Nellie. Yes I knew her." "Her brother was with my brother at the law school." "Yes. I know her brother is a lawyer." "People get so lost, don't they? I'm out now of everything." "Yes. People do get lost." "Jim here says he's taking the car abroad if he sells Farrand and he wants a chauffeur. I said, I'd do the driving. I'm rather good at engineering. I mean a motor isn't." "No, not exactly engineering." "But Jim says if he pulls this deal off, he's going to Europe." Jimmie Farrand paid no attention to them. He was sorting out things from a cupboard at the room's far end, old gloves, a broken oar, some fishing tackle. "It must be rather terrible giving up things."

Her said "It must be rather terrible giving up things" while an odd elation caught Her seeing Jimmie chuck old treasures aside, as if to make a barn fire. Baseball gloves, tennis rackets, things split and splintered. "Mim kept everything." Jimmie Farrand drawing near them said, "Mim kept everything," as if Mim were some sort of sister or even sweetheart. Mim was something that had had a new lease of life, someone grown up with a grown-up son (Jimmie was grown up) who was dancing on the Lido (Jimmie had told Her) and who tired out Kitty. Mim was someone who had grown-up children, who was dancing. Europe in consciousness became a place for grown-up people. Gloves, tennis rackets, what was America? A carnival and boys (from Yale) standing on tip-toe to blow out candles … a carnival or desks with stooping shoulders.

Gart and the formula and Uncle Sam pressing people down in test tubes. Europe was a room painted over with bright figures and within it people dancing … "Why don't you come with us? You could join Mim in Venice."

It was odd the moment you gave quite in to people, people came right, came just in true perspective. It was like that dreadful Perseus at the old Academy who had goose wings on his sandals. People of the world brought things in just perspective. Harold Grim brought things in true perspective. He didn't care (he did care) about the rice paper, about expulsion from his college. It meant everything and it meant nothing. There was nothing in America for them but rows of desks and stabilization and exact formalization (Uncle Sam pressing things down in test tubes), there was nothing but standardization or dancing at a carnival. In between there were no nuances (for them). For them there were no nuances. Things would change; for them it was formalization and exact fitting to one type. College, school, failures and the exact presentation of one type. Jim and Grim and Her. "Yes, it would be funny." Jimmie Farrand all sophistication was explaining how they could join up with the Wetheralls, Mrs. and Dot and all go together. Her could be one of them. His mother wanted someone. His mother must have someone with her for the winter. She wanted someone to be with her. Would Her talk it over with her people? Jimmie Farrand went on sorting trash out of the hidden cupboard. Grim said, "We've all got to the end of something."

No. She wouldn't let Grim or Jim see her across the meadow. It was just what she didn't want. No, really. She wanted just that plunge into grey dusk, just that finding foothold on the half frozen path to help her. "I feel just that walk home is going to change everything." Grim said he didn't like it and Jim said "She was always like that. Her knows her own way." Her left them standing in the doorway, a feeling of elation caught at Her, a sort of atavism having to do with Olympia. "Games," she said to herself, "I suppose it's the casual way he hurled things about that brought back things." Things brought back became a sort of hecatomb, a heap of things, things, all having set symbolism, having some sort of office. Formalization of the lacrosse rackets, crossed above the mantel, the great glove like a Pentathlon boxer's, the several kinds of running shoes and even the old snowshoes. Things piled up became a sort of hecatomb for some god. Zeus or one of his fleet sons. Hermes more exactly.

Grim and Jim stood there like two gatekeepers, opening a gate, swift thought that so exactly saw things; Jim so swift seeing so exactly. Thought drove Her forward like the avid pulse and beat of some motor in a beached yacht. I have been here, really stagnant. Things come right when you really don't hurt people ... I hurt Eugenia. I am sorry. I was terrible to Minnie. Feet pulsed forward, drove Her homeward, her feet were winged with the winged god's sandal. Everything will be right. I'll get the money they said they'd give me for my trousseau. I was really going to keep it for the nursing. The money *is* mine. Gran left it for my marriage ... this will be my marriage. The thought sustained Her. Practical and at one with herself, with the world, with all outer circumstance, she barged straight into Mandy in the outer hallway. "Oh, Miss. I thought you was back long since. I done left Miss Fayne all alone upstairs in your little workroom."

A Postlude

Fifty years after the events of Hermione, *the author wrote as follows in* End to Torment, *her memoir of Ezra Pound:*

I did not see him [Ezra Pound] at the time of my first confinement, 1915. I lost that child. The second was four years latter, 1919. He hurtles himself into the decorous St. Faith's Nursing Home, in Ealing, near London. Beard, black soft hat, ebony stick—something unbelievably operatic—directoire overcoat, Verdi: He stalked and stamped the length of the room. He coughed, choked or laughed, "You look like old Mrs. Grumpy" (or some such) "in Wyncote." Wyncote was where the Pounds had lived, outside Philadelphia. True, I wore a becoming (I thought) black lace cap. Naturally, I looked no sylph. He seemed to beat with the ebony stick like a baton. I can't remember. Then, there is a sense of his pounding, pounding (*Pounding*) with the stick against the wall. He had banged that way, with a stick once before, in a taxi, at a grave crisis in my life. This was a grave crisis in my life. It was happening here. "But," he said, "my only real criticism is that this is not my child."

...

The first time, in the taxi, was before I was married. Frances Gregg [Fayne Rabb] had filled the gap in my Philadelphia life after Ezra was gone, after our "engagement" was broken. Maybe the loss of Ezra left a vacuum; anyway, Frances filled it like a blue flame. I made my first trip to Europe with her and her mother, summer 1911. Frances wrote, about a year after her return to America, that she was getting married ("When this letter reaches you, I shall be married.") She said that one of the objects of her marriage to this English University Extension lecturer—or in fact the chief object—was a return to Europe so that she could join me; we would all go to Belgium together where "Louis" was lecturing.

I found Ezra waiting for me on the pavement outside the house, off Oxford Circus, where I had a room. His appearance was again unexpected, unpredictable. He began, "I as your nearest male relation …," and hailed a taxi. He pushed me in. He banged with his stick, pounding (*Pounding*), as I have said. "You are not going with them." I had seen them the day before at their hotel, off Victoria Station. It was all arranged. Ezra must have seen them afterwards. "There is a vague chance that the Egg," (he called her), "may be happy. You will spoil everything." Awkwardly, at Victoria Station, I explained to a married Frances, with a long tulle travelling veil, that I wasn't coming. I had changed my mind. Awkwardly, the husband handed me back the cheque that I had made out for my ticket. Glowering and savage, Ezra waited till the train pulled out.

Afterword

"Mythology is actuality, as we now know" —H. D., *The Gift*

Hans Christian Andersen's "The Little Mermaid" tells the story of a young mermaid who falls in love with a human prince. She drinks a potion that gives her legs to live with him on land—but in exchange, she loses her beautiful voice in perpetuity, and can never again return to the sea. When Hermione Gart's overbearing fiancé refers to her as Undine—a water spirit from a German legend that inspired Andersen— and his mother slyly comments, at a party, that she resembles a mermaid in her green dress, Hermione reacts with justifiable alarm. To a student of myth, these remarks are clear warning that their marriage will risk the submersion of her identity into his, and curb her burgeoning ambitions as a writer. *Hermione* is about a woman's search not for feet but for a voice: it is H. D.'s reckoning with her family and formative relationships, and the story of her "own first awakening"—gradual and painful—as a poet.

H. D. finished writing *Hermione* in 1927 at the ornate chateau on the shores of Lake Geneva where she had lived, on and off, since 1921. Since the birth of her daughter Perdita in 1919, H. D. and her partner Bryher had lived a peripatetic life, moving across Europe as work and whim took them, with Bryher caring for Perdita to give H. D. time and space to write. Bryher had fallen in love with H. D. as a poet of crystalline precision: before they met in 1918, she had memorized H. D.'s first collection *Sea Garden*, spare, musical lyrics conjuring wild borderlands inhabited by gods and nymphs. But over the 1920s, H. D. turned—privately—to prose, to relive and unravel a series of highly distressing events during her first decade in Europe. A sequence of novels—*Palimpsest, Asphodel, Paint It Today*—explored the inner life of a writer uncertain of her status as a woman artist in a male-dominated world. Each covered the same narrative, contracted or expanded in tellingly shifting ways: her arrival in London in 1911 and her immersion in the circle of Imagist poets around Ezra Pound; her marriage to the poet Richard Aldington, his military service, infidelity and their separation; her brief affair with the musician Cecil Gray and her pregnancy (he left her as soon as he found out); and her meeting Bryher in the depths of despair and together forging a new, matriarchal family. By 1927, H. D. was ready to delve further back into the past: to her youth in Philadelphia, and the complex events and inner turmoil that preceded her departure for Europe.

Hermione was never published in H. D.'s lifetime, but its manuscript—along with most of the other unpublished novels she wrote in the 1920s, many with "destroy" scrawled over them—was among the papers she donated to Yale University's Beinecke Library at her death in 1960. Penciled on the title page was a list of dramatis personae, designating for posterity the real people—and events—that lay behind the fiction, as if her characters were actors in a play. Hermione, a young woman who has recently dropped out of Bryn Mawr after failing in Algebra, is Hilda Doolittle herself. Carl and Eugenia Gart are her parents, Charles and Helen Doolittle—he a professor of astronomy, affectionate but forgetful; she a talented musician who gave up her work at her husband's bidding ("Your father likes the light concentrated in a corner. He can work better if I'm sitting in the dark," she tells her daughter). The magnetic, mysterious Fayne Rabb is Frances Gregg, a student at the Pennsylvania Academy of Fine Arts who lived with her widowed mother and was often mistaken for H. D.'s sister. And George Lowndes, Hermione's debonair fiancé, is Ezra Pound. H. D. had first encountered Pound at a teenagers' Halloween party in 1901, and he had swiftly appointed himself responsible for her aesthetic education, plying her with poetry books (Morris, Rossetti, Swinburne) and declaiming his own sonnets to her on walks in the woodland or sitting aloft in the branches of the maple tree in H. D.'s family's garden. H. D.'s family were shocked at Pound's sudden return to Philadelphia, in June 1910; they remembered him as an imperious and dangerous figure who had left for Europe two years earlier under the shadow of a scandal (he had lost his job teaching French at Wabash College after his landlady discovered a woman in his room). Their engagement, though short-lived, placed Pound at the head of a series of men H. D. came to call her "initiators." Writing to her friend Norman Holmes Pearson in 1950, H. D. described Pound's influence as "the scorpions sting or urge that got me away": "at that time," she added, "it was essential."

As the novel opens, Hermione is lost and alone: an "odd duckling" in the family, a disappointment to herself and others. Her nickname—Her—casts her in grammatical terms as a generic female object, rendered anonymous and "clutching out toward some definition of herself." None of the women in her immediate family offer Hermione a model for the independence she yearns for. The walls of her family home seem designed to constrain her: she feels trapped behind high hedges, just as her spirit is stifled by the Victorian conventions that govern life inside. Everything changes when she receives a letter announcing the imminent return from Venice of the "immensely sophisticated" George Lowndes, who arrives determined to "dynamite her world away for her." His strong opinions help mask her own indecision; his irreverence towards her hometown's hypocrisies emboldens her to separate from the world she knows. Yet over the course of their reacquaintance—as he tells her what to read and how to see, blithely dismisses her poetry as "rot," and insists she run away with him to Europe—Hermione comes to fear that by surrendering her future to George, she's swapping the restrictions of her family home for a life where her own interests and desires still remain of secondary importance. He "wanted Her, but he wanted a her that he called decorative," Hermione realizes; her wavering poetic voice is in danger of being "smudged out."

"Perhaps, there was always a challenge in his creative power," H. D. wrote of Pound in her memoir *End to Torment*, written during an intense period of analysis in 1958, while Pound was incarcerated in St. Elizabeths Hospital. It was Norman Holmes Pearson who encouraged H. D. to record her memories of Pound, convinced the process would offer her "a kind of catharsis" towards the end of her own life. She reported back that she enjoyed recalling "the early American scene, when almost everyone I knew in Philadelphia was against him"—but rifling through her memories reaffirmed the sense, apparent thirty years earlier in *Hermione*, that had they married "Ezra would have destroyed me and the centre they call 'Air and Crystal' of my poetry." *End to Torment* takes the form of journal-like reflections from the present, as recollections of her "inner schism"—caught between her parents and Pound—float back into her consciousness. On its eventual publication in 1979, *End to Torment* was appended with the twenty-five poems Pound wrote as a teenager, titled *Hilda's Book*, in which she is a silent addressee: the only time she speaks is as the mythological Daphne, warding off Apollo's assault by transforming into a tree. In a way, *Hermione* is

H. D.'s answer to *Hilda's Book*: Hermione's challenge is to assert herself as a woman and as a writer before she becomes a captive muse to another poet who refuses to hear her voice.

"Names are in people, people are in names," goes the mystical refrain that occurs several times in *Hermione*. Names, and naming, were a longstanding preoccupation of H. D.'s ("Hermione" offers a coded key to the character's autobiographical roots, recalling the daughter of Helen in Greek myth, and the mother of Perdita in *A Winter's Tale*). It was Pound, famously, who was responsible for H. D.'s use of her initials for her published writing. One afternoon in the autumn of 1912 he picked up a sheath of poems over tea at the British Museum, exclaimed "But Dryad, this is poetry," scratched out a few lines and added at the bottom—sweeping her up into the movement he was currently promoting—"H. D. Imagiste." Despite the end of their fleeting engagement, Pound had been eager to draw H. D. into London literary circles, introducing her to poets and literary editors at the regular teas and cocktail parties where he presided and untiringly promoting her work with his contacts. Though grateful for his support, H. D. never felt comfortable with the public association of her name with his "Imagist" label, and as she gradually distanced herself from Pound, the problem of names persisted. Each of her unpublished prose manuscripts is attributed to a different author—Delia Alton, Edith Gray, Rhoda Peter, Helga Dart, Helga Doorn—as if she herself is playing a part, slipping on a new mask for every fresh dive into the depths of the past. "I find it increasingly difficult to remain MYSELF when writing," she wrote to one editor. In a way, each of her autobiographical novels marks a new effort to regain control over her past, to explore who she might be beyond the identity ascribed her by her father (Hilda Doolittle), by Pound (H. D.), or by the law (Mrs. Richard Aldington). Freedom, for H. D., lay in a refusal of fixed labels: the ability to shift between places, forms and styles, to experiment, to defy expectations. As she recast her life over and over, the texts forming a palimpsest, H. D. stepped outside of the myths and names imposed on her by others, and took control of her own legend. "It is obviously Penelope's web that I am weaving," she wrote.

Hermione is perhaps the most radical of all her novels in its triumphant refusal of what the poet Adrienne Rich called "compulsory heterosexuality." Hermione's realization that "sister love" could offer greater fulfillment than an engagement to George Lowndes deftly subverts the traditional "marriage plot"—it displaces Pound's hold on H. D.'s "origin story," insisting that her poetic vocation was awoken long before Pound "named" her in the museum tea shop. H. D. met Frances Gregg in 1910, and immediately sensed she had found a spiritual soulmate: in *End to Torment* H. D. describes how Gregg filled the gap in her life after Pound's departure for London in February 1911 "like a blue flame." In *Hermione*, Fayne Rabb is the first to take Hermione's writing seriously, showing that her work will be a way—the only way—to achieve the self-knowledge she is lacking: "Your writing is the thin flute holding you to eternity. Take away your flute and you remain, lost in a world of unreality." Together, Fayne and Hermione read Swinburne's *Itylus*, the story of love between the sisters Procne and Philomel, claiming—and subverting—a place in the history of Romantic literature for themselves. Up in Hermione's small workroom, Fayne creates a febrile atmosphere of desire and creativity that spurs, rather than stifles, Hermione's creative powers. George dismisses their bond as "witchcraft," an accusation H. D. picks up in *Asphodel*, her sequel to *Hermione*. The women's relationship—their "concentric intimacy"—is defined by the image of two convex mirrors placed back to back, in which Hermione does not see herself reflected as she is, but merges, thrillingly, with Fayne's body. Yet this image of total oneness is tempered by Hermione's growing fear that the closeness is too much, that it threatens to "drown" her. Drawing on Plato's dictum that we spend our lives seeking the other half that was sundered from us in a previous existence, Hermione comes to realize that artistic freedom will be achieved not by allying with a more forceful other, but by learning to know and understand herself.

H. D. sailed for Europe in 1911 in the company of Gregg and her mother. *Asphodel* explores Hermione's exhilaration at life in London ("Can you see how London at least left me free?" H. D. wrote to Bryher in 1924), and her disappointment when Fayne chooses to return to America rather than stay and share a flat together as they had planned. "We can't creep back into our mothers, be born again that way," Hermione insists. "We must be born again in another way." But shortly after her departure, Fayne writes to inform Hermione that she's engaged, completing the betrayal that began, in *Hermione*, with her intimacy to George Lowndes, who breezily let them both know he preferred Fayne's poetry to Hermione's. In her diary of these years, Gregg wrote of "Two girls in love with each other, and each in love with the same man. Hilda, Ezra, Frances." Gregg's marriage to Louis Wilkinson confirmed the dissolution of this uneasy triangle: when she invited H. D. to join them on their honeymoon in Belgium, it was Pound who intercepted H. D. on her way to Victoria station, and insisted she stay behind for her own sanity. Gregg remained a crucial figure in H. D.'s emotional life, but it was not until she met Bryher that H. D. found a relationship which met both her artistic and emotional needs. In her novel *Paint it Today*, their bond is represented by the open landscape of a natural paradise where women worship Artemis and where childbirth represents the culmination of a powerful creative force.

Paint it Today and *Hermione* are the most overtly lesbian of H. D.'s novels: in both, heterosexuality is a societal force to be rejected once the protagonist has come to understand how her desires and sense of self are shaped by the narrow expectations of those around her. That these texts remained unpublished in H. D.'s lifetime is perhaps not surprising: she and Bryher tended to disguise their relationship in public, and paid close attention to the obscenity trial that engulfed Radclyffe Hall's 1928 novel *The Well of Loneliness*, which depicted a doomed relationship between two women (condemned on the grounds that it condoned "unnatural practices"). The novel H. D. did publish in 1960, *Bid Me to Live*, erases the two relationships with women—Frances Gregg and Bryher—that are central to other versions of this story. Instead, *Bid Me to Live* focuses on an emotional tussle with a character based on D. H. Lawrence, an intriguing episode absent from H. D.'s previous novels. As in *Hermione*, the central struggle of *Bid Me to Live* is that of a woman writer searching for creative autonomy while men attempt to control her and her work. Yet paradoxically H. D. is still, too often, defined by her relationships with famous men, obscuring her position in queer history and undercutting her own importance as a multidisciplinary avant-garde artist of extraordinary range and power.

A line in *Hermione* encapsulates the spirit of H. D.'s prose oeuvre: "All your life you will retain one or two bits of colour with which all your life will be violently or delicately tinted." *Hermione* is an explosion of colour: H. D.'s writing is hallucinogenic and incantatory, rendering the contours of Hermione's psyche in prose as beguiling as her heroine's dilemma. H. D.

spent the rest of her life processing this first sexual and artistic awakening—through analysis (including with Sigmund Freud) and through writing. Her memoir *The Gift* delves further into her maternal heritage, exploring the mystic traditions and affinity for the supernatural she inherited from her grandmother, as well as returning—with more sympathy than the narrator of *Hermione*—to her sense of loss at her mother's squandered musical talents. Her epic poem *Helen in Egypt* is perhaps the apex of her achievement, a revision of the myth of Helen of Troy in which the beleaguered Helen, through a process of psychoanalysis and communion with characters from her past (in particular her mother) comes to reshape her own identity, which had been fragmented by her false appropriation into other men's stories. *Hermione* is H. D.'s rejoinder to mythic authority: her portrait of an artist groping her way slowly towards self-expression ends with her sexuality and artistic powers awoken, ready to name herself so all the world might know who she is.

FRANCESCA WADE

New Directions Paperbooks—a partial listing

Kaouther Adimi, Our Riches
Adonis, Songs of Mihyar the Damascene
César Aira, Ghosts
  An Episode in the Life of a Landscape Painter
Will Alexander, Refractive Africa
Osama Alomar, The Teeth of the Comb
Guillaume Apollinaire, Selected Writings
Jessica Au, Cold Enough for Snow
Paul Auster, The Red Notebook
Ingeborg Bachmann, Malina
Honoré de Balzac, Colonel Chabert
Djuna Barnes, Nightwood
Charles Baudelaire, The Flowers of Evil*
Bei Dao, City Gate, Open Up
Mei-Mei Berssenbrugge, Empathy
Max Blecher, Adventures in Immediate Irreality
Roberto Bolaño, By Night in Chile
  Distant Star
Jorge Luis Borges, Labyrinths
  Seven Nights
Beatriz Bracher, Antonio
Coral Bracho, Firefly Under the Tongue*
Kamau Brathwaite, Ancestors
Basil Bunting, Complete Poems
Anne Carson, Glass, Irony & God
  Norma Jeane Baker of Troy
Horacio Castellanos Moya, Senselessness
Camilo José Cela, Mazurka for Two Dead Men
Louis-Ferdinand Céline
  Death on the Installment Plan
  Journey to the End of the Night
Rafael Chirbes, Cremation
Inger Christensen, alphabet
Julio Cortázar, Cronopios & Famas
Jonathan Creasy (ed.), Black Mountain Poems
Robert Creeley, If I Were Writing This
Guy Davenport, 7 Greeks
Amparo Davila, The Houseguest
Osamu Dazai, No Longer Human
  The Setting Sun
H. D., Selected Poems
Helen DeWitt, The Last Samurai
  Some Trick
Marcia Douglas
  The Marvellous Equations of the Dread
Daša Drndić, EEG
Robert Duncan, Selected Poems

Eça de Queirós, The Maias
William Empson, 7 Types of Ambiguity
Mathias Énard, Compass
Shusaku Endo, Deep River
Jenny Erpenbeck, The End of Days
  Go, Went, Gone
Lawrence Ferlinghetti
  A Coney Island of the Mind
Thalia Field, Personhood
F. Scott Fitzgerald, The Crack-Up
  On Booze
Emilio Fraia, Sevastopol
Jean Frémon, Now, Now, Louison
Rivka Galchen, Little Labors
Forrest Gander, Be With
Romain Gary, The Kites
Natalia Ginzburg, The Dry Heart
  Happiness, as Such
Henry Green, Concluding
Felisberto Hernández, Piano Stories
Hermann Hesse, Siddhartha
Takashi Hiraide, The Guest Cat
Yoel Hoffmann, Moods
Susan Howe, My Emily Dickinson
  Concordance
Bohumil Hrabal, I Served the King of England
Qurratulain Hyder, River of Fire
Sonallah Ibrahim, That Smell
Rachel Ingalls, Mrs. Caliban
Christopher Isherwood, The Berlin Stories
Fleur Jaeggy, Sweet Days of Discipline
Alfred Jarry, Ubu Roi
B. S. Johnson, House Mother Normal
James Joyce, Stephen Hero
Franz Kafka, Amerika: The Man Who Disappeared
Yasunari Kawabata, Dandelions
John Keene, Counternarratives
Heinrich von Kleist, Michael Kohlhaas
Alexander Kluge, Temple of the Scapegoat
Wolfgang Koeppen, Pigeons on the Grass
Taeko Kono, Toddler-Hunting
Laszlo Krasznahorkai, Satantango
  Seiobo There Below
Ryszard Krynicki, Magnetic Point
Eka Kurniawan, Beauty Is a Wound
Mme. de Lafayette, The Princess of Clèves
Lautréamont, Maldoror

Siegfried Lenz, The German Lesson
Alexander Lernet-Holenia, Count Luna
Denise Levertov, Selected Poems
Li Po, Selected Poems
Clarice Lispector, The Hour of the Star
  The Passion According to G. H.
Federico García Lorca, Selected Poems*
Nathaniel Mackey, Splay Anthem
Xavier de Maistre, Voyage Around My Room
Stéphane Mallarmé, Selected Poetry and Prose*
Javier Marías, Your Face Tomorrow (3 volumes)
Adam Mars-Jones, Box Hill
Bernadette Mayer, Midwinter Day
Carson McCullers, The Member of the Wedding
Fernando Melchor, Hurricane Season
Thomas Merton, New Seeds of Contemplation
  The Way of Chuang Tzu
Henri Michaux, A Barbarian in Asia
Dunya Mikhail, The Beekeeper
Henry Miller, The Colossus of Maroussi
  Big Sur & the Oranges of Hieronymus Bosch
Yukio Mishima, Confessions of a Mask
  Death in Midsummer
Eugenio Montale, Selected Poems*
Vladimir Nabokov, Laughter in the Dark
  Nikolai Gogol
Pablo Neruda, The Captain's Verses*
  Love Poems*
Charles Olson, Selected Writings
George Oppen, New Collected Poems
Wilfred Owen, Collected Poems
Hiroko Oyamada, The Hole
José Emilio Pacheco, Battles in the Desert
Michael Palmer, Little Elegies for Sister Satan
Nicanor Parra, Antipoems*
Boris Pasternak, Safe Conduct
Octavio Paz, Poems of Octavio Paz
Victor Pelevin, Omon Ra
Georges Perec, Ellis Island
Alejandra Pizarnik
  Extracting the Stone of Madness
Ezra Pound, The Cantos
  New Selected Poems and Translations
Raymond Queneau, Exercises in Style
Qian Zhongshu, Fortress Besieged
Herbert Read, The Green Child
Kenneth Rexroth, Selected Poems
Keith Ridgway, A Shock

Rainer Maria Rilke
  Poems from the Book of Hours
Arthur Rimbaud, Illuminations*
  A Season in Hell and The Drunken Boat*
Evelio Rosero, The Armies
Fran Ross, Oreo
Joseph Roth, The Emperor's Tomb
Raymond Roussel, Locus Solus
Ihara Saikaku, The Life of an Amorous Woman
Nathalie Sarraute, Tropisms
Jean-Paul Sartre, Nausea
Judith Schalansky, An Inventory of Losses
Delmore Schwartz
  In Dreams Begin Responsibilities
W. G. Sebald, The Emigrants
  The Rings of Saturn
Anne Serre, The Governesses
Patti Smith, Woolgathering
Stevie Smith, Best Poems
  Novel on Yellow Paper
Gary Snyder, Turtle Island
Dag Solstad, Professor Andersen's Night
Muriel Spark, The Driver's Seat
Maria Stepanova, In Memory of Memory
Wislawa Szymborska, How to Start Writing
Antonio Tabucchi, Pereira Maintains
Junichiro Tanizaki, The Maids
Yoko Tawada, The Emissary
  Memoirs of a Polar Bear
Dylan Thomas, A Child's Christmas in Wales
  Collected Poems
Tomas Tranströmer, The Great Enigma
Leonid Tsypkin, Summer in Baden-Baden
Tu Fu, Selected Poems
Paul Valéry, Selected Writings
Enrique Vila-Matas, Bartleby & Co.
Elio Vittorini, Conversations in Sicily
Rosmarie Waldrop, The Nick of Time
Robert Walser, The Assistant
  The Tanners
Eliot Weinberger, An Elemental Thing
  The Ghosts of Birds
Nathanael West, The Day of the Locust
  Miss Lonelyhearts
Tennessee Williams, The Glass Menagerie
  A Streetcar Named Desire
William Carlos Williams, Selected Poems
Louis Zukofsky, "A"

*BILINGUAL EDITION

For a complete listing, request a free catalog from New Directions, 80 8th Avenue, New York, NY 10011 or visit us online at ndbooks.com